HEART OF DEFIANCE

RYAN KIRK

WATERSTONE
MEDIA

For Micah

1

Bai came to awareness slowly. Her head hurt, pounding as though she'd been hit by a rock. She took a deep, shuddering breath, groaning with agony.

It felt like a boulder lay on her chest, her lungs tightly constricted, unable to expand.

She clawed her way to wakefulness, fighting against the pull and temptation of endless rest. She coughed and spit, her mouth dirty, dust thick in the air.

Bai tried to remember. Where was she? What had happened? Her mind spun in circles but provided no answers. She felt as though she was waking from a deep slumber, dazed and disoriented. Yet this waking came with enormous pain.

She was not in her bed, and no answers came, no matter how much time passed. Each breath came a little easier, but her memories were as elusive as ghosts.

Bai scrunched her eyes and blinked them open. She was face down in the grass, green blades gently stabbing at her face. She groaned again, every passing moment bringing another wave of needle-like pain. Her entire body felt like it was being poked at with thousands of tiny pins.

It would be easier just to lie there, to close her eyes and return to sleep, maybe to never wake again. Her eyelids drooped and she forced them to stay open, the effort no less than carrying a full bucket of water from the well to her home. Her body protested every movement. Perhaps if she just rested for a little while longer. She surrendered to her exhaustion, her eyes closing as she took a long, deep breath.

She saw her mother's serious face in her mind's eye, the memory flooding her with distress. *Something* had happened. If she hurt this badly, was her mother okay? Was her mother even near?

The questions demanded answers, forced her to open her eyes. She pushed herself up to her hands and knees, her head swimming with even that small feat. She shifted her weight back and sat on her knees, her back straight, just the way her mother had taught her.

Bai looked around, catching her breath from the exertion. She didn't recognize her surroundings. At times, the scene hinted at past familiarity, but that was impossible. She'd never seen devastation like this before. Not even in her nightmares.

The buildings around her had been flattened, as though a giant hand had come from the sky and slapped them down. Broken timbers and collapsed roofs were all that her tired eyes could make out.

After a few seconds, she had to close her eyes again. Sleep demanded its due. Her arms hung limp at her sides, and although she knew she needed to stand, to search the area for answers, the very idea of that level of exertion made her want to collapse in exhaustion.

But she'd been tired before. Often, she and her mother

had worked late, mending clothes that others had needed stitched immediately. They'd worked through the night, dim candles and the moonlight pouring through the open window their only sources of illumination. Bai had suffered through sleepless nights before and still worked without problem the next day. Why was she so tired now?

And why couldn't she remember? The longer she remained awake, the more that question frightened her. Her other memories seemed fine. She remembered the weathered lines of her mother's face, aged too early from a life of labor and fear. She remembered the feel of silk against her hands as she worked the fabric into a design suitable for some of the wealthiest men and women in Galan. So why didn't she know where she was or what had happened?

Bai pressed her eyes together, willing her full memory to return, but fortune did not smile on her. After a dozen frustrating seconds of blinding nothingness, she gave up and opened her eyes again.

When she did, she realized that there *was* something vaguely familiar about the place where she sat. Her mind wasn't tricking her. She knew this place. She fought her way to her feet. She wobbled for a moment, her balance not quite centered, before the world finally steadied.

Bai slowly turned around, focusing not on the destroyed buildings but on the spaces between them. Off in the distance, familiar mountains stabbed into the cloudy evening sky. They were the same mountains she had looked at every day of her life, appearing no different than before.

Her stomach twisted, realizing a sickening thought moments before she was consciously aware of it. Her gaze traveled down to the ruins around her, marking out the locations of the foundations. She knew this place.

This was home.

She was in the market square of Galan, a place where she'd spent no small part of her life.

A wave of nausea threatened to send her back to her knees, but she put her hands on her thighs, barely managing to remain standing. Her stomach heaved, but nothing came out. They hadn't had much money for food lately.

New memories surfaced. Boys playing catch with a ball in this square. Her mother had sent her out to purchase supplies, and there had been someone else. An angry man?

The memories stopped there, a solid door slamming between her and the knowledge of what happened. She poked, prodded, and pushed, but her memory refused to cooperate.

Her dry mouth brought her attention back to the moment. She was thirsty, as though she'd worked all day in the sun without so much as a sip of water. There would be water skins back at their house, only a block away.

Bai's heart pounded. Her mother!

She turned around, dreading the answer. No houses stood for at least three blocks. Bai scrambled over and around the broken buildings. There was no clear path to where her house had once stood. Broken wood trembled under her heavy, unbalanced footsteps.

As the shock wore off, she noticed more details. She had thought she was alone, but that wasn't quite true. There were bodies, covered in dust, all around her. She saw limbs and faces, a few of them immediately recognizable. Why hadn't she seen any bodies in the square? With a mounting sense of terror, she struggled forward.

Finding her house wasn't as easy as she'd expected. When all the buildings had collapsed, the narrow separation that existed between the homes had been destroyed. Small pockets of individual lives had been replaced by one communal disaster.

She saw the neighbor next door, the young boy who had believed that someday he and Bai would marry. He'd courted her endlessly even though she was ten years older than him. She'd tolerated his affection, smiling and nodding when he spoke about their future together. She'd thought of it as harmless fun, and observed that the dream had given the young boy a hope for his coming days. His unblinking gaze now stared endlessly at the sky, a thin layer of dust obscuring his brown eyes.

Bai found her house, or what remained, at least. Seized by a sudden burst of energy, she frantically threw aside rubble, searching the ruins for an answer. She tried to call out for her mother, but the words caught in her parched throat. She focused on digging, the broken wood tearing through her calloused hands.

Had the bandits done this? She'd heard plenty of rumors over the years of the men and women who lived high in the mountains, somehow exempt from monastic oversight. Patrols rarely ventured that way. Outside of the farms and forests that buffered Bai's village from the mountains, there was little of the empire beyond her home. Sometimes, one heard stories of the bandits coming down from the mountains, killing and slaughtering innocents. She'd always dismissed such stories as fancy, but who else could have done something so terrible?

Or had it been the temperamental monks? They had the power to do something like this. Bai loathed and feared the monks in equal measure. Their demands, as of late, had become increasingly onerous. Perhaps they had simply decided to destroy Galan. She couldn't imagine why, but who knew what madness lay in the heart and mind of a monk?

Her thoughts came to a crashing halt when she uncovered a hand, one of the fingers bent permanently at an unnatural angle. For a few moments, she stopped digging, afraid of what she might uncover. Then she came to her senses. Perhaps there was still hope. She threw some of the broken wood behind her, grunting with the effort as she pulled debris off the victim.

Bai sank to her knees when she uncovered more of the arm. A bracelet rested on the wrist, a bracelet that Bai had made and given to her mother on her fortieth birthday. She uttered a wordless cry and grasped the hand. It was cold to the touch, lifeless.

She clasped the hand with both of her own, tears soaking into the dust below. Her mouth hung open, a silent scream of loss ripping her heart in half.

Now she was alone.

Her mother had been the one who kept her safe, had taught her how to survive in a heartless world. She'd chiseled Bai into stone, quiet and nearly impervious to the trials of life.

But even stone could shatter.

A sudden shiver seized Bai, causing her to release her mother's hand and wrap her arms tightly around herself. A glance at the sky told her night was coming. She'd left home in the morning, she remembered. Had most of the day passed?

She realized then that the sounds she'd grown up with, the sounds of people bustling back and forth, were gone. Outside of the whisper of the breeze cutting through the broken homes, there wasn't another voice to be heard. No cries of agony marked the places where victims lay. She was alone, completely. No one else had survived.

Why? Why did she have to continue to suffer when her mom had gone on without her?

Her limbs felt like tree trunks rooted to the ground, but beyond her exhaustion and the fresh cuts on her hands, she wasn't even injured. How had she lived when all that she loved and knew had died?

Then she heard voices. It took her a few seconds to realize what they were. It seemed like a lifetime ago that she had heard someone else speaking. She licked her lips and swallowed, preparing to yell for them. Then a terrible thought occurred to her. What if she was listening to the bandits from the mountains, back to finish whatever horrible work they had started? Or worse, what if they were monks?

Even if the voices were benevolent, what good would her yelling do? Everyone was dead. Rescuers would discover the same soon enough, with or without her.

A memory of her mother came back to her. A memory from the day Bai had been beaten for trying to defend a household servant. The servant, a young boy, had been accused of muddying the master's boots. Bai had known the accusation wasn't true. The master's son had worn the boots and gotten them dirty. She'd spoken up in the servant's defense and had coughed up blood for two days as her reward. The master hadn't taken kindly to her pointing fingers at his son.

Bai's mother had tended her well enough, but her words had been stern.

"You need to learn silence, little one," she had said as she bathed her daughter that night. "The best servant is invisible. If people don't see you, and if they don't hear you, they won't hurt you."

Her mother had been right, as she always was. Speaking out now would be just as foolish. Who knew what trouble she would court if she brought people's attention her way?

Bai looked around. The voices came closer, some of them shouting. She didn't have much time. Before she left, she pulled the bracelet from her mother's wrist. It seemed pitifully little, but Bai wanted something to remember her mother by.

She found a gap, a dark shadow where she could hide. It would have to do. She scrambled and squeezed in, curling into the fetal position so she wouldn't be seen.

Bai fought to calm her ragged breathing. With every passing second, she became more convinced that the voices were after her. They sounded angry, and they kept coming closer. Bai closed her eyes, hoping she wouldn't be found.

2

Delun stared across the stone courtyard at his opponent, a monk wearing simple training robes. Though the monk tried to look outwardly composed, Delun could easily see the small physical tics that betrayed the boy's true feelings. He saw the monk's eyes dart back and forth, noticed that the monk was breathing quickly through his mouth even though the match had not yet started. Delun imagined he could almost feel the monk's elevated heart rate.

Just as telling as the monk's fear was the attitude of the circle of monks surrounding them, each holding a shield of energy. Though he couldn't afford to give the circle the same attention he did the monk in front of him, Delun was observant enough to notice the sly grins, the mirth in the eyes of the onlookers as they glanced back and forth. Several of them were a moment away from laughing out loud. Many of them had been through this trial themselves and delighted in being a part of the circle rather than inside it.

Beads of sweat gathered on the young monk's forehead,

even though the air was cool, thanks to the elevation of the mountains.

Delun knew his reputation well enough. He rarely sparred with other monks anymore for that very reason. The others sparred to train, but Delun had left the walls of the monastery often enough to see the foolishness in that approach. Sparring to train ingrained bad habits. A killing blow was withheld. Punches were pulled. The body remembered. These were mistakes that could get him killed on the other side of these thick stone walls.

Delun didn't spar to train. He sparred to win.

The other monks knew that fact well. They'd been on the receiving end of enough of his beatings to understand. Now, sparring Delun had become something of a rite of passage, an unofficial test for young monks about to take their final vows. Survive Delun, the argument went, and you could survive anything.

Delun loathed the practice. It wasted time and there was much to be done. But Taio, their abbot, had insisted on this concession to the other monks. It built community and strengthened the order. Delun didn't agree, but he never disobeyed a request from Taio.

The young monk's weight shifted and Delun focused his attention sharply on the boy. The monk's energy grew as it was focused. The hopeful warrior made two signs with his right hand and a single sign with his left. Delun fought the urge to shake his head. The boy was far too eager and too confident in his own superiority. Hearing rumors of a strong opponent didn't dissuade a young man. It only encouraged him. Delun understood. He'd been a young man with a point to prove once, too.

He still wished the trainees would exercise more restraint.

Ever since the Battle of Jihan, twenty years ago, single-handed techniques had become standard in the monasteries. Before, a single-handed technique had been considered inferior. With rare exceptions, they generated less focused attacks and shields, and were typically weaker than a sign's two-handed counterpart. The only advantage had been that a monk could prepare two techniques at the same time.

Prior to Jihan, no one had used two single-handed techniques simultaneously in combat, though. It was thought doing so required too much focus. On the rare occasions when monks had dueled, only two-handed techniques had been used.

Sometimes all it took to change the world was for someone to demonstrate what was possible.

In Jihan, two masters had fought, masters who had both been able to summon two single-handed techniques with ease. Since then, hundreds of monks followed in the footsteps of those infamous warriors.

Delun considered such a path a mistake. The true path sat, as it often did, between the extremes, a place of balance. Using two single-handed techniques could be useful, and should be trained. But Delun believed that in battle, such techniques should only be used by masters to whom such techniques had become as natural as breathing.

The monk in front of him was a perfect example. He had an attack and a shield prepared, but both were weak, and even though only a second or two had passed since the trainee formed the signs, he was already struggling to maintain the focus required to hold such techniques. Far better to commit to one move done well than two performed poorly.

The monk leveled his right hand at Delun, aiming his

attack. Delun stood perfectly still, balanced exactly between his feet. He made no move to defend himself. But if the trainee believed Delun was unprepared, the boy was a fool.

Delun saw the way the monk braced himself, giving Delun a moment of warning.

It was all he needed.

Delun slid to the side as the monk released his attack. The energy manipulations of the monks were invisible to the eye, but Delun could feel the wave of energy tear through the place he had just stood. The attack glanced off his shoulder, barely affecting his balance. The rest of the energy wave was absorbed by a monk in the circle, holding a shield to keep the sparring match from destroying the rest of the monastery.

These trials were no picnic for the monks in the circle either. They all used the first and easiest shielding sign to create the circle of shields, but maintaining it for the duration of the combat, especially if one was absorbing blows, was no small feat. That was why a group of monks stood behind the circle, ready to step in and replace a friend at a moment's notice.

Delun stepped toward the boy, closing the distance with precise, calculated steps. The younger trainee, fearing an imminent attack, held up his left hand and released the shield he had prepared.

To the boy's credit, his attack and defense had been perfect. The boy followed his training, and his master should have been proud of the boy's responses. But Delun didn't fight like a monk, and existed to remind the monks there were other paths to victory. If he believed this trial accomplished anything, it was to prove, as physically and dramatically as possible, that the monks weren't as infallible as they thought. If he could open their eyes, this farce was worth it.

He'd expected the shield. As a child, he would have responded exactly the same. He planted his left foot in front of the shield and spun around it.

The first sign of the shield only protected a small area. The trainee brought his shield around, following Delun's movements, keeping it between the two of them.

Delun stopped his spin with his back to the trainee. He didn't attack, but moved his own right hand quickly through the first two focusing signs of an attack. He wanted to hurt the boy, not kill him. His life was too valuable.

The trainee, confused by the lack of a strike and Delun's sudden stillness, dropped his shield. Delun assumed the boy had simply lost focus, his mental energy already consumed by the effort required to use two techniques at once. This mistake wasn't terrible. The boy had already started signing a second shield with his open hand.

But a single mistake in a single moment was enough to lose a fight. Delun had been patiently waiting for it, had felt it coming.

The trainee realized the consequences as Delun twisted around. Too late, the monk felt Delun's own power. The young monk attempted to finish his shield, but Delun didn't leave him enough time. Delun turned enough so that he could point his right hand at the monk and released his attack, directly into the trainee's torso.

The blast threw the monk backward, crashing against the shields of the monks behind him. The young monk's eyes went soft for a moment, and Delun worried he'd hit the boy too hard.

Then the monk recovered and everyone in the circle

relaxed. A few of the monks chuckled softly, and Delun heard one monk say to another, "I thought he'd last longer."

Delun walked over to his sparring partner and offered his hand. The younger monk took it, and Delun pulled him gently back to his feet. Delun gave the monk a questioning glance.

The trainee had a sheepish grin on his face. "I'll have bruises, but I'll be fine."

Delun gave the monk a short bow, which was returned with slightly more respect. Then he turned to walk to his quarters.

He was stopped before he could make it three paces beyond the circle. Another monk, acting as a messenger, had been waiting for just this moment. "The abbot wants to see you."

Delun nodded his acknowledgement and changed direction toward the larger building in the center of the monastery. He was approaching his thirtieth birthday, and the monastery high in the mountains above the town of Two Bridges had been his home for almost twenty of them.

The monastery had a long and distinguished story, but its most recent history had catapulted it to its unique status in the monastic system. Twenty years ago it had been burned to the ground, its previous abbot killed, the whole incident a prelude to the Battle of Jihan. Taio, their current abbot, had returned from Jihan and rebuilt it.

Damage from the fire was still evident. Blackened stones formed the foundations of some of the buildings, and the wood showed far less age than most monasteries. The logs had been hauled up one by one from the forests far below. The resulting architecture struck a discordant note, one that Taio frequently acknowledged. The burned stones reminded them of their past, but the new walls kept them focused on building a better future.

The monastery at Two Bridges was unique among monasteries. It only accepted trained monks, and its purpose was simple: to protect the monastic system at all costs.

The monks at Two Bridges didn't patrol the roads or wander the lands, as so many of their peers were supposed to do. They weren't focused on maintaining the peace of the empire, at least not directly. In the twenty years since Jihan, the threats against the monasteries had only grown. Delun and his peers fought against those forces. No work was more meaningful.

Delun found Taio in his study. The man sat, stiff as a board, studying the most recent batch of messages he had received. When Delun bowed and entered, Taio motioned for him to take a place across the table.

Delun kneeled and Taio poured him a cup of tea. Delun's eyes flicked over the messages, but he refused to read them. Their contents were for Taio, who would tell him what he needed to know.

"How long did the fight last?" the abbot asked.

"Not long."

"Your thoughts?"

"He needs experience." How many times had Delun said those very words in this room? Almost a dozen monks had gone through their unofficial rites with Delun, and almost every time Delun's answer was the same. The monks didn't lack for strength or dedication, but until they spent more time out in the world, traveling and adapting to situations, training alone would never suffice.

Taio nodded, accepting the advice as he always did. For a moment, Delun wondered if Taio would ask more questions about the trainee. Instead, the abbot slid a note across his desk to Delun, spinning it so Delun could read it. Delun took in the information with a glance. His eyes wandered back to the abbot. "How certain are you of the information?"

"As much as I can be. The source has proven trustworthy in the past, and the information matches my own thinking. The west is a hotbed of seditious activity, which makes it ideal for rebellious ideologies to take root."

Delun didn't need to ask what his task would be. It was always some variation of the same theme, and he was given a wide latitude to handle situations as he saw fit. He was the best at what he did.

"You'll leave in the morning. I'm coordinating fresh horses for you along the entire route."

Delun's eyebrows raised in surprise. He currently sat on the opposite end of the empire. The fresh horses would make the trip several times faster, especially if there was a carriage. But the expense was considerable, to say the least.

The abbot answered the unspoken question. "The Golden Leaf is perhaps the greatest threat I can foresee to monastic stability. If this tip is accurate, you might be able to cut the head off the snake. It's worth the cost." Taio gave a slight smile. "But I can't afford to bring you home the same way."

Delun nodded. The way he saw it, his role in life was straightforward. He owed Taio his life and more, and he'd gladly follow the abbot's orders, no matter the risk. If Taio wanted something done, Delun would see it through. There was never any point in questioning the abbot.

"Is there anything else I should know?"

Taio thought for a moment. "I've been hearing rumors of this Golden Leaf for years now. It's been hard to separate fact from story, but the sheer prevalence of rumors worries me. I know you will be, but remain vigilant. If half of what I've heard of them is true, they may be far more organized and dangerous than any group you've encountered before."

The abbot handed over a sealed note. "This orders any monastery to provide whatever aid you require. It will be obeyed."

Delun took the note, folding it neatly into his robes. He was about to stand when he saw a flicker of doubt cross over the abbot's face. He'd known Taio too long to let that pass without remark. "What?"

Taio hesitated for a moment before answering. "It might be nothing. But there are other rumors from the west, coming from high up in the mountains where no law reaches. I suspect someone lives up there, someone even you don't want to tangle with. I don't know if his presence and the Golden Leaf are related, but I would be very afraid if they were."

Delun's curiosity was piqued. Who would be so strong as to concern Taio? The abbot knew well Delun's skill and strength. "Who?"

Taio shook his head, unwilling to say more. "A ghost of the past."

3

The voices circled around Bai, close enough now that she could make out their words.

"Did you find someone?"

"No survivors here."

"Search that building. Move closer to the square."

The voices all sounded low and gravelly. Buried in her small cave, Bai couldn't decide if they were distraught or calm. The men, whoever they were, kept their voices even. She pushed herself deeper into the shadows, a sharp point digging into her back. She welcomed the pain, so long as it kept her out of sight of the men searching the area. Her fingers squeezed tightly at the bracelet like a scared child clutching onto their parent.

At first, Bai hoped the men would move on quickly. Once gone, she could decide her next steps. She had no money, but her skill as a seamstress was known in town. There would be work for her. Would someone shelter her, at least until she could purchase a house? She had no answers to any of her questions. Her mother had always been the one to worry about such things.

There were kind people in Galan, though. Some gave her mom more money than the work required. The baker sometimes let them take a loaf without paying. Bai forced herself to hope.

Her town would help her.

The voices drew closer, and the memory of her mother's calming guidance came back to her, the same advice Bai had heard her whole life. "Never let them see you, my dear. Attract no attention and you'll come to no harm."

The repeated thoughts of her mother brought tears to Bai's eyes. As thirsty as she felt, she was surprised she could cry. Her last memory of her mother would always be that arm, sticking out of the rubble, cold and lifeless. She choked back a sob, breathing in a cloud of dust.

Her reaction was immediate and uncontrollable. She coughed, then immediately covered her mouth, gripping so tightly nothing could escape. She cursed to herself, hoping against hope she hadn't been heard.

"Over here! I thought I heard someone!"

Footsteps approached. Bai considered showing herself, but her mother's advice made too much sense. She had no guarantee these were villagers here to help. The men could be here to finish the destruction they had started. She could feign death, or at least unconsciousness. Perhaps that would be enough for them to leave her alone.

She closed her eyes and stilled her breathing, her tired lungs burning with the need for more air. Dust tickled the back of her throat. If only she could cough one more time, she could clear the tickle, but she didn't dare. The men were already too close.

A single man stopped in front of her hiding place. From the sounds he made, Bai guessed that he had spotted her. She held her breath and willed herself to perfect stillness.

Though her eyelids were closed, she could detect the light of the lamp as it was held close to her. She couldn't hold her breath any longer, and finally had to exhale and inhale. She made the actions as slow as possible, but her efforts were doomed to failure.

The loud voice in front of her almost made her jump. "I found someone!"

Bai figured she had no choice but to continue her ruse. If they were villagers here to help, they would help regardless of her condition. If the men meant harm, perhaps her feigned unconsciousness would keep her safe.

She wanted to open her eyes to see if she recognized anyone. Recognition meant safety. But she didn't dare.

Voices called back and forth, the men spreading news of a survivor. Before long, Bai guessed that there were at least five men in front of her hole. They discussed among themselves whether it made sense to pull her out, or if it might cause more harm.

Eventually the harsh voices were joined by one a softer one. Bai kept her eyes closed and her breathing as slow and steady as possible. She heard the sounds of feet shuffling and then a new presence knelt down in front of her. She couldn't put the words to her feelings, but somehow she knew this man wasn't like the rest. His presence was lighter.

Gentle fingers prodded around her ribs and felt along her neck. Bai almost tensed up at the touch, just barely managing to keep her reaction under control. It had been years since any man had touched her. Her mother said that men were just another opportunity to court trouble they couldn't afford.

Bai assumed the man was a doctor. After a few moments of silently examining her, he told the men it would be fine to move her. Several strong, firm hands wrapped themselves around her arms and legs and pulled her gently out of the hole.

Bai was almost convinced, but decided to play out the ruse. Her heart beat lightly in her chest. No doubt, these were villagers.

She would be safe.

She was laid softly on flat ground and she heard the doctor's voice calling for space. She sensed the man kneel down next to her, that same gentle presence again. Soon, the unmistakable pungent scent of smelling salts came wafting through her nostrils. No matter how strong her control might have been, there was nothing she could have done in the face of such an odor.

Bai coughed and opened her eyes, tears trickling down her face from the force of the aroma. She blinked rapidly, not needing to fake her disorientation.

She got her first glance at the men. Almost immediately she recognized some of them from around town. She had made the robes several of them now wore. The looks on their faces ranged from confusion to fear, hatred, and sorrow.

Of course, the disaster had affected them all. She wasn't the only one who had lost a loved one. Their town wasn't that large, and everyone would have known at least one of the lost. She saw the storm of her own emotions reflected on the faces of those who stared at her.

Another man entered the circle, younger than many. "I don't think there are any other survivors."

Looks passed between the men, about her. Bai felt her heart pounding faster. What did it mean that she was the only one who had survived? More people stared at her severely.

She understood, intuiting the feelings none of them

dared speak aloud. She'd always understood people, sometimes better than they seemed to understand themselves. They hated her for surviving. Hated her for being the one who still drew breath when those they cared for no longer did. She hoped they would treat her kindly enough, but nothing she could do would diminish that hate.

Only time would allow it to fade.

Bai looked for one friendly face, someone she could connect with, someone who might shelter her. She had never known many of the townspeople as more than acquaintances or clients. Her days were spent indoors, hidden from the world, buried deep in the work her mother gave her. She wasn't invited to meals, had no childhood friends to lean on. It had always been her and her mother.

Now it was just her. She started to cry again.

A hand gently squeezed her shoulder, and Bai realized that the doctor had been speaking to her. "I'm sorry, girl, but what is the last thing you remember?"

Bai thought of her mother, sending her out for errands that morning. "Mother. She wanted me to pick up fabric at the market."

More looks passed between the men in the circle around her. Even the doctor looked disappointed. She didn't have the answers they sought. "Are you sure you don't remember more?"

Bai squeezed her eyes shut, trying to remember, the same door as before blocking her memories. "I think there were some boys playing ball in the square."

Off to the side, a man listening suddenly broke down in tears, his neighbors extending comforting arms around him.

The doctor nodded, as though Bai had said something important. She didn't think she had, though. "Can you stand? I'll take you someplace where you can rest. Your memories will return in time."

Bai, with the help of several men, got to her feet. She leaned against one of her rescuers, grateful for the sturdy support. She felt as though she would collapse again if left on her own. Even her eyelids felt heavy. Though she didn't dare confess her worry to the doctor, she feared she wasn't well.

The doctor led the way as they left the market. The going was slow, the men struggling to support Bai's unsteady weight as they moved across the rubble. Eventually, shattered houses and collapsed roofs gave way to unbroken road, and their pace increased.

Though the streets looked familiar, Bai couldn't say where they were going. Her mind felt so tired, and all she could think about was finding a place to lay her head, to rest as long as needed. Before long they were in front of a big, squat building. Some part of her recognized it, knowing she had seen it before, but she couldn't place it. She was brought into the building and into a small room, complete with a bed and bedpan.

The room was warm, and as the doctor sat her down on the bed, one of the men that had escorted them left and came back with food and drink. Bai gulped at the water greedily, the water soothing her scratchy throat, but found that she couldn't eat much food. The doctor watched everything she did with a curious eye.

Soon they were joined by another man. Bai recognized him, though it took her a few moments to place his face. It was the elder of their town.

The title was a bit of a misnomer, a holdover from when small towns and villages were governed by the oldest living citizen. The man in front of her was not the oldest in town, but had been chosen from among the willing elders to lead the town in important matters. He was well regarded.

The doctor glanced over at the elder, and Bai noticed for the first time the elder's eyes were red-rimmed. "She claims she doesn't remember anything."

The elder glared at her, as though the force of his will would uncover the mystery of what had destroyed the town market. Bai felt guilt lodge itself deep in her stomach, twisting it in knots.

"I'm sorry, sir. I wish that I remembered more, but I don't. I'll keep trying."

The elder gave her a gruff nod, and Bai saw the same hate in his manner that she'd seen from so many of the other men. From the elder, the hate seemed particularly sharp. She guessed he had lost someone particularly important.

The doctor, content with the care he had administered, stood up. "We'll leave the food and water here for you. Let us know if there is anything else you need."

Bai bowed toward the men. They were kind to care for her after the disaster. Kind to give her shelter. Her hope had not been misplaced.

Without another word, they stood and stepped out of the room together, closing the door behind them. Bai heard the sound of wood scraping on wood, the sound not quite registering in her confused state. She looked at the door, perplexed by the iron bars embedded in the thick wood.

She knew where she was.

Terror beating in her heart, she found the strength to stand and walk to the door. She pressed her face against the iron bars just in time to see the men turn the corner and move out of sight. She pushed against the door, looked for any sort of latch that would open it, but she found nothing.

Gritting her teeth, she planted her shoulder against the door and shoved with all her remaining strength, but the door didn't give at all.

Feeling her strength fail her, Bai returned to the bed.

She'd been betrayed. But why would the village lock her away? She summoned the energy to scream for help.

But her mom's advice echoed in her thoughts. So long as Bai was quiet and obeyed, the men would eventually let her out. Perhaps they were only trying to ensure her safety. She wouldn't anger them by making a scene.

4

Delun grew increasingly certain that he wasn't making his journey to the western edges of the empire alone. He'd already seen two men three times on the road, and thought he'd recognized a third man as well. As he rode in the small carriage, he considered his evidence.

He'd first noticed the men in Two Bridges, the small town directly beneath Delun's monastery. Monks coming and going often attracted attention, but Delun made a habit of noting those whose eyes followed him too closely. He attributed his continued survival to his awareness, noticing threats before they could strike.

In Two Bridges two different men had followed him, switching off between one another so as not to arouse his suspicions. Had they been better at their craft, the technique might have worked. Both of them were amateurs, though. They followed too closely and were too obvious, their gazes always pointed in his direction. Delun wasn't that interesting.

At first, he hadn't paid them much mind. More monks were reporting this type of behavior, and Delun himself had been subjected to it countless times in his travels. There were groups trying to track monks' movements. The trend was worrying, but no specific incident elicited much concern. Delun assumed that once he began his journey west his tails would disappear.

He'd been wrong. He'd already put leagues between Two Bridges and his destination, and he still spotted the men on occasion. As the carriage carried him, Delun considered the implications. He'd been moving without stop for over a day now. Thanks to the carriage, he could sleep while traveling. The conditions were far from ideal, but he'd slept in worse.

Taio had spared no expense to ferry Delun quickly across the empire. More than the abbot's dire warnings, the carriage and fresh horses were perhaps the greatest indicators of how much value the abbot placed on the information he'd received. Normally, he would have been content to let Delun walk.

While Delun slept and rested, the men following him struggled. Delun assumed they didn't have advance knowledge of his route. No one should know the ultimate destination besides Delun and Taio. If the men knew, it seemed unlikely they'd expend the effort to follow him. He almost felt sorry for them. They had ridden through the night and no doubt had to purchase new horses.

He suspected that if he simply continued on he would eventually outride them. They had to be exhausted, and if their funds weren't already depleted, they must be close. Horses were not cheap.

Delun looked down at the copy of the letter he had made in the abbot's study. The letter stated that the seditious organization known as the Golden Leaf was based out of a small city in the west named Kulat. Delun only possessed a passing knowledge of the city. It was one of the larger cities near the western edge of the empire, and its most strategic value was the fact that it was out of the way. There was a larger monastery inside the town and a few smaller ones scattered far and wide around the area.

Beyond the work of the monasteries, Delun assumed the empire wouldn't pay much attention to the area, which made it a reasonable place for an organization like the Golden Leaf to hide. The lord of that region of the empire, Lord Xun, was considered an ambitious man. He was an excellent administrator and had favor in the eyes of the emperor himself. Thoughts of the Golden Leaf, the empire, and the monasteries swirled in his head, the connections not quite solidifying yet.

The question that loomed over all of Delun's thoughts was if the letter and the men following him were connected. Delun didn't believe in coincidence, and it seemed suspicious to attract this amount of attention just as he drew this assignment.

The Golden Leaf had been a rumor for years. Like many other groups that'd popped up over the last decade, they claimed they wanted to burn the monastic system down. They'd never been much of a threat. Delun had his finger on the pulse of all rebellious activity, and he didn't know of any actual attacks the Golden Leaf had committed. But they were unique in that all the attempts to squash the rumors about the organization had resulted in failure. At times, Delun had almost dismissed the group entirely, but the persistence of the whispers indicated some truth the monasteries hadn't yet ferreted out.

Delun folded the letter. The only way to answer his questions was to ask them directly. He glanced out the window. At the moment, the road behind him was clear.

That wasn't too surprising. The reason Delun had noticed the tails in the first place was when he'd asked the carriage to stop and the pursuers had accidentally ridden too close. They had played their parts well, giving Delun a short bow as they passed, seemingly uninterested in him. But they were the same men from Two Bridges.

The sun was setting, and the outlines of a plan formed in Delun's mind. He leaned out of the carriage. "Let's stop for the night at the next village that has a decent inn."

The driver looked hesitant, the order contradicting his command to ferry Delun with all possible haste. But he accepted the change. Few openly questioned the request of a monk. Delun figured he could sacrifice one night of travel to learn more of the men who followed him.

The carriage came to a stop outside of a small inn located near the heart of a town. Delun rented a room for the night, ensuring it possessed a window that looked out on the streets. Before long he was perched next to the window, his room dark, watching the few people below. The town was quiet tonight, the road nearly empty. It made the gathering of the three men in the alley across from the inn all the more suspicious.

Delun stole out of his room, exiting the inn near the rear where the stables were. From there he made a wide circle until he was behind the men, on the other end of the alley from them. He stood behind a corner, listening to their conversation with ease.

He was convinced these men knew little about their craft. They'd made no effort to encircle the inn, nor had they placed anyone in the common room to mark his comings and goings. The final fact that damned them was that they spoke normally in the alley, making them painfully easy to eavesdrop on. Delun was almost disappointed by the lack of challenge they presented.

"Wherever he's going, I suspect he will continue to have fresh horses. We can only keep up with him for another day or two before we run out of money." Delun marked the speaker as the tallest of the three. He spoke with an air of authority.

"What should we do?" asked another, small and thin.

The tall man didn't answer for a moment. "We'll follow as best we can. When we can't any longer, we'll send a bird with everything we know."

The third man, who appeared to be the muscle of the group, spoke softer than the rest. "We could kill him."

"You want to try your skills against this one?" asked the tall man, clearly incredulous.

The small man chimed in. "Of course he does. That monk has it coming to him, after all he's done."

Delun frowned. So they weren't just following him because he had left the monastery. They knew who he was.

The tall man calmed the other two. "Perhaps it might come to that, but I do not think he is as easy a target as you think."

The third man's response was almost instant. "A knife across a sleeping man's throat kills a monk just the same as a farmer."

Before, Delun had debated the best course of action. Now, he had no question. These men weren't just following him, they spoke like practiced criminals, men seriously contemplating the killing of a monk. They had sentenced themselves to death with their own words. His duty, as one who upheld justice in the empire, was clear.

Delun stepped from around the corner, making his

movement sudden enough that it would draw their attention.

The tall man cursed and the other two turned around to see what had alarmed their leader.

Delun savored the looks of fear on their faces. For all their bravado a moment ago, when real danger appeared, they knew how little weight their words carried.

He had expected the third one to strike first. Of the three, he seemed the most eager for violent resolution. The monk arched an eyebrow in surprise when it was the small one who darted at him, daggers appearing in his hands as if by magic.

Delun stepped back to avoid a slashing cut aimed at his face, then stopped and grabbed the man's second arm as he stabbed at Delun. He executed a quick reversal, jamming the dagger into the man's own shoulder. The small man's eyes widened with pain and Delun shoved him down.

Delun didn't have time to finish the kill. The third man slashed at Delun with a sword, forcing him to back up again. The alley just wasn't wide enough for him to move the directions he wanted. Delun saw the way the man stumbled forward, the power of the strike pulling him off-balance. The man might be a murderer, but he certainly wasn't a trained warrior. He handled the blade like a man who only knew the pointy end was supposed to go in the opponent. There was no grace or style to his movements.

The small man was getting to his feet, though. Soon it would be two against one, and Delun didn't need that complication. He waited for the swordsman to swing again, then stepped easily inside the man's guard and chopped viciously at the man's throat. His quick strike was true, and the man dropped his sword as he gasped for air. Delun threw an elbow into the man's face and borrowed the sword.

With a blade in his hand, he slapped aside the small man's incoming dagger and stabbed him through the heart. The man never had a chance. Like his burly companion, he lacked the training necessary to be a threat. The third man rolled on the ground, trying desperately to find air. Delun drove the sword through the man's chest and into the dirt below, putting an end to his struggles.

Delun turned to see the tall man standing at the mouth of the alley, his sword drawn, but his body frozen. It seemed he had lost his courage. That was a shame. From his stance, Delun could tell the man had received more training than the other two combined. If they had all attacked together, Delun might have had a real fight on his hands.

Hate glowed in the man's eyes, and Delun figured it would only be a moment before anger overwhelmed fear. He'd seen the same reactions often enough.

His hands held behind him, Delun made the first sign for an attack, feeling the energy build up near his hand. He would have preferred to use only his bare hands, but something in the man's stance persuaded him preparation might be worthwhile.

The tall man darted forward, his body balanced over his feet at all times. He led with a series of thrusts. In the alley, against an unarmed opponent, the technique was excellent. The man never lost his balance, never gave Delun an opening to attack. The sharp steel of the blade cut the air between them, creating an impassable barrier. Delun retreated a few steps before deciding he wouldn't win this exchange without his gift.

Changing his tactics, he formed the second sign and held his hand out in front of him.

The tall man stopped attacking the moment he realized what he was looking at.

Delun released the attack, the wave of energy crashing over the other man, sending him tumbling back several paces. To the man's credit, though, he hung on to his sword.

The tall man struggled to his feet, but Delun had no intention of allowing him a chance to regain his balance. Honorable combat was a lie. Victory or defeat was all that mattered. He stepped up close to the man, and before he could swing his sword Delun had thrown him down the alley again.

The man fought his way to his feet as Delun approached. This time the man swung wildly, but Delun was prepared. He blocked the strike with a quick one-handed shield, using the sign of the first attack to focus his energy in his other hand and release it.

The tall man slammed into the wall of the alley. This time, though, Delun didn't release the attack. He kept the pressure on the man, rendering him immobile against the wall. Maintaining the attack, Delun reached out with his free hand and wrested the sword from the man's grip. With careful precision, he drove the sword through the man's shoulder and into the wall behind him, pinning him there.

The man gritted his teeth in agony but refused to scream. Delun didn't mind. Less attention usually made this sort of work easier. He released his attack, satisfied when the man's weight settled on the sword. Delun walked down the alley and found the small man's clean dagger. Short blade in hand, he turned back to the tall man.

"Now," he said, "I have some questions for you."

5

Bai didn't feel well. Her skin felt clammy to the touch and she couldn't stop shivering, even though she didn't think it was that cold in her cell. She had lost all track of time inside the dark, windowless room, but when she'd woken up for the third time, it had been to someone dumping a bucket of cold water on her. They hadn't asked any questions. They'd just poured the bucket out, making sure every drop fell on her, then left without another word. Since then, she'd felt her health slip away.

To fight the growing panic, she imagined the blossoming spring outside. The end of winter was always one of her favorite times of year, with small green plants budding through freshly thawed ground. If she focused, she could almost make herself believe she was there. She could almost feel the heat of the sun on her skin.

Almost.

A grating sound from outside the door spiked her heart rate. The fear, beating hard in her chest, caused her limbs to tingle with terrible expectation. When the door to the cells didn't open, she breathed a long, slow sigh of relief.

Her days in the cell had not been pleasant. At first they had asked her questions. They all had so many, but she had no answers. Though she was certain days had passed, her memories hadn't returned. She still remembered her mother sending her to the market, and she was convinced she remembered a group of boys playing catch.

After that she knew only blackness and the terror of waking up in the ruined square. She couldn't explain why she alone had survived, and without so much as a cut. At times, she desired the truth as much as those who questioned her. She told herself she wanted to know what happened. She wanted to know what killed her mother.

The accusations leveled against her were horrible. Bai knew from their questions that they believed she had been working with a monk. Their ruthless logic was clear. Only a monk possessed the power to destroy so much of the town. If she had been left alive, it meant she had been involved.

She refused to believe them. She hated the monks as much as anyone in her village. They took food and money and provided little in return. They were little more than thugs with the backing of the empire. The nearest monastery was several days away, in the town of Kulat. If a monk did make it all the way to Galan, it was only to procure supplies. They didn't keep the roads and towns clear of crime, and they rarely offered aid. The idea that she would work with one of *them* made her stomach queasy.

And yet, she didn't have a better answer. The only other explanation she could think of was luck, and the rest of her life disproved that idea easily enough. Luck had never been her companion.

At times, when she had the strength to face the truth, she admitted that some core part of her was okay without knowing what had happened. She couldn't imagine a reason for being alive that didn't terrify her. Perhaps it would be easiest to let the truth hide in the unreachable blackness of her memory.

Her ruminations ended abruptly when she heard the heavy key in the door that led to the cells. As far as she knew, she was the only prisoner, and the thick walls meant no sound other than her own breathing echoed in the hall. The sound of the key, soft as it probably was, sounded like thunder to her ears.

The door opened and daylight speared into the hallway. She closed her eyes against the brightness and scrambled back into the corner of her cell. If it was daytime, it meant that Wen was probably on duty.

Her heart thudded in her chest and she looked desperately around the room for something to defend herself with. The reaction was instinctive but futile. She closed her eyes again, curling into a tiny ball, hoping that maybe this time it would be enough to cause him to lose interest.

Bai heard his footsteps, slow and ponderous, and she knew her cause was hopeless. They stopped, right outside her cell door. She cracked one eye, keeping the slit narrow enough that hopefully he wouldn't notice.

Her breath caught in her throat, even though she knew what she'd see.

Wen stood there, his face still a mask of cold rage as he stared in at her.

Bai didn't know how long the stare lasted. She refused to look, knowing what she would find and not wanting to offer any encouragement. She held her knees tightly to her chest, hoping that this time he would go away.

Her body tensed up uncontrollably when she heard him lift the bar that blocked the door to her own cell. She wanted to cry, but tears refused to come. Tears would only make him more angry.

Bai knew Wen's sister had lived near the market square. She had died that day. Wen had volunteered to help watch Bai in prison.

She forced herself to look up. He hated it when she cowered, and sometimes it made what came next worse. He held a tray of food in his hands, a simple bowl of rice with a few vegetables. Her stomach growled. How long had it been since they'd brought her food? From the pain in her belly, she guessed at least a day or two.

"Hungry?" Wen asked. His voice was surprisingly gentle.

Had something happened? Had they figured out who caused the disaster in the market? For the space of a heartbeat, she dared to hope.

Bai nodded quickly. Wen smiled and grabbed the bowl from the tray, extending it in her direction.

She reached for it, uncurling from the corner.

Wen's smile never faltered.

He turned the bowl upside down and dumped the rice on the dirt floor of her cell.

For a long moment, nothing happened. Bai fought the tears that threatened to fall. The food was so close she could smell it.

"Aren't you going to eat?" Wen asked.

A sinking feeling of dread came over her.

"If you don't want the food, I can get a broom and sweep it away. But I thought you were hungry."

Wen's voice sounded understanding, caring almost. Every word cut as sharply as a blade.

Wen nodded, as though this was what he'd expected. "Fine." He turned to leave.

Bai, suddenly certain that if she didn't eat now, she

wouldn't for another day or two, scrambled forward on hands and knees and started picking the rice up from the ground and putting it in her mouth. She tried not to think about what she did.

Wen towered above her, chuckling. Bai tried to ignore him, pretended as though he wasn't there.

He made that difficult when he started pouring cold water on her back. "Figured you might be thirsty, too."

She'd eaten several handfuls of rice when he delivered a powerful kick to her side. She went tumbling across the small cell, thunking into the sturdy stone walls. She groaned, trying to keep down the little food she'd eaten.

Wen stepped toward her and lifted her chin in his hands. He stared at her, cold and implacable as a frozen mountain lake in the dead of winter. "You know what? *Everyone* wants to know what's in your head. We've received word from both the monastery and Lord Xun. Each is sending someone to talk to you. Lord Xun, in particular, was certain that the man he's sending would get answers out of you. In fact, he ensured it."

Bai hadn't thought it was possible for her to dread her future more. She'd heard rumors of Lord Xun's questioners, same as anyone else. They were said to be the very best at what they did. The idea of one of them coming here to visit her turned her insides to ice.

But the monks were still worse.

Wen drew a knife out of his belt. It wasn't big, but the edge looked honed to a fine point. He held it up close to her face. "You know, I was thinking of killing you myself. The elder is insisting that we care for you until we find out the truth of what happened, but I think he's wrong. I think you know, and you're not telling us."

He flashed the knife in front of her, causing her to flinch

back, but his hand held her face immobile. He let her get a good look at the edge before putting it away. She almost wished he hadn't. The knife held a promise she now desired.

"I want you to stay alive until they get here." Wen stood up. "So eat up. You're going to need your strength."

He took one step back, and for a moment Bai thought he was going to turn to leave. Instead, he stepped forward and launched another kick into her stomach, doubling her over and leaving her gasping for breath.

She heard her cell door shut and the wooden beam settle in front of the door. A candle had been left outside the door, casting the barest shadow of light into the cell.

Slowly the pain subsided and Bai crawled to the rice, picking it off the floor and eating it.

AGAIN, she didn't know how much time had passed. She could feel the bruising from where Wen's kicks had landed, and the rice had done little to sate her appetite. Since Wen's last visit, she'd wondered if she should try killing herself.

She had no desire to die, but the future promised nothing but agony. A monk and a questioner? Either would mark the end of her life as she knew it. For days now she had held out the hope that if she simply didn't cause a problem, they would let her go and she could find a way to move on.

That idea sounded naive now. She had no future and no desire to suffer. Her mother, the only person who had cared for her, was gone.

Why fight?

She couldn't answer the question, but she couldn't bring herself to plan her own end, either. Some spark refused to give in, even though doing so made the most sense.

Bai sat on her bed, occasionally shaking as another chill ran through her body. With little food and drink, perhaps the decision wouldn't be hers to make.

Suddenly, the stillness of her contemplation was interrupted by a quick series of scuffling sounds from outside the door to the cells. Bai instantly became alert. The sounds had only lasted a second or two, then silence once again descended on her ears.

Then she heard the unmistakable sound of the key in the lock. After her time in confinement, she'd come to recognize the ways people turned keys. The elder fumbled a bit, his age and poor eyesight causing him to miss the lock once or twice before he got the key in. Wen snapped the lock open as though he had won a fight against it. The man who watched her in the evening also opened the lock quickly, but not with the same force as Wen.

This sound was unlike the others. The bolt slid slowly, so softly that Bai almost wasn't sure the lock was turning. But the sound of the door opening was unmistakable. Someone was entering the prison, someone Bai didn't think she knew.

A sliver of moonlight poured through the open door, barely illuminating the passageway. If Bai's eyes hadn't already been so used to the darkness, she didn't think she would have noticed the light. A shadow crept into the hallway with a smooth and easy grace.

Bai pressed herself to the small window in the door, staring out for any clue as to who was there. Then the shadow approached the door and Bai realized the person outside might not be friendly. She scrambled back to her corner again, huddling down as deep into the shadows as she could.

The shadow, whoever it was, crept down the hallway.

They seemed to be checking every cell, and Bai's stomach twisted into knots. Eventually, the shadow stopped in front of her cell. Despite Bai's attempts to hide, she knew she'd been spotted. But old habits died hard. She cowered in the corner as the intruder lifted the bar off the door and opened her cell.

Bai looked up, confused by the sight in front of her. A woman's silhouette stood tall in the doorway.

"Bai?"

Bai nodded, then realized the movement might not be visible in the darkness. "Yes?"

"My name is Hien. Care to get out of here?"

Unknown futures danced in front of Bai. Instincts long embedded told her to stay, to wait out the storm. But a part of her knew that was foolish. If she remained, she had no future.

She stood up and followed the stranger into the night.

6

Delun detested mystery. He accepted the fact that much of life was outside his control. No matter how much he might wish differently, he knew he couldn't make people act the way he believed they should. He could intimidate them for a time, or coerce them in other ways, but given enough time they would eventually return to the behaviors of their past. People were always resistant to change.

But while he could live with a lack of control, lack of knowledge itched at him like a tick burrowing under his skin. Delun believed that everything was knowable. While there were plenty of mysteries in the world, he believed they would all someday be solved and that the people of the empire would live in a state of perfect knowledge.

It made his current lack of information all the more frustrating. Several days had passed since he had stopped for the night to interrogate the leader of the men following him. He'd put more leagues behind him than he cared to count, the unfamiliar scenery of the western lands hiding the answers he sought. Despite the measures he had resorted to, he still knew far less than he desired.

The tall man, although willing, hadn't had many answers. Flashes of memory sometimes troubled him, the actions he had taken with the knife unforgettable, and perhaps unforgivable. Sometimes, to maintain justice, one had to embrace the darkness that lived inside. Delun had struggled and made his peace with that fact long ago. He had used the borrowed dagger to great effect, and by the time he was finished, he was certain the man had divulged everything. In exchange, Delun had granted the tall man the final quick release he desired.

Unfortunately, the sacrifice had been for little gain.

The group following him had been common criminals from Two Bridges. One drunken night at the Old Goat, a seedy tavern near the edge of town, the men had been approached by a beautiful woman. They started talking and the group realized they shared one trait in common: a deep distrust of the monasteries.

They'd been given Delun's description and more money than any of them had ever seen at one time in their lives. Their instructions had been simple: follow him and report on his movements. Some of the money was theirs to keep, but the rest was for expenses. They were to send birds to Kulat as often as possible, the messages marked with the symbol for "truth." They were promised more money within the month.

Of course the men had taken the work. Their story, such as it was, ended there. The man had heard of the Golden Leaf, but knew nothing more than the organization's name and reputation. Delun had pressed those questions, but when it was over, he was certain the man had told the truth. His tails had been hired help and nothing more.

He only had gathered two useful pieces of information. The first was that whoever had hired the criminals knew Delun, at least by reputation. They had spared little expense to have him watched. Why? The second piece of information was that some of his answers sat hidden in Kulat. Delun had considered several deceptions, knowing that whoever was watching him was expecting messenger birds. Unfortunately, each deception added more complications than necessary. When he reached Kulat, perhaps he could use the information to his advantage, but until then, it was just another brush stroke in a painting he didn't comprehend yet.

Delun pushed his thoughts aside as he looked out over the majestic landscape revealing itself before him. He'd been lost in his thoughts for days now, his mind having little to occupy it within the cramped confines of the carriage. He'd been on the road almost nonstop since his confrontation, pausing only for the occasional needs of the body. Not only had Taio wished for all possible speed, Delun had an instinctive feeling about this assignment. This one mattered, more than they usually did.

They had rumbled through a great forest for the past several days, riding between enormous trees that towered over the carriage and blocked the sun like giants of legend. The air had the deep earthy scent of pine, tinged with a sweetness that permeated the carriage and his thoughts. The smell was almost enough to relax the tension in Delun's back. Delun hated the forest, hated having his line of sight constantly interrupted. Reasonably, there was little chance of being attacked, but his caution never wavered.

The thick forest began to thin as they traveled farther west. Those trees that still blocked his view were younger than the ones near the center of the wood, the forest slowly conquering more territory inside the empire, growing ever larger. The western edges of the empire, so far removed from Jihan, were far less populated. When he could get an uninterrupted view of the landscape, Delun saw range and farmland as far as his eye could see. Cows and sheep roamed in herds, and more than once Delun smelled the pungent aroma of droppings where the herd had come close to the road.

This place wasn't for him. He felt at home in the monastery above Two Bridges, high in the thin air of the mountains. He didn't care for the lowlands, filled with people and activity. Fortunately, he could just make out the tops of the mountains far to the west, only a day or two beyond his destination. Those were the mountains that scared even Taio. Perhaps, someday, Delun would carry his work into those high passes.

They had just passed an intersection for another road heading north when a surprising sensation struck Delun. There was another monk nearby, off the road. Someone nearly as strong as he was.

Delun imagined a map of this region of the empire. He'd committed several to memory before leaving his monastery. He suspected, though he hadn't seen a sign, that the road they'd just passed led towards Galan, one of the last small towns before truly reaching the edges of the empire. If his position was accurate, there was no monastery nearby, no reason for a monk to be off the road.

There were no coincidences.

Delun leaned his head out of the carriage and asked for the driver to stop. A few moments later Delun stepped out, stretching as he allowed his senses to take in the surrounding area.

The road here, as it had been for the past several days,

was quiet. Tall grass surrounded him, coming up almost to his chest in places. Bugs, newly hatched in the warmth of spring weather, flew around him in patterns beyond his comprehension. He could smell the horses pulling the carriage and the scent of his own body, locked in the carriage for days. A bath would be one of his first responsibilities once he reached Kulat.

Delun glanced at the driver and ordered him to wait. He didn't expect violence, but it was always best to be prepared, so far as he was concerned.

The presence off the road was as strong as ever. A monk with that strength would have a difficult time hiding from other gifted warriors. Delun knew the problem firsthand.

There was little point in subtlety. Delun could feel the other monk, and he had no doubt the other monk could feel him. Delun backtracked a few hundred paces down the road, away from the carriage. Then he stopped and waited for the other monk to show himself.

It only took a minute. Delun raised one eyebrow in surprise when he saw the man. He wasn't sure he had ever seen a monk who looked quite as intimidating as this one. The man stood at least a head taller than Delun and appeared to be almost as wide as the road. Yet there wasn't the slightest amount of fat on the man. He looked as though he ate leather for breakfast.

Appearances weren't everything, though Delun appreciated the man's clear discipline. One didn't obtain a body like that by chance. Although Delun was fairly certain he would win a duel, it wasn't a risk he felt like taking. He gave the monk a short bow. "My name is Delun." He paused, but when there was no response, he continued, "It's a pleasure to meet you."

The other man squinted at Delun, clearly deciding

whether or not he was a threat. That, in itself, was an interesting piece of information. Monks didn't fight with one another, at least not in any way that mattered.

The man shifted, and Delun saw that the man's left hand was holding a second sign of shielding. The other monk was expecting him to fight, but why? Delun kept his hands at his sides, his palms open toward the man. He prepared no attack.

If it came to a fight, Delun would be outmatched, at least for the first precious seconds. It would take him a few moments to collect his strength, moments that might mean the difference between victory and death. But he refused to fight another monk unless he had good reason. Why didn't this monk feel the same?

The tense moments ticked away, and eventually the other monk reached a decision. He didn't release his sign, but he bowed in return. "My name is Kang. I do not recognize you."

"I'm from the monastery above Two Bridges."

A flash of recognition crossed over Kang's face. Everyone had heard of the monastery above Two Bridges. Most monks held their brothers in Two Bridges somewhere between awe and fear. The man pondered the information for a few moments. "Are you here because of what happened in Galan?"

Now it was Delun's turn to be silent. Galan? He hadn't heard a thing about Galan in his travels. If not for committing the maps to memory, he was pretty certain he wouldn't have ever heard of the small town. Of course, if something had happened and word was spreading, Delun wouldn't have known. He'd spent his last days practically locked in a carriage. He shook his head. "I'm not. What happened?"

Delun could see the question on Kang's lips. If Delun wasn't here because of Galan, why was he here? But few monks questioned the actions of the monastery above Two Bridges. "We're not sure. There are rumors that a monk destroyed the town market and the area surrounding it. Citizens are angry and blaming the monasteries. My abbot believes that the rebels who hide up in the mountains are responsible. He sent me to investigate and attempt to calm the town."

Delun measured the man again, wondering if anything about him could be considered calming. He spoke well and his eyes were sharp. This man wasn't just strong, he was thoughtful as well. Now, he understood why Kang had been off the road. If the rumors were true, not all monks could be trusted. Delun pitied any rebel monk who tried to stand against Kang. No doubt that was the true reason the man had been chosen. Delun wouldn't have been surprised to find that Kang was the strongest monk in the entire western empire.

On the other hand, the damage described by Kang was impressive. Delun thought he *might* be able to duplicate such a feat, but it would take everything he had. If the rumors were true, the implications were considerable.

Delun glanced at his carriage, waiting patiently to carry him to Kulat. Then he looked at Kang, on the hunt for the solution to a new mystery.

There were no coincidences. If the Golden Leaf was active in this area, could they have staged the attack to place the blame on monks? The idea sounded outlandish at first, but there seemed no reason why it couldn't be possible.

Delun gave a hint of a grin. "Would you have any interest in working together? I think that if we were to combine our abilities, we might get to the bottom of this problem faster."

Kang finally released his shield. In the same way Delun had judged him, the monk seemed to be taking the measure of Delun. Finally, he nodded. "Will you kill whoever is responsible?"

Delun didn't even hesitate.

"Gladly."

7

B ai woke up warm and content. The air smelled fresh and sweet, filled with the scent of pine trees in spring. The contentment lasted only a moment before her body was wracked with a coughing fit that bent her in half. Her stomach hurt when she coughed, and her memory returned to her, splashing over her like familiar buckets of cold water.

She remembered being imprisoned within the town's cells, being beaten and threatened by Wen. For a second, panic pressed against her chest, challenging her breath, but it passed as she bolted upright and took in her surroundings.

Bai wasn't in the cells anymore. Instead of tight walls, she now had endless space. Tall evergreens surrounded her, and the sounds of birds chirping settled her fears. She had been rescued.

An old, dented metal cup was held out toward her. Steam curled around the edges, and Bai reached for it gratefully.

"Careful, it's warm."

Bai paused for a second, then grabbed the cup by its lip.

Gingerly, she pressed one of her hands against the bottom of the cup, feeling the warmth of it seep into her hand. She wasn't sure she'd ever welcomed a sensation so eagerly. She wrapped both her hands around the worn metal and brought it close to her chest, as though the cup could warm her entire body. She took a sip, the tea grassy and fragrant. "Thank you."

The woman next to her nodded. Her name returned to Bai.

Hien.

Bai had never met a woman like Hien. She wasn't certain very many people had.

From a glance, Hien looked middle-aged. Bai guessed the woman was a little older than her mother, somewhere above forty. But though some of her hairs were beginning to turn silver with age, Bai recognized a predator when she saw one.

Perhaps it was her own history of avoiding confrontation, but she'd developed a sense for people predisposed to violence. It was something in the way their eyes studied the world, the way they held themselves. There were people who weren't afraid to exert their will upon others, with force if necessary.

Most often, those people were richer men. Bai had come across plenty of those, even in her small town. They believed, perhaps rightly, that their money gave them authority. Bai knew to bow meekly and escape their notice as soon as possible.

Hien had something of the same look, but had something more, too. From the way she moved, like a wraith in the night, to the basic fact that she had rescued Bai from a prison with the same attitude that she prepared tea. She radiated strength, and Bai had never met a woman like her.

She'd also never met a woman who carried so many weapons. Back in town, a few of the girls she knew carried small daggers, more as a threat than anything else. Most of them would have dropped the blades at the first sign of trouble. But Hien carried enough steel to supply Kulat's entire city watch. As Bai sipped at her tea, the older woman pulled blade after blade from various hiding places, examining them in what appeared to be a daily routine. Most went back into their hidden sheaths, the motion so smooth Bai almost couldn't follow. Some kissed a whetstone before being returned.

Hien held the blades like mothers held newborn babies. Bai could think of a child or two that received less attention than Hien's steel.

Hien noticed Bai's gaze, focused on the blades as they flashed in and out of the late morning sunlight. "Want one?"

Bai shook her head. Her mother had despised weapons, saying they gave people a sense of power they didn't deserve. Bai figured if she held the daggers she was more of a danger to herself than to anyone else.

Hien shrugged and returned to her routine.

Lost in her own thoughts, Bai remembered the escape from the evening before. Hien had taken her from the cells, and they'd passed the inert form of the night guard. Had Hien killed the man? Bai couldn't recall. She hadn't been paying close enough attention.

Outside of the cells, they had made their way out of town. Hien led the way, always scouting ahead and telling Bai when it was safe to move. Bai couldn't remember much in the way of details. She had just followed. Eventually they had crossed the outskirts of town and reached a wooded area. Hien made Bai an impromptu bed and Bai had fallen asleep almost instantly.

She realized now how much she had taken on trust. Granted, Hien had helped her escape, but Bai didn't even have the slightest clue where she currently was, or where they were going.

Another coughing fit passed over her, violent and sudden. Hien looked over at Bai, a concerned expression on her face. "How are you feeling?"

Bai wanted to say she felt fine. The answer was the expected one, after all. But Hien didn't seem like the type of woman who had much patience for social niceties. "Not well," Bai admitted.

Hien was silent for a moment, then stood up. "You should get some rest. I was planning on moving this afternoon, but perhaps we can afford to wait a while. I'll scout the area, maybe try to catch some more food. Until then, you should eat as much of this as you want." The mysterious woman reached into a large pack Bai was certain she hadn't been carrying the night before and pulled out dried meat, cold rice, and some assorted vegetables.

Bai stared at the feast, her mouth watering at the sight alone. How long had it been since she had seen so much food in one place? With a start, she realized she didn't even know what day it was. She'd lost all track of time in the windowless cells.

"I'll return before too long. Is there anything else you need?"

Bai looked down at the pile of food in front of her. She couldn't think of anything.

Hien gave her a knowing smile. "Don't eat too much, too fast. Your stomach won't be ready for it."

With that, the enigmatic woman was off, slipping through the spaces between the trees without so much as a sound. Bai wondered briefly where the woman was off to, but quickly lost interest as her gaze fell back to the food arrayed in front of her.

She began with the dried meat, the salted beef alone causing her eyes to water with joy. Despite her desire to gorge on everything in sight, she followed Hien's advice, chewing slowly and working her way through the food one mouth-watering bite at a time.

She was surprised when she felt full much sooner than she expected. Looking down at the food, it looked as though she'd barely eaten anything at all. Bai found a water skin near the food, sipping the cold liquid with incredible delight.

Her stomach full, Bai felt an overwhelming exhaustion come over her again. She'd only been awake for an hour at most, but she didn't question the urge. She ducked deeper into her blankets, now warmed by the sun high in the sky, and fell asleep again.

She awoke to a gentle hand on her shoulder. Bai blinked away the sleep from her eyes and saw Hien standing over her.

"Do you think you're good to walk?" Hien asked.

Bai didn't want to get out of the warm blankets, but the tone of Hien's voice told her it was more a request than a question. "I think so."

"Good. Let's get the rest of this packed up and we can get moving."

Bai slid out of the blankets, immediately overcome by longing for the warmth of the covers. It was so cold. Too cold for the season, she thought.

Hien handed her a heavy cloak, which she gratefully accepted.

Bai noticed that the rest of the camp had already been packed. Hien had waited to wake her until they were almost ready to travel. Bai felt grateful. She needed the sleep.

Hien folded and packed away the blankets, then slid the pack onto her back. "Ready?"

Bai suddenly realized she had absolutely no idea what was happening. "Why do we need to leave?"

Hien took off, not answering Bai's question until they were moving. Bai noticed the subtle manipulation. If they were already moving, Bai would be less inclined to stop. Had Hien answered the question first, Bai might have been unwilling to start.

Regardless, Bai didn't know what else to do at the moment besides follow, so she did. Once they were away from the campsite, Hien answered her question. "The villagers are looking for you. I hoped they would search in all directions, giving us some more time. Unfortunately, they've guessed our destination, which means they came closer to us faster than I'd hoped. If we hadn't been so far off the trails, they might have found us. We'll have a bit of a hike in front of us, I'm afraid."

Bai took all this in. She wasn't sure exactly what she wanted, but she knew she didn't want to go back to the cells. Thoughts of her nights there made her think of the man who'd been standing guard when Hien arrived. "Did you kill the man on night watch?"

"No."

Bai bit her lip. She wasn't sure how many more questions Hien would tolerate. Bai also didn't want to upset her. But she did need at least one more answer.

"Where are we going?"

"Up the mountains."

Bai walked a few more steps before realizing the import of Hien's words. That was why she'd been cold. Thoughts tumbled after one another, and a new fear took on sharp edges. Bai stopped in her tracks, not sure she wanted to follow Hien another step.

Hien noticed immediately. The woman's senses were as honed as her steel. Her look wasn't angry, exactly, but Bai could only think about just how dangerous this woman was. The words escaped from her before she could stop them. "You're a rebel."

Hien frowned, as though she'd been insulted. "I live freely, if that's what you mean."

"Why?"

"Why what?"

The questions poured out of Bai now. "Why did you come to save me? Why are you taking me up to the mountains? Why is this happening?"

Hien looked past Bai, as though scanning the trees for enemies. Eventually, her posture relaxed a bit and she dropped into a resting squat. Bai knew it was another trick of perspective. By making herself small, she appeared less threatening. Bai knew it was a trick, but it worked. She stepped closer, almost instinctively, to hear what Hien's answers would be.

The warrior took a deep breath. "I live up in the mountains, with the 'rebels,' as you call them. Perhaps we are that, but we live in peace, just outside the rule of the empire. The man who leads us was a monk a very long time ago."

Hien saw Bai's reaction and extended a hand in a calming gesture. "He's not like any monk you've ever met. I can promise you that. He felt what happened down in Galan and asked for me to scout the area."

Bai got the sense that Hien wasn't telling the full truth, but she let it go for now.

"I reached Galan a few days ago. I saw the damage that was done and heard that they had locked you up because they believed you were involved. There were many stories and rumors, but no facts. Then one night I heard the man named Wen bragging to some of his friends in a tavern about how he was treating you. I decided to break you out."

"Just because you heard Wen bragging in a tavern?"

Hien looked off into the distance, her gaze unfocused. "You could say I've made something of a life out of helping women in difficult situations."

Bai wasn't convinced. People simply didn't act that way.

Hien shrugged, as though she'd experienced exactly the same reaction a dozen times before. "My decision was easy. I believe the man who leads us can help you, no matter what you decide to do."

Bai considered. "I'm free to leave, if I want?"

Hien looked hurt. "Always. If that's your choice, you can take the cloak and whatever food and supplies you can carry." She looked back into the trees they'd come from. "But I would ask that you make your choice quickly. Our pursuit is approaching, and our journey will be difficult if we avoid the well-known trails into the mountains."

Bai couldn't see the pursuit Hien was talking about, but she found she trusted the other woman. She even trusted that she could leave if she wanted.

What did she want?

The question was one she hadn't had to answer often. Her days had always been set by necessity and tradition. Hien would give her the supplies to run wherever she wanted. Bai wasn't naive enough to believe she could return home now, but the empire was vast.

On the other hand, Hien believed that answers lay in the mountains above. Bai had been raised to fear the rebels who lived there. Given Hien's particular set of skills, perhaps such fear wasn't unfounded. But Bai's curiosity was overwhelming. And it was the easiest path. Hien would protect her and guide her.

"Let's go," she said.

8

Delun didn't take long to decide that Kang was less than ideal as a traveling companion. Kang spoke little, and when he did, his sentences were terse, as though speaking were a chore he had no desire to complete. Delun, who'd been stuck alone in a carriage for almost two weeks, craved company that Kang refused to provide.

Fortunately, with the carriage at their disposal, the trip to Galan only took a day. They rented two rooms at the only inn in town, agreeing to begin their investigation the next day. The prices were too cheap to be believed, and Delun didn't miss the fear within the innkeeper's eyes as he passed over their keys.

He thought about sitting down in the common room and listening to local rumors, but seeing the looks that the other patrons gave him when he entered, he decided a more productive route would be to simply get a full night of rest. He'd been able to sleep in the carriage as it carried him overland, but the rest had hardly been pleasant. A night of uninterrupted sleep would do wonders.

He noticed that Kang didn't seem to pay any particular

attention to the sullen stares turned his way. Delun almost asked why, but given the quality of Kang's responses to earlier questions, Delun decided to hold on to his inquiry. He was used to not being loved thanks to his monastic robes, but this open fear and hostility was a degree worse than his usual welcome.

Delun slept soundly, and the next morning he and Kang made their way to the market square. With the village as small as it was, it wasn't hard to find. Kang led the way.

Delun tried to keep his expression neutral, but he couldn't help but widen his eyes when he saw the devastation in front of him. Kang had told him the square and some of the surrounding area had been destroyed, but this was beyond what Delun had imagined.

Two facts were immediately apparent. A strong monk had done this. As Delun stood on the edge of the circle of destruction and looked around, he imagined how much of his own energy something like this would take. He didn't like the answer.

Delun kept his eyes on Kang. The man's expression was also neutral, and Delun had the feeling Kang knew more than he was letting on. He followed the larger man deeper into the devastation.

At first, he'd expected to find damage from multiple attacks. That idea died quickly. All of the buildings had collapsed outward, from a central point that Delun imagined was the market itself. One blast had done this.

He thought of Taio's warning about the rebels up in the mountains. His abbot had been frightened of the power that resided up there, and Delun now thought he knew why. If one man was capable of this, what were the limits of his strength?

The ruins of the market were empty. Delun expected to

see workers clearing the rubble and starting to rebuild, but his expectations were disappointed. Even the untrained knew that the gifted had caused this to happen. The power of the monks, a mystery to most, carried a stigma that took time to overcome.

Delun's memory went back, too far. He remembered another scene of devastation, another place where it had taken years to rebuild.

Jihan.

There, the buildings he had grown up around were left abandoned, in some cases for months. Whether they acknowledged it or not, people didn't want to be anywhere near the places where the gifted had fought.

In time, money had changed minds, as it often did. Jihan continued to grow, even after the battle. Property was too valuable to be wasted, and people eventually overcame their initial reluctance. Buildings were repaired, or torn down and rebuilt completely. Eventually, time erased the damages of the past.

But it had taken substantial time in Jihan, and it might take even longer here. Delun forced himself to the present. Galan was hardly a bustling city. Perhaps this would be the blow that killed the town completely. He could see a future in which one family after another, not wanting to live near the site of the disaster, moved to Kulat.

He sighed. Such problems were not his to worry about. His mission was to find and eliminate the Golden Leaf. If they had anything to do with this disaster, his motivation just became sharper. He wasn't certain, though. In some ways, black powder could duplicate the strength of a monk, but black powder left unmistakable traces. This hadn't been staged as a monk's attack, it had been a monk's attack. Did the Golden Leaf have monks working for them? The idea unsettled him, almost more than the damage itself did.

He picked his way among the ruins, working toward the epicenter of the blast. The destruction of so many of the buildings had been complete. He had expected to see damage, but not like this. The more he saw, the less certain he was that even he could have done something of this magnitude. He grew more and more sure that he was weaker than whoever had caused this. That thought worried him, chipping away at his confidence. Even if he found the guilty party, would he be able to deliver justice to everyone who had died here?

Delun took a deep breath. He closed his eyes for a few seconds, following the movement of his breath and centering himself. When he opened his eyes, he started taking in the scene as an investigator. He would bring some measure of peace to the victims of this tragedy.

Closer examination revealed more information. The extent and nature of the damage meant that this had been an unfocused attack, a pure explosion of energy in its natural form. Most monks increased their power by focusing it, but unless a new technique had been discovered, Delun didn't think that was the case here. The strength required to do this without focusing was beyond considerable. Delun shook his head, refusing to follow that train of thought any further.

He let his eyes wander over the scene, soaking in the details as they came to him. His eye found a patch of green and he frowned, stepping closer.

The patch was near the edge of the market square. Delun wondered at that. If the attack had been intentional, wouldn't the monk have stood directly in the center of the market? He studied the ground with a careful eye. The green patch was a little less than two paces in diameter. All around it, the grass had been stripped from the ground by the power of the blast. This patch, then, was where the attack had come from.

In a perfect world, he would have been the first person here. He could have tracked footprints, at least for a while, in the dirt. As it was, though, at least a few days had passed, if not more. Delun realized he didn't know exactly when the attack had happened. Since then, dozens of people had been through the square, erasing much of the evidence Delun desired.

He looked around, wondering what other information he might find. He wasn't sure what else there was to learn. A monk had done this—a monk of incredible power. Delun would have assumed he would know of a monk of this strength, but apparently that wasn't the case.

Delun was about to speak with Kang, who was also making his rounds of the destroyed market, when he noticed something else. Another patch of undisturbed ground, smaller than the first. The grass would have been easy to miss. It sat in the shade of a building's foundation, barely visible from most of the destroyed market square. Delun approached it and crouched down. The grass here was undisturbed, and the corner of the foundation stood while the rest of the building had crumbled. He frowned.

He stood up and turned to Kang. "What aren't you telling me?"

The monk's look of surprise only lasted for a moment. Kang shrugged, as though the information didn't matter much. "Two of our monks were in town when the incident occurred. Neither of them returned."

Delun wanted to yell at the man, but it would do no good. Monasteries had a long history of holding on tightly to their secrets. Sometimes, when one got used to living behind a veil, the practice became ingrained. Still, it burned at him that Kang hadn't shared the information earlier. The more information Delun had, the more he could uncover.

"Was either of them capable of something like this?"

Kang shook his head. "As far as anyone knew, both were fairly weak."

Delun took in the entire scene again. "I believe one of your monks might have survived." He pointed to the ground he stood next to. "Someone set a shield here."

Kang strode over and confirmed Delun's observation. But it only led to another question: if one of the monks had survived, why hadn't he returned to the monastery?

"Anything else you care to tell me?" Delun asked.

"One of the monks wasn't popular within the monastery. He was considered old and soft by many of us. The other was a young man, filled with promise. There is not much more of them worth noting."

Delun nodded. "I'm not sure there is much left to learn here. Shall we visit the girl?" Kang had spoken of there being a survivor in the wreckage, now kept under lock and key in another part of town. The townsfolk suspected her of being involved with the disaster. If nothing else, perhaps she would be able to give a more detailed description of what had happened here.

Kang agreed, and led the way to the cells.

Once there, they found a commotion. Men were running back and forth, and horses passed by them, galloping too fast to be safe in town.

Kang and Delun shared a glance, and Delun gave Kang a small nod. The man was local to the area and would have better luck getting information. Besides that, he was more intimidating than most. The gathering of men would be far more likely to answer his questions than Delun's.

They stepped forward and Kang took charge. "What's going on here?"

One of the men, older than the rest, stepped forward. Delun assumed he was the elder of the village. "Last night, someone attacked the guard and helped the girl escape. We've been searching the area between here and the mountain. Someone just returned with news. A campsite was found, northwest of town, in the woods. There's no real trail, but it confirms our suspicion. The girl was working with the rebels. I just sent out a group of men to retrieve her."

Kang towered over the elder. "And even though you knew of our arrival, you didn't care to inform the monks of this?"

Delun had to give Kang's intimidation credit. The man cowered beneath Kang's shadow. "I'm sorry. I thought this was something we could handle ourselves. I didn't want to trouble you."

Delun's eyes narrowed as he watched the exchange. There was an undercurrent here he couldn't quite place. Like Kang, he had little doubt the elder of the village knew of their arrival. The presence of monks stirred up a commotion even in cities. Here, it would be all anyone would talk about. And yet the town had hoped to hide the escape from the monks. Why? Lack of trust? The involvement of the Golden Leaf?

There were more mysteries here than answers.

Kang turned to Delun. "Thoughts?"

Delun glanced around at the men. Most of the activity in the area had stopped, every eye turned on the monks.

"It seems to me that any further answers most likely exist with that woman."

The elder interrupted. "Masters, if I might suggest an idea? It looks like the fugitives have taken to difficult parts of the woods. My men know the area. Perhaps we can be of assistance."

Delun and Kang glanced at one another. A look was enough to know they felt the same. Kang turned back to the elder. "You're dealing with powers beyond your comprehension, old man. Tell us where the campsite is, and we'll find that woman."

9

B ai stopped, bent over, and struggled to get air into her lungs. She gasped at the cold mountain air, wondering if she had made the right choice. Was her answer worth this much suffering?

Night had fallen, and had Bai not been hiking up the mountain with little rest, she probably would have felt the chill of the high air seeping into her bones. But they had charged up the mountains since Bai had woken that afternoon. Occasionally Hien permitted a short break, but they were never long enough. The warrior pushed them hard.

Bai willed her legs to move, but they wobbled underneath her. About a dozen paces ahead, Hien looked back and saw that Bai had paused again. "Let's take a break for a bit," she said.

Bai nodded, trying to express her gratitude even though she couldn't get enough air to speak. She knew breathing was more difficult the higher one climbed, but she had never experienced the problem firsthand.

Hien turned and came to where Bai sat. The action,

small as it was, impressed Bai. Had she been in Hien's shoes, she wouldn't have given up a single step in elevation. Hien wasn't even breathing hard. How could she be so strong?

Bai worried the other woman judged her harshly. Although Bai could make out a thin sheen of sweat on Hien's forehead, the woman didn't look nearly as ragged as Bai felt. Even though she was almost twice Bai's age, she was far stronger. It made Bai cringe, knowing Hien wasn't exhausted even though she carried the pack.

They shared a water skin, although Bai noticed she drank considerably more water than Hien. The woman almost didn't seem to be human.

Eventually, Bai's breathing returned to normal. "I think I'm ready to continue."

Hien didn't reply, and Bai looked up to see a concerned look on Hien's face. The older woman cursed under her breath.

"What's wrong?" Bai asked.

"Someone is following us."

Bai couldn't hide her surprise. "How?"

Hien didn't answer the question, and Bai turned to look down the mountain. In the darkness of night, she didn't see anything. "Where?"

Hien pointed and Bai followed her finger.

There, off in the distance, a small point of light danced among the trees. Bai hadn't noticed it before. As she watched, she could see that it was coming up the mountain, coming in their direction. It looked a ways away, though.

Hien shrugged off her pack. "Do you need any more food before we go?"

Bai debated, then grabbed one strip of dried meat. She wasn't hungry now, but she figured it couldn't hurt. Hien handed her the water skin. "We won't have time to stop for more food or drink. This will need to last most of the night."

Bai slung the skin over her shoulder. Her body immediately protested at the added weight, but she didn't complain. It wasn't that heavy.

Bai glanced at the light below once again, wondering how far behind them it was. In the darkness she found it difficult to judge distance.

When she turned back to Hien, she saw the other woman was stringing a bow. A small quiver was pulled out of the pack and arrows were unwrapped. In a few moments Hien had donned the additional weapons and discarded the rest of the pack. She looked more like a warrior than ever before. Bai couldn't be sure, but she thought she saw a hint of eagerness in the other woman's eyes.

Without a word, the two women resumed their trek up the mountain. Bai had expected Hien to push them harder, but their pace remained unchanged. Every step took them higher, and although Hien glanced down the mountain constantly, Bai could almost convince herself they weren't being pursued.

Bai had lost all track of time when they finally stopped to rest again. She was higher than she had ever been, but that was about all she knew. Her world had shrunk to the ground in front of her. All that mattered moment-to-moment was the next step. She placed each one carefully, ignoring the burning pain in her legs as they kept climbing. The trail was steeper now and there was little flat ground to be found.

"Look over there," Hien said, pointing.

Bai looked and saw a cluster of lights, off in the distance and a little below them.

"That's the main trail to the pass," Hien explained. "It

looks like the town has sent a number of people after us. They're waiting. It's a faster route, and one I'd hoped to take."

Hien's finger traveled down to the other light, directly below them. Bai wasn't sure if it was her imagination or not, but the light seemed closer. "I think that's a different group."

Bai cursed. She rarely did, as her mother had believed that cursing drew too much attention. But it felt good. "Is everyone after me?"

Hien gave a grim smile. "Probably. At least in the region."

Bai looked up at her, understanding something new about her companion. "You're enjoying this, aren't you?"

Hien didn't answer, but her smile suddenly didn't seem so grim. She turned and pointed up the mountain. "Can you see our trail and where it leads?"

Bai studied the mountain. With Hien's help, she found she could see the trail above. It led to a notch in the rock above them.

"I want you to follow the trail. Move as quickly as you can. I'll catch up to you soon."

"What are you going to do?"

Hien gave her a blank look, as though the question needed no answering.

Bai looked at the bow and understood. Her eyes widened. "What if they're monks?"

Hien gave a small shrug. "What if they are?"

Bai stood openmouthed. She couldn't believe Hien. Was the woman mad? No one took on the gifted. Those who did had nothing but an early grave waiting for them. And yet she looked as calm as though she had just announced she was going to pick up bread from the market.

Bai wanted no part of what was coming. With a nod to

Hien, she resumed her trek up the trail. Before she'd gotten more than a few steps she heard Hien call after her.

"Bai?"

"Yes?"

"Don't stop, no matter what."

Bai nodded and continued. Hien's words sounded ominous, but Bai refused to think about them. Hien was competent. Whatever she had planned, she wasn't going to sacrifice her life for Bai's.

At least Bai hoped not.

She grimaced and pushed up the trail. At first, she tried to pick up her pace. The notch above her was where she would find her answers. All she had to do was reach it. But the trail became a series of switchbacks, and although the notch looked close, she quickly realized there was plenty of distance to go. She now understood the wisdom in Hien's slow but steady approach.

As she pushed higher, she wanted nothing more than to stop and rest, but Hien's words kept coming back to her. One step at a time, she ascended the trail. Occasionally she found the energy to look below, but there was little to see. The night wasn't perfectly dark, but even with the sliver of moon and the stars, Bai couldn't see anyone below. The light, which had once indicated their pursuit, was gone.

She had too many questions. She understood almost nothing of what was happening. All she could do was keep pushing forward. Keep pushing forward and hope.

Bai heard the sound of feet behind her, and Hien reappeared. If possible, she looked even more concerned than before. Regardless, Bai's heart leaped when she saw the other woman.

"What happened? Did you kill someone?" Bai realized

how harsh her voice sounded, and wished she could take the words back. But Hien didn't seem to notice.

"I don't think so." She studied the ground below them. "I think those are monks."

Bai's heart stopped. "Are you sure?"

"I think my first shot was high. My second was good, but it stopped before it hit them."

Bai squeezed her eyes tightly together, willing her life to be different. This couldn't be happening, not to her. No one attacked the monks, and no one did it with the casual indifference that Hien possessed. Why wasn't she afraid? She almost sounded disappointed she hadn't killed a monk.

"Keep moving," the other woman said. "We're almost there, but I think I angered our pursuit."

Bai obeyed, not knowing what else to do.

Far below them, the mountain exploded without warning. Rock shattered and cracked, the sound assaulting Bai's ears, all the more painful in the silence of the night. Before she could even decide what to do, Bai had curled into the fetal position.

A hand grabbed roughly at her cloak and hauled her to her feet with an ease she wouldn't have thought possible.

"Run!" Hien shouted.

For two long heartbeats, Bai stood there, frozen, unable to comprehend what was happening.

Again, rock suddenly cracked. This time, the sound came from directly below them. Imagining the path collapsing, Bai finally ran. She cursed as she came to the next switchback. Looking up, she saw the notch just four turns above them. So close, and yet they ran back and forth, targets for those below.

Another wave of energy slammed against the rock, this time in front of them. Bai swore she could feel it. A small section of trail collapsed, falling hundreds of feet to a gentler slope below. Bai had no trouble imagining that being her body.

"You have to jump," Hien said.

The gap wasn't large—no more than a pace or two at most. But they were high, and the path narrowed the higher they got. Bai knew she could jump the gap, but terror froze her feet in place.

She heard the twang of a bowstring behind her, and she turned around to see Hien aiming down the mountain. "They're catching up, Bai. We don't have much time."

Even now, Hien's voice was steady.

Bai looked up. For the first time, she realized that even the notch above might not provide the safety she thought it would. The monks behind them wouldn't give up. The thought was almost enough to sink her to her knees in resignation.

Then Hien's bow sang again and Bai suddenly felt ashamed of herself. This woman had risked her life—was risking her life—to save Bai. She at least deserved Bai's best effort.

Before she could convince herself otherwise, Bai ran up the switchback, leaping over the gap and landing clumsily on the other side. She turned around to see Hien right behind her, clearing the short gap with ease. Another attack hit behind them, widening the gap another foot. Now Bai was less certain she would have been able to jump it.

Fear gave her legs the energy she needed. They made it to another switchback and then another. Bai didn't look behind her or down the mountain, her eyes focused only on reaching the top.

The path seemed strangely silent. Bai shouted back at Hien. "Why aren't they attacking?"

"I don't know and I don't care," Hien replied. "Keep moving!"

Suddenly, they were at the top. Bai hadn't even realized they were on the last rise. Granite crags rose up on both sides of them, but a flat, narrow trail ran between the rocks. Bai had never been overjoyed by flat ground before, but she was now.

The trail was narrow, barely wide enough for two people to pass shoulder to shoulder. Hien squished around Bai and led the way. They had barely made it a dozen paces when a man stepped in front of them, coming around a bend. His pace was quick, but he looked surprisingly calm.

What Bai didn't understand, though, was how *bright* he looked. She didn't have any other words to describe it. As Hien passed, a look traveled between them. The man nodded, and Hien pulled Bai through.

Bai twisted her head to get one last look at the man before they turned the bend. He stood peacefully about twenty paces from the summit, waiting for the monks. She realized then that he was waiting for a fight with some of the strongest people in the empire.

And he had been smiling.

10

Delun held the arrow in his hand, studying it. The deadly shaft was a reminder that for all their strength, monks weren't invincible. He hadn't had any premonition that he was in danger. They had been hiking quickly up the mountain, following an intermittent sense of power high above them. An arrow had suddenly split the air between them, and Delun had barely gotten a shield up in time to stop the second. The second shot had struck his barrier no more than a second after he formed it, the arrowhead a mere hand's width from his chest.

Whoever was above them was an incredible shot, and quick with a bow. Since the attack, Delun and Kang had taken turns holding a shield above them. When one got tired, the other took over. The idea had been Kang's, and he seemed to have some experience coordinating his actions with other monks. Delun made a note of the fact for later. Most monks tended to work alone.

Kang threw a number of attacks at the path above when it wasn't his turn to hold the shield. Delun eventually stopped him, realizing that Kang was tearing up the path. At times, Delun thought he saw glimpses of movement up above, but it was too dark to be certain.

They took a short break as they neared the top of the mountain pass. Kang, probably because of the amount of energy he'd used attacking and holding the shield, was concerned about having enough strength to fight when they reached the top. Delun was less patient and less exhausted, but he also didn't have any desire to fight alone. He remembered the damage in the town below, and if he was going to fight that power, he wanted Kang by his side.

Still, his patience was wearing thin. He was certain they'd begun catching up to the fugitives, and every moment they caught their breath was distance lost. He stood up. "Let's go."

Kang, for all his strength, looked winded by the effort he'd sustained. But he stood up all the same.

Just then, Delun felt a power near the top of the mountain like he'd never felt before. It was strong, but there was a quality to the energy he couldn't quite articulate. The power felt endless, yet also contained. Delun couldn't describe it, but he knew with utter certainty that it was enough to have leveled Galan.

Kang's eyes were as wide as Delun imagined his own were. The other monk stepped forward first, though. Delun's heart raced, but not because of the altitude. He clenched his fist, feeling as powerless as when he'd been a child. Even with Kang by his side, he wasn't sure they had the strength to win a fight, if it was a fight that waited for them.

Delun leaped over a gap in the path, glancing at the fall below as he did. He was glad he'd managed to stop Kang before the monk had gotten too ambitious. Much more damage and the path would have been lost entirely.

He was near the top when he realized Kang had fallen

behind. Even though Delun hadn't run, he'd moved quickly, and was only a few dozen paces away from the notch the path led to. Kang was two switchbacks below. Unlike Delun, he wasn't accustomed to high altitudes.

Curiosity overrode caution, and Delun stepped into the notch to face the power that was so unlike anything he'd ever sensed.

A lone man stood there, possibly twenty paces away. In many ways he seemed remarkably average. His height and size weren't worth mentioning, and while he looked strong, in other circumstances Delun would barely have noted it. The man certainly wasn't built like Kang. He looked to be somewhere in his forties, with some of his long black hair beginning to turn gray.

While the man's appearance wasn't remarkable, his presence was. His face was calm, with a hint of a smile tugging at the corner of his mouth. Was this what Taio feared so greatly? When Delun looked at the man, he felt as though he'd just bathed in a cool mountain spring. A sense of peace emanated from him.

Delun took another step forward and the stranger shook his head. "I am sorry, monk, but you are not permitted here."

The statement was calm, but it carried the weight of command. The words stoked the fire always burning in Delun's heart. "I am permitted wherever I like."

He took another step forward. The stranger raised an eyebrow. "You're not from here."

"No. My name is Delun, and I come from the monastery above Two Bridges."

A flash of a deeper smile passed over the man's face, but it was gone in a moment. Delun took another step forward, unsure of what to make of his opponent.

"I wouldn't recommend coming any further," the man said.

Delun, tiring of the man's idle threats, stepped forward again.

Suddenly, he was thrown backward, the man launching into the first two-handed attack with a speed Delun had never encountered before. He'd gone from stillness to action in a moment, catching Delun completely off balance. Delun's feet clawed helplessly at the ground, and he became suddenly aware that he was approaching the notch with incredible speed. If he didn't land on the path, it was a long way down.

The attack dissipated, allowing Delun to land on quickly backpedaling feet. Only a few more feet and he would have been doomed.

Delun looked at the man. He was standing as still as a statue, that same sense of peace emanating from him. If not for the very obvious evidence to the contrary, Delun would have said the man hadn't even moved.

The attack had been brilliant, and beyond anything Delun had encountered. The attack had been a first-level move, one of the first taught to new recruits at the monasteries. Most people were lucky if they could knock over a cup with the attack. It focused a monk's power, but not to a killing blow. It certainly didn't pick men up and throw them back.

Everything about that attack sent a message. The other man didn't want to kill Delun. If he had, Delun had little doubt the man could have sustained the attack for the extra few seconds it would take to throw him over the side. He'd also given the monk a very personal taste of the strength he was up against.

Delun registered all of that, but that wasn't the

information he fixated on. The man had used an attack taught by the monasteries. At one point in time, he had been a monk.

The anger he'd felt before engulfed him, jumping past every bit of self-control he possessed. The man had betrayed his oaths! Delun's fingers danced an intricate pattern, focusing an attack with both hands.

The stranger remained still, watching Delun's preparation with interest. He didn't seem concerned in the slightest.

Delun stopped at the fourth sign. Undefended, it could kill a man, but he was beyond reason. He extended one arm, yelled, and released the attack.

Energy surged out of his hand, but the man seemed unperturbed. As Delun's hand came up, he formed the first shield.

Delun grinned in feral satisfaction. The first shield had no hope of standing against an attack as focused as this.

His attack connected, and Delun could feel the energies collide. He grunted, putting more of himself into the strike. He wouldn't allow the stranger to make more than one mistake.

Without warning, Delun's attack unraveled. He blinked, confused.

In front of him, the man stood tall, still holding his shield. Delun's effort hadn't even managed to wipe the serenity from the man's face.

Delun didn't bother trying to understand what happened. If the attack didn't work, he would try a new approach. He sprinted at the man, wishing that he had more space from side to side. As it was, he was something of an easy target. Fortunately for him, the man didn't attack. Delun focused on his left hand, still holding the fourth sign.

With an effort, he made the fifth. Delun rarely practiced the move, too powerful for most uses.

He came in jabbing with his free right hand. In terms of the fight, the jabs, even if they landed, wouldn't do much. They were a distraction, designed to break the other man's focus and make him think about meaningless attacks. The man evaded with an ease that spoke of long years of practice. Delun threw in a few quick low kicks with the same purpose. None of them connected.

But he had gotten close, and the man had to be focusing on the physical attacks if he was dodging them so easily. Delun brought his left hand close to the man's sternum, feeling the rush of triumph.

He looked up, just in time to see the man still smiling. In one of his hands he held the sign for the second shield. Delun realized it too late, his attack already released. The energies met and swirled, visibly bending the air in the space between them. To Delun's senses, it looked as though a sun had been born in the small space.

The shield didn't give, and the resulting force blasted Delun back. He felt his body floating in the air for an endless moment, wondering if he'd just killed himself. Then the ground rushed up to meet him. He relaxed his muscles and let himself skid to a stop.

Above him, the stars in the sky were starting to dim, overwhelmed by the first hints of the rising sun. He blinked once and the pain came. He felt the dirt and rock in the cuts in his back, the trembling in his arms from exhausted muscles. Like an untrained recruit, he had put too much of his energy into those attacks.

Grunting, he worked himself to a sitting position just as Kang came over the rise, a look of panic on his face. No doubt he'd never felt so strong a fight. Delun also saw a flash of recognition on Kang's face. He knew this man.

Delun stood up, collecting himself. This fight wasn't over. The man had won the first round, but he wouldn't win the next. Not with Kang here.

"Together," Delun said.

He charged the man again, ignoring the ache in his muscles, forming the signs for an attack and a shield in his hands. Behind him, Kang hesitated for a moment, then followed suit.

They came in fast, but the man stepped back into the first two-handed attack once again. He thrust out his hands and released his attack. This time, Delun got a shield up in time, but the force of it still knocked both him and Kang back. What were the depths of power this man possessed?

Delun dropped his previous strategy. With Kang, perhaps they could simply go toe-to-toe with this man. He looked over. "Give it everything."

Kang looked uncertain, but he followed Delun's lead as they both gathered and focused their energies. Delun made it to the strongest two-handed signs he could create. Kang did the same. Delun felt his partner's full strength for the first time. They were very closely matched.

The mysterious man still stood, motionless. He didn't even seem concerned by the enormous energies arrayed against him. Together, the two monks easily could have recreated the damage in the town below, with power left over.

"Now!" yelled Delun.

They both attacked, the waves of energy barreling toward the man like an unstoppable river. Nothing could survive such power.

Delun felt another power, even more focused, pressing

against his own. His eyes widened and he pushed, giving as much of himself as he dared. He groaned as he searched for more strength. The energies broke upon one another with an audible crack, but no wave of force washed over him. For all his effort, nothing had resulted.

How?

Nothing could have survived that attack. But Delun had been defeated.

He collapsed to a knee, noticing for the first time that the stranger had a sword in his hand.

Delun's heart raged, but his body and soul had nothing left to give.

The stranger knew forbidden techniques, skills denied to the monks for the safety of all. The stranger needed to face justice.

Delun refused to surrender. There had to be a way. He got to his feet and began making the first sign in his right hand. Even that took more than he cared to admit. One way or another, he wouldn't be leaving the top of this mountain alive.

"Delun." It was Kang.

The monk looked over at his partner. The man had suffered a cut, a gash that ran all the way across his torso. It wasn't deep, but Delun understood the importance immediately. Not only had the man blocked their attacks, his own had been strong enough to reach Kang.

Delun looked over at the stranger. He didn't even look winded.

Reason warred against rage. He would kill this man, but not today. Without Kang there was no chance.

Despite his anger, his mission was more important. He still had work to do.

The fact stung at his pride. Without another word, he

and Kang turned and started working their way back down the mountain. The man watched them go, also silent.

As they dipped below the notch and out of sight, Delun made an oath to himself. If it was the last thing he did, he would kill that man.

Justice demanded no less.

11

B ai woke up in a bed, far nicer than the one she had slept in at home. The covers were thick, protecting her from the cool air, and the mattress was soft. She huddled deeper into the covers, soaking in the warmth with a contented sigh.

How long had it been since she was allowed a full night of sleep? In the cells down in Galan, she had been woken up a few times a night by the night watchman, and the cell had never been terribly comfortable to begin with. Sleep had become something of a treasure.

Careful to keep herself deep under the covers, she stretched, feeling the aches and pains that her body had accumulated during the past few weeks. So far as she could tell, she was fine. She had plenty of bruises and scrapes, but was otherwise unharmed. Considering all she had been through, she was going to count that as a victory.

Her last memories from the night before were vague and distorted by exhaustion. Hien had brought her here, and there had been other people, all of whom had treated her kindly. They had shown her to a bed and that was the last of her recollection. What had happened to the monks chasing her?

Bai didn't want to let this moment go, so she pushed the question aside for the moment. She relaxed into the bed.

As she rested, sounds began reaching her, giving Bai an idea of the place she'd come to. She heard a few children shouting, and she imagined they were playing some sort of game. Occasionally a deeper voice would interject, and hints of conversation sometimes trickled through her open window.

When she took a deep breath, she was greeted by a variety of pleasant smells. Somewhere nearby beef was cooking over a fire, and Bai thought she detected the faint smell of incense nearby.

She was in a village. That much seemed obvious. But what kind of village? If they had climbed into the mountains, it stood to reason this was the home of the rebels that terrorized the region. And yet, even from her bed, it didn't feel like a place of rebellion. She had expected something more military, or perhaps more monastic. Instead, it felt like a home.

Bai let her mind wander, half-hoping that she would fall back asleep even though it was clearly sunny outside. She thought of Hien and the strange man they'd passed on the way in. Despite the violence that surrounded her, she felt safe.

She was just about to drift back to sleep when she heard the door to her room open. Her first instinct was to hide under the covers and pretend to sleep, but these people had been kind to her. They deserved better. She pulled the covers down so her head poked out above them.

The air outside was startlingly cold, and her first impression of the woman who entered was that she was just as cold. Cold and beautiful, like a mountain peak at sunset. The woman moved with impossible grace and set down a tray carrying tea, bread, and butter. When she spoke, Bai was surprised her voice wasn't as icy as expected. "It's good to see you awake. I understand that you've been through a lot, but there is much to decide."

Bai nodded, not sure what the woman was getting at.

"My name is Daiyu, and I function as the elder in this village."

Bai's eyes widened a hint with shock. Daiyu didn't look much older than Hien. Was she among the oldest in the village?

Daiyu caught Bai's look. She gave a hint of a smile, an action that seemed to warm the entire room. Bai began to believe that she had mistaken this woman.

"No, I am not technically an elder here. But our circumstances are unique, and most of the decisions regarding the running of the village fall on my shoulders. I do not always make my decisions alone, but my word carries weight. Do you understand?"

Bai nodded, even though she didn't understand. A woman, in charge of an entire village, acting as an elder? It was as if she had climbed the mountains and found herself in a new world, resembling the one she knew superficially, but completely different underneath.

"Good. Now, let us speak for a moment. Why are you here, and what do you want?"

Bai blinked, confused by the questions. "I'm here because you sent Hien and she rescued me."

Daiyu gave Bai a look that made her feel as though she had answered the question incorrectly. "My husband sent Hien, but rescue was never part of the plan. That's a decision we've already disagreed on. But I want to understand you. Why did you follow Hien up here? No doubt, you considered different destinations. Hien told me she made it clear you could leave if you wished."

Bai's mind raced. She had just followed Hien, hadn't she? Then she thought back to their conversation at camp. Hien had told her she could leave. She hadn't just blindly followed. She had chosen.

"I hoped there might be answers here."

Daiyu's gaze was sharp. "What kind of answers do you expect to find? You call us rebels down in the valley, but we haven't had any dealings with the empire for years."

Bai's heart sank. She didn't think Daiyu was lying. What if they didn't know anything about what happened down in the village?

Then another more frightening thought occurred to her. What if they did? If Daiyu was lying, Bai had put herself in incredible danger by coming to the very village where the attack had come from. Why hadn't she thought of that before? Bai was the only witness to what had happened, and she'd possibly walked right into the den of the enemy.

But that didn't make sense. Hien could have killed her at any point in the journey. It would have been far easier than saving her. She had to trust these people.

Even though Bai hadn't spoken, Daiyu looked as though she had found her answer. She stood up. "Everyone who lives in this village is here for a reason. If you haven't already figured it out, you are the most sought-after person in the western empire right now, and everyone knows you're here. I'm not going to throw you out. But unless you want to put everyone here at risk, I would consider leaving. You are a danger to us all so long as the empire knows you hide here."

With that, she stood up and left, leaving the room even colder than before.

The warmth of the bed still called to Bai, but the lure of food was even stronger, and her bed no longer seemed quite as welcoming. She pulled herself from the covers and dressed in clothes that had been provided for her. She sipped at the tea and bit into the bread eagerly. For all of Daiyu's cold demeanor, the food she brought told another story. The tea was fragrant, with just a hint of sweetness beneath the grassy green flavors. The bread was fresh and warm, the butter rich. All in all, it was the best breakfast Bai thought she'd ever tasted.

She'd barely finished when there was a knock at her door. She looked up, surprised that someone would knock. No one had shown her that courtesy in ages. Even her mother hadn't, back when they'd lived together. "Come in."

The door opened slowly, and the man from last night stepped in. Something about him still seemed to glow, but the effect wasn't as distinct as the night before. He looked well-rested and relaxed, and unlike Daiyu, seemed to radiate a gentle peacefulness that warmed the room. He looked at the few crumbs that remained of breakfast. "How was it?"

"Incredible." Bai suddenly remembered her manners. "And thank you, for everything."

The man nodded and gestured to the balcony of the room. Bai led the way, finally getting her first view of the village in the full light of day.

Galan and Kulat were the only other towns she'd ever been in, and this village was nothing like either. Houses and huts were at all different elevations, and ladders, stairs, and poles connected everything. It was one of the most vertical places she'd ever encountered. As she watched, children scampered up the ladders with delight, and women carried baskets on their backs as they followed.

Even from a glance, she could tell that life in this village was not easy. And yet, she didn't see discontent on the faces of anyone who passed. Even at home in Galan, most people looked like they were simply trying to make it through the day.

The man let her look for a few moments before he spoke. "You've spoken with my wife already."

It wasn't a question, but a statement, giving her an opening to respond to. "You're Daiyu's husband?"

The man smiled deeply, as though the title brought him great joy. "I am. My name is Lei."

Bai couldn't help but study the man. Instinctively, she wondered what drew the two of them together. At first glance, they seemed too different to be husband and wife. At the same time, she already guessed at the strength of their bond. This village was theirs.

Lei caught her glance and read it correctly. "I assume she told you that she wants you to leave?"

Bai nodded.

"I hope you'll forgive her. She can come off as quite cold at times, but underneath, she cares. Perhaps even more than I do. You'll never guess this, but when we came here, we were hoping to start an inn. Instead, we founded a village."

Bai pulled her gaze from Lei and out to the village. Her curiosity was overwhelming. How had all of this come to pass? Why did everyone consider them rebels? What she saw in front of her directly conflicted with the years of stories she'd heard, and she didn't know which was more real.

"The truth is," Lei continued, "Daiyu would love to help you. Thanks to Hien, we've offered shelter to no small number of women over the years. But you've guessed how many people are interested in you, and your presence here endangers the rest of the village. Daiyu is torn between wanting to help you and protecting this village."

Pieces shifted in Bai's perception, and suddenly Daiyu made more sense, from the cold exterior to the warm bread. Surprisingly, she felt a measure of respect for the other woman.

"Where's Hien?" Bai asked.

"Probably at home, resting. She returned to where we crossed paths last night after she dropped you off. She was worried that I might need help. We didn't get back until early this morning, and her, myself, and Daiyu needed to speak. Hien's not great at sleeping in, but I wouldn't be surprised to find her relaxing in her garden. You're more than welcome to go see her, of course. You're free to go anywhere."

Bai appreciated the offer, but something else stuck in her mind. "What about the monks who were following me?"

Lei waved his hand away dismissively. "They returned to Galan, I assume."

Bai looked at him suspiciously. "Why?"

"I can be very persuasive."

She didn't buy the glib answer. "Why?"

Lei gave a small sigh. "They tried to fight their way past me, but I held them off."

She looked at Lei again. This man had fought off two monks on his own? That, more than anything else, stretched her belief. But he didn't seem like he was lying.

They stood in silence for a few minutes. Bai had a hundred questions she wanted to ask, but none of them seemed quite right.

Lei broke the stalemate. "Why did you come to us?"

Bai bit her lip. She was getting tired of this question.

Why did anyone do anything? "I hoped you might have answers."

He looked at her then, his gaze boring into her like a miner digging for gold. She felt vulnerable under that gaze, even though she felt no danger. "Why did you really come to us?"

Frustration boiled up in her. What were he and his wife going on about? Were they privy to some secret of hers? "I came up here because I didn't know what else to do!"

Lei nodded. "Closer."

"What do you want me to say?"

"The truth. You came up here because it was the easiest choice to make. You knew if you left Hien you'd be captured. Maybe you're curious about what happened in Galan, but it wasn't curiosity that drove you."

Bai clenched her fist. She hated Lei's words. She had come here for answers! She had!

Lei stood up straight and looked over the village one more time. "Unlike my wife, I have no reservations about allowing you to stay here. But your time of easy decisions is coming to an end. Every choice you make from here on will have tremendous consequences. If you're going to stay here, I think you'll find answers, but I'm not sure you're going to like them. If you stay, I want you to be prepared." He walked to the door.

She couldn't let him leave on that note. "What do I need to be prepared for?"

He looked over his shoulder at her. "Truth doesn't care for our feelings. If you find the truth, you'll be freed from ignorance, but the burden of knowing might destroy you."

12

D elun woke up the next morning, and for a single moment he felt a surge of peace. Tall evergreens stood all around him, and the fire crackling to his side had kept him warm all night long. The birds chirped their morning song and not a single human voice could be heard.

Then he glanced over and looked at Kang, and his fury returned. He clenched his fists, fighting the urge to kill the man where he lay.

He knew the desire was irrational. Kang had fought by his side. He hadn't done anything wrong.

But Delun hated that the man had been the one to urge retreat. Although Delun recognized it as the rational decision, he hated that Kang had been so willing to bend when the time came.

Kang didn't look like he would wake anytime soon, and Delun needed to work off some of his anger. Anger led to poor decisions. He'd almost sacrificed his life for nothing last night because of it. Delun walked a ways from the fire, basking in the sensation of the cold mountain air against his skin. He warmed up with the routines he had been taught in the monasteries as a child, the simple forms that gradually became more complex.

He ran through the basic forms first, repeating them until his body was loose, limber, and warm. Then he moved on to more advanced movements, working up a pleasant sheen of sweat. He eventually came to the forms that used energy manipulation, but he stopped there. Perhaps it was paranoia, but he didn't want to let Kang sense exactly how strong he was.

When he returned to the fire, Kang was just beginning to wake. The hour was late for a monk, but the night had been long and exhausting. Picking their way down the trail was almost as dangerous as their ascent. The damage they caused to the trail had become a significant obstacle given how exhausted they were. Delun had barely been able to stand, supported more than once by the larger monk.

Delun saw Kang glance at him, a glance that was every bit as curious as Delun's. They'd put off having this discussion earlier, but now the questions had become too pressing.

Delun knelt across from Kang, alert for any shifts in the man's energy. He suspected Kang was doing the same. He opened the conversation before Kang could begin. "You knew him."

Kang hesitated for a moment, then nodded. "His name is Lei. He and I have met before."

"You didn't think to mention him?"

Kang scratched at his chin. "I didn't think it was necessary. I thought we would catch the woman before she reached the village. She moved faster than I expected."

Perhaps there was some truth to the statement, but Delun still felt as though Kang was holding on to his secrets too tightly. He waited. Silence was often the best way to promote conversation.

Kang gave in. "I hoped we could catch them before they reached the summit. I knew Lei was up there, and I didn't want to fight with him."

Delun shook his head. "What do you know about him?"

"Not much. He's the strongest man I've ever met, without equal as far as I know. He rarely comes down from the mountains, though."

Delun thought Kang was missing a rather obvious observation. "And he knows how to use weapons."

Kang nodded.

Delun waited for more, but Kang didn't look like he had much left to add.

"Perhaps you'd care to tell me how a man of that strength, who can wield weapons with our gifts, is living freely in the mountains?"

Kang sighed. "It's a bit of a story. Shall we walk?"

Delun looked up at the mountain. "I think this is where I need to be. I need to know what that girl knows, now more than ever."

Kang followed Delun's look. "If she's up there, you won't get to her."

Anger surged within Delun and Kang held up his hands in a placating gesture. Coming from the large man, the movement looked almost foolish. "I'm only telling you the truth. Maybe you can talk your way past Lei, but given your attitude and the way you attacked him last night, I doubt it. You can't fight him and win, and if you want more monks, they are several days away, and that's if you manage to somehow convince the abbot, which I don't think you'll be able to do."

"At the very least," Delun replied, "I should be here to watch for the girl to return."

Kang shook his head. "I doubt she'll be down soon. There aren't many friendly people down here, as I see it. We can talk to the elder below. If she does descend, we can have a bird within an hour."

Delun considered Kang's words. He wasn't sure he liked the man, but he spoke the truth, at least as far as Delun's options went. He had run straight into a mountain he couldn't climb alone. He couldn't think of a way around it now, but perhaps there were other options open to him. "What do you suggest?"

"You said you were here to investigate the Golden Leaf, correct? Come with me to Kulat and resume your investigation. Perhaps there you will find some of your answers."

Delun took a deep breath as he looked once again at the mountains looming above them. He hated the idea of retreat, but sometimes, he acknowledged, there was no better option. He wanted an hour alone with the woman to find answers, but that day was not today.

"Very well. Lead the way."

The two of them put out their fire with water from a nearby stream, then began walking toward the road that would take them down to Galan and eventually Kulat. They walked in silence for a few minutes before Delun prodded Kang.

"Lei's story?"

Kang sighed but acquiesced. "Some of this is only legend and speculation. Lei's been here longer than most of us. I've only been a monk here for about five years, and am originally from further south."

Even that was curious, but Delun let it slide for now. The person he really wanted to know about was Lei.

"As far as I know, Lei came into the area about seventeen, maybe eighteen years ago. He might have been living here before then, but I doubt it. We would have known. There are all sorts of rumors about his arrival, and I don't know how many are true. Some say that he killed an abbot, others say that he destroyed a crime boss. The monastery doesn't have any records of an abbot being killed in this area, and my own abbot claims the story is a myth. Regardless, the first stories of Lei are pretty old. Personally, I tend to think he cleared out crime in this area. You'll note the triads are barely a presence here."

Delun listened intently. He didn't like the speculation, but at least the time frame of Lei's arrival seemed fairly certain.

"Eventually, Lei came into conflict with the monastery at Kulat. My abbot was a monk there at the time, and he said that there were a few open battles. He never got into specifics, but made it clear that no matter how many monks attacked, Lei never had a problem fighting them off."

"Really?" Delun had a hard time believing that. Lei had been strong, but that strong?

Kang shrugged. "That's what I've heard. I'm inclined to believe it. Kulat is a decent-sized monastery, and we have many monks who are talented, but against someone like Lei? They wouldn't stand a chance."

Delun supposed his own perspective was skewed. He'd never come across a man who so openly flaunted the power of the monasteries. Closer to Jihan, such a man certainly would have been killed by now.

"Why didn't your abbot summon more help?"

Kang shrugged again. "I've never asked, and the abbot

from that time has long since passed away. I suspect that the old abbot and Lei either came to an agreement, or the abbot simply decided the cost was too great. This wasn't that long after the battle of Jihan, and I suspect attitudes were different then."

Delun conceded the point. It grated, but he could see where a weak abbot would make such a choice.

"Eventually, I came to Kulat and made a name for myself. I was the strongest warrior they'd seen in some time, and by then, the abbot I now serve was in charge. When they had trained me as much as they thought was necessary, I was sent into the mountains to kill Lei."

Delun approved of this new abbot. He, at least, seemed to have the right idea.

"That was four years ago now," Kang continued. "I made my way into the mountains and Lei came down the path to meet me. I never made it as high as I did with you. No doubt, he sensed my presence and came down to greet me."

Kang paused.

"And?" Delun demanded.

"We didn't fight," Kang confessed. "I could tell, even then, that my ability paled in comparison to his. We introduced ourselves, exchanged a few words, and then I hiked down the mountain, defeated without even making a single sign."

Delun wanted to be angry at the other monk, but he heard the shame in the man's voice. Kang still carried that burden.

"Since then, I've done nothing but train harder to beat him. Last night, with you, I thought I had my first real chance."

Kang left the rest unspoken.

Delun let Kang's story soak into his thoughts. Part of him

was still angry that Kang hadn't given more of himself, but he understood Kang had simply been more rational in the heat of battle. Only one question still bothered him. "If your new abbot wants him dead, why haven't you gone to greater lengths?"

Kang gave a grim smile. "Now that answer I know. For my abbot, the cost is too great for too little benefit. For the most part, Lei stays up in the mountains. Sometimes we can feel incredible surges of energy from that direction, but we never hear any complaints from Galan. Occasionally strangers wander up the mountain, and they never come back down.

"But the village and Lei don't cause trouble, at least as far as I know. They branded Lei a rebel after his actions when he first arrived, and most townspeople tend to attribute every disaster to him, but there's never been any evidence we can find. He leaves us alone and we leave him alone. It's a thorn in the abbot's side, but removing that thorn would cost the lives of far more monks than he is willing to spare. The way my abbot sees it, there are far more effective things a monk can be doing."

Delun wasn't sure he agreed. The law was the law, and Lei was clearly in violation. And yet part of him understood the reasons Kang gave.

"But you don't think Lei had anything to do with what happened in Galan?"

Kang didn't answer for a few seconds. "No, I don't think so. He's strong enough, certainly. In fact, he's one of the only people strong enough that I can think of, except the two of us. In others' eyes, that might be evidence enough, but I don't accept it. As far as I know, Lei hasn't come down in years, and although I can't prove this, my instincts say that he's fundamentally a man of peace."

"With that power?" Delun remembered the battering he'd taken, and he hadn't gotten cut up as badly as Kang.

"With that power, he could have easily killed us both, and if my memory serves, you attacked first." He pointed at his cut. "Do you know what this means to me?"

Delun shook his head, unsure where Kang was going with the argument.

"I can't use weapons, but I've heard how incredibly difficult that power is to control. Fighting against both of us, he managed to use just enough force to destroy our attacks without killing us. I sensed that he didn't put all of his power into that move. He held back, and he had enough control to leave us both alive. This cut tells me that even after an additional four years of training, I'm nowhere near strong enough to take him on. It also means that I've gone to fight him twice, and both times I've walked away with my life. In my eyes, that means I owe him, not once, but twice."

Delun's objections were silenced by the conviction in Kang's tone. He didn't see the world the same way, and after a few moments, Delun had to say something.

"But he can't continue to disrespect the monasteries like that. If he doesn't respect us, who will?"

Kang looked over at Delun, as though asking himself a question. "You believe in the monasteries, don't you? More than most."

Delun nodded, glad the other monk finally understood his perspective.

Kang's face broke out in a wide smile. "Come, then. I know exactly who you need to meet."

13

B ai looked around her room, her eyes resting on the small sack of belongings she possessed. Everything inside had been given to her by Lei and Daiyu, including the small sack. Their hospitality, especially considering her circumstances, was unbelievable. They generously furnished her with food and supplies, and if she rationed the food well, she suspected she could make it to a place where no one would look for her.

She'd thought long and hard on Lei's words to her. Somehow, he knew something about what happened in Galan. Something he refused to simply tell her. Given that he had fought off the monks for her and welcomed her into his village, she suspected that if he feared to tell her what he knew, there was good reason for it.

Bai slipped her mother's bracelet off her wrist and looked at it. It was her only true possession. She smiled sadly, knowing exactly what her mother would tell her to do right now.

Leave.

Hide.

Build an existence somewhere far away, just as Daiyu had suggested when she brought the pack.

Bai had been packed for a while now, but she made no move to leave. If she waited much longer, she'd have to stay overnight. More than once she'd picked up the bag and walked to the door, but that was as far as she'd made it.

Doubt gnawed at the edges of her mind. She hated all of this. She hated the burden of choice. If she left, she could hide, but she would never know what happened. Then she thought of Lei's words, and she wasn't sure she wanted to know.

She couldn't will her feet to move, no matter how much she ordered them too.

A knock on the door startled her. She hadn't been expecting company.

"Come in."

The door opened and Hien stepped into the room. She looked down at the sack and then at Bai. "So, you are leaving."

The warrior made no attempt to disguise the disappointment in her voice, and Bai felt suddenly very selfish. This woman had risked her life to bring Bai to a place of safety. Bai was spitting in her face by leaving again so soon. She hung her head in shame.

"Want to take a walk? Get out of this room?"

Bai shook her head. If she didn't leave soon, she worried she would remain forever.

Hien, however, didn't see it that way. "There isn't much difference between leaving today and tomorrow, if it gets that late. Anyhow, wouldn't you rather sleep in a warm, comfortable bed for one more night?"

Hien's argument was compelling. And the woman had risked everything for her. Without her, Bai would still be imprisoned, suffering indignities at Wen's hands. She owed the woman more than she could repay. Reluctantly, she agreed.

Since waking up, she hadn't been much out of her room. She'd found Daiyu after she made her decision to leave. Daiyu, unsurprisingly, had been pleased by Bai's choice and agreed to put together everything she needed. The sack appeared shortly thereafter, almost as though Daiyu was ready for Bai to leave already.

Hien led Bai into the village. They walked for a few minutes in silence, Bai taking in the sights and sounds of village life. In some ways, it reminded her of Galan. People went about their daily work. Some young children played in the street under the watchful eyes of their mothers.

There were differences, too. Everyone greeted one another kindly. No one stood on streets to beg or sell their wares. As near as Bai could tell, there was no market. She wondered a little at this but held her tongue. Galan wasn't large, but it held far more people than this village. She'd never been someplace so small.

The spaces between the buildings were often too narrow for a proper road, and most people walked on well-worn dirt and stone trails. Because there weren't roads, the smells of spring embraced them. Mountain wildflowers bloomed next to walking paths, and Bai paused at a few to deeply inhale the sweet scents of the plants.

Overall, the village felt like the most peaceful place Bai had ever been. Considering her whole life to that point had been spent in either Galan or Kulat, she supposed it wasn't that much of a claim. Still, it hardly seemed like the center of rebel activity that it was made out to be.

"What's on your mind?" Hien asked.

"This place isn't what I expected."

Hien grinned a little at that. "Yeah, we hear that a lot from new visitors. As you might guess, the monasteries don't really like Lei, so they spread rumors about us."

Bai couldn't help but ask the question directly. "But aren't you rebels?"

Hien shrugged. "I suppose it depends on who you ask and what you mean. We don't live under the protection or laws of the empire, so maybe we are. But, for the most part, we also don't interfere with affairs down below. We mostly keep to ourselves, which is why we're here in the first place."

"You rescued me," Bai pointed out.

"And Daiyu has lectured me plenty about that," Hien retorted. "We aren't completely isolated. I couldn't sit still in this village for more than a week or two without losing my mind, but I still call it home. Lei often asks me to keep an eye on happenings in the empire. I'm not sure that he'd ever come down himself, but he worries constantly."

Bai digested that information, wondering what to make of it.

"Do you want to know something interesting?"

Bai did.

"Your name. I knew another Bai, a long time ago. In many ways, she's the reason I'm here. I'm not much for superstition or fate, but your presence here, it makes me think there's a larger order to things."

"Who was she?"

Hien paused and stared off into the distance for a moment. "Lei had a brother once, a man named Jian. He was a monk. I worked with him once in Jihan. It was the work that eventually led to him being murdered. But he was in love with a woman named Bai. She worked at a brothel in Jihan and I helped her escape to a sanctuary."

Her voice was terse, but Bai felt the emotion behind it. "That's how you met Lei?"

Hien shook her head. "No, that didn't come until much later."

"How did saving the other Bai lead you here?"

Bai could see that Hien was lost in the vast corridors of her past. "When I was younger, I only looked out for myself. I discovered I was good at killing when I was pretty young. When I took Bai to the sanctuary, it was the first time I'd done something because I thought I should, not because I was getting paid for it.

"Eventually, I found myself doing that more and more. That was what led me to Lei, but that's a story for another time. It's enough to say that I helped him create this little village, even though he did most of the work."

Bai was dying to ask questions, but Hien was clearly in no mood to answer them.

"I didn't visit you to talk about myself. You're planning on leaving, on finding someplace to hide?"

Bai couldn't convince herself to say the words out loud. She nodded, feeling the blood rush to her cheeks in shame.

Hien's voice was soft. "I don't blame you, you know."

Bai looked up, surprised.

"Hiding seems easier, a lot of the time. Most of the people here are hiding in one way or another. I am, too, if I'm honest. But you can't hide here. Here you'd be forced to search for answers and find the truth. If you want to hide, you need to run."

Bai hadn't expected such understanding from Hien. She seemed too strong to understand such concerns.

"I'd ask you to reconsider," Hien said.

Bai actually took a step back, surprised by Hien's forthrightness. "Why?"

"Because, although our circumstances are very different, I've been where you are."

They paused at a small garden. Bai could feel Hien's need to tell her story. She gave Hien the silence and time she needed.

"I was kicked out of my home when I was fourteen," Hien confessed. "My parents loved me, I think, but they couldn't live with who I was. They forced me to leave the home and ordered me never to return. I spent some time on the streets of Jihan, which wasn't a good time. I made a lot of mistakes and got hurt. That was when I killed my first man and realized it didn't bother me."

Bai stared at Hien. Again, her statements were short and terse, but they masked an ocean's worth of emotion. Her heart went out to the other woman, but she also knew Hien would accept no comfort.

"I spent years in hiding. All sorts of people were looking for me. Criminals, jealous lovers, you name it. I left destruction wherever I went."

Hien paused as she kneeled down to look at a new blooming flower. "I moved around, every couple of weeks at most. I was good at hiding, at blending in to new places. But, Bai, it's hard. You're always looking over your shoulder, no matter how safe you think you are. Your past is always haunting you. Living in hiding is no way to live. Even now, up here, protected by Lei, I wake up in the middle of the night worried that someone is outside my window, hunting me."

Bai struggled to believe that claim. Up here?

Hien noticed her expression. "I really upset some people, Bai. It's not out of the question. That's part of the reason why my heart breaks for you. No one knows for sure what happened down in Galan, but if anyone can help you find the answers, it's Lei. He's one of the best men I've ever known, and I think you've figured out he knows something. You don't have to live your life in hiding."

Hien's shoulders relaxed a little, as though she had finally let go of the burden she'd been carrying for too long.

The words hit Bai like sledgehammers to the stomach. Not just because she suspected that Hien was right. Because there was someone here, someone who barely knew her, who cared this much about what happened to her. Mother had cared, in her own way, but not like this.

"I'm scared," Bai admitted.

Hien nodded. "There's nothing wrong with being afraid. But if you give in to fear today, you'll give in to it tomorrow, and the day after that. I won't tell you staying is the easiest path. But it is the better one."

They stopped outside of a building and Hien gestured to the ladder leading to the third level. "Care to come into my house?"

Bai's curiosity was overwhelming. She followed Hien up the ladder to a balcony that overlooked the village. The sun was starting to set, casting long shadows that made the houses look like giants. They admired the view for a few moments, then Hien led them into the small room.

Bai hadn't been sure what she'd expected, but Hien's place didn't seem much like Hien. Scrolls and artwork hung from the walls, and a kettle of water was boiling over the fire. Another woman was in the room, folding clothes. Hien introduced her as Ling.

Hien took her over to a small dresser, where a comb sat. Hien picked up the comb with reverence and handed it over to Bai. "This was a gift given to me by the Bai I was telling you about."

The comb itself was unremarkable. Only Hien's attitude toward it marked it as something of value.

"Do you know what I think about when I pick up this comb?"

Bai shook her head.

"It's been over twenty years since I helped the other Bai. I haven't kept track of her, but I know that for twenty years, she's been free, thanks to a decision I made. I would like to think she's done something with her life—maybe helped someone else out, or made a name for herself. Or maybe she's just been able to live a life of normalcy, starting a family with a man who cares for her.

"I know it's tempting to make the easy decision today. But if you make the hard one, who knows what possibilities await? If you run, you'll be hiding until you die, and I'd hate to know that was the path you chose to take."

Bai finally broke down, the last of her flimsy barriers collapsing. She held up her hands in surrender. "Fine, I'll stay, at least for a while."

"That makes one of you," Ling said, her voice bitter.

Bai looked at Hien, a question in her gaze.

Hien gave a short sigh. "Lei is worried about the monastery at Kulat. He's asked me to go observe, to see what I can find out."

Bai couldn't help it. She laughed.

"What's funny?" Hien asked.

"You've spent all this time convincing me to stay while you're planning on leaving."

Hien rolled her eyes. "I'm coming back, within a week or two at most."

Eventually Bai's laughter faded. She felt good, better than she had in a long while. When had she last laughed?

"I'll let Lei know you decided to stay," Hien said. "He'll probably want to start training sometime soon."

Bai's lightheartedness faded instantly. She thought immediately of the fact that she was in a rebel village. "Training?"

Hien's smile fell. "He didn't tell you?"

Bai shook her head. She had no idea what Hien was talking about.

Hien looked uncertain, like she'd said too much. She met Bai's gaze.

"Bai, Lei thinks you're gifted."

14

The carriage ride back to Kulat was more pleasant than the trip to Galan had been. Kang, who had once been so stingy with his words, now spoke freely. Delun got the impression that he had passed some sort of test with the big monk. Unfortunately, Kang's topics of conversation were somewhat limited.

Kang loved to talk about training.

After making sure the elder of Galan was very clear they expected word of any news, Kang and Delun had the horses saddled and got on the road. Since then, Delun had debated diet, exercise regimens, mental techniques, and even morning routines with Kang. The man's fascination with training seemed deeper than an ocean.

Delun was fascinated by Kang's obsession. It wasn't that he didn't have some interest in Kang's views. Like any monk who sought to improve his skills, he was always open to learning new techniques and practices. But the monasteries had been around for over three hundred years, and Delun was fairly certain that in that time every possible variation of training had been experimented with. The techniques widely used were used because they worked.

A few major training systems had developed over the centuries. Delun would describe Kang's as pushing until the breaking point, day after day. It was, unfortunately, a fairly common system. The practice *could* create strong warriors. Delun had met a few in his travels, and Kang was certainly among the strongest monks he'd ever met. If not supervised properly, though, it could destroy a warrior. Fortunately, most abbots who supervised such training knew just how far they could push their students. Kang's abbot seemed to know exactly what he was doing.

Occasionally, Delun attempted to steer the conversation to other topics, but Kang kept asking him questions about his own training, surely disappointed in the answers. Delun believed in the practice of consistency. He never trained as hard as Kang, but he also never missed a day of practice, no matter where life took him.

Eventually, Delun gave up trying to discover anything useful about the situation in Kulat from Kang and enjoyed the scenery as he traded training tips with Kang. It wasn't terribly difficult. Kang was nothing if not sincere, and Delun often developed a bond with those who practiced their craft with deliberate care.

When they arrived at the outskirts of Kulat, Delun asked the carriage driver to stop. They got out of the carriage and Delun had the driver ferry his limited supplies to the monastery. The driver bowed and took off deeper into town.

Kang looked at Delun, curiosity in his eyes. Delun had offered to let the man ride the carriage all the way, but Kang had elected to remain with his new friend.

Delun gestured at the town. "I like to get a sense of a place before I begin working there. Different towns have different flavors, different practices that offend. One can't experience a place without slowing down, which is exactly what I intend to do."

Kang gave Delun a look that implied the older monk had lost his mind, but said nothing. Youth was wasted on the young, Delun figured.

They made their way into town. It didn't take Delun long to decide Kulat was far different than most towns he'd been in.

The white robes of a monk were always conspicuous, and people everywhere reacted in different ways. Some reacted with awe and respect, as they should. Others cowered in various degrees of fear. Such reactions weren't ideal, but they would do. In Kulat, Delun saw little of either reaction. Instead, he saw anger. A lot of it.

His instinct was to ask Kang, but knew that was foolish. From the look on his new friend's face, he didn't even recognize the glares he was getting. Either he was completely oblivious or had lived with them for so long he had gotten used to them. Neither boded well for Delun's work.

Kang led the way to the monastery while Delun continued to observe. He saw plenty of black looks. A few women hugged their children closer, and a few particularly bold men spit on the street where he and Kang had just passed. In other towns, Delun might have done something about the open disrespect, but here he feared he would start an incident. The problems in this town went deeper than just the Golden Leaf.

Eventually they approached the tall white walls of the monastery. Kulat had grown up right around the monastery walls, something Delun was seeing more and more of. Hundreds of years ago, most monasteries had been founded well outside of towns and cities. The separation was considered beneficial for both the monks and the civilians. But the population of the empire had grown, and more monasteries were being swallowed by towns. Not for the first time, Delun was grateful his own monastery sat high in the mountains, far removed from such a fate.

Their robes gained them easy admittance to the gate and Delun passed into another world.

Immediately he felt his body relax. In his travels, he had been to dozens of monasteries. All of them differed, of course, but there was an air about them that was constant and refreshing. In the monasteries, discipline and order ruled. Here, the course of the empire was maintained.

The monastery in Kulat was yet another blend of comforting similarity and striking difference. Though the day was late, the monks still stood in rows, practicing their forms together. Delun glanced at their technique. Most monasteries maintained high standards, and this one was no different. In fact, as he watched, he realized the technique of most of the monks was nearly flawless. Punches were sharp, and no monk trained with less than complete focus.

Delun stopped, impressed. He nodded at the man at the head of the group. "Is that your abbot?"

Kang's admiration was evident. "Yes. That is Guanyu."

"He's an excellent master."

"I agree. It was the quality of his teaching that brought many of us here."

Delun frowned, a thought occurring to him. There were a lot of monks here. Too many, actually. Kulat was a town of a few thousand people, based on the last census. The monastery shouldn't have more than a dozen monks. Delun supposed if they were drawing from the surrounding area that number might bump up to twenty, but surely no more.

A quick glance told him almost fifty monks trained within these walls. That made it almost as large as the monastery in Jihan, the largest in the empire. For a small town in the middle of the sparsely populated western empire, that made little sense. Delun almost asked Kang, but that was perhaps another question for the abbot.

The abbot spotted them and finished instructing the form. Then he bowed to Kang. Without a word passing between them, Kang stepped up and took the role of teacher as the abbot came and joined Delun.

The abbot bowed. "You must be Delun. My name is Guanyu, and I am the abbot here in Kulat. Taio told me to expect your coming, but I expected you several days ago."

Delun bowed, slightly deeper than the abbot, to show him the proper respect. "I am. On the way, I came across Kang and we traveled to Galan together."

"Ahh," the abbot said. "And were you able to uncover what happened there?"

Delun shook his head. "No. The situation in this region is far more complex than I was led to believe. Also, I am sorry. I understand that you lost two monks to the attack."

The abbot's face darkened. "One was an old fool I was happily rid of, but another was young and strong. He believed in our cause, and had a bright future ahead of him. He'll be sorely missed."

Delun caught the abbot's turn of phrase. "Your cause?"

The abbot gave a grim smile. "Are you a student of history, Delun?"

"Not particularly. I know more than most, but I've always had my focus set tightly on the present."

"A worthy goal. But history has much to teach us. Do you know how empires crumble?"

Delun had to admit he did not.

"There's more than one danger, unfortunately, but the one that concerns me most is the danger of the frontiers, the places empires pay too little attention to. Perhaps a piece of land is lost here, or a village rebels there. No single incident is large enough to attract the empire's attention. But piece by piece the empire falls away, doomed even before it is aware of the threat."

"You worry about that here?"

"Constantly. We are not a populated area, nor do we create much wealth. The people here tolerate the rule of the empire, but they don't embrace it. It is a different, far less civilized world out here. Is this your first visit west?"

"This far, yes."

"I won't belabor the point. The nearest lord is two week's march away at best. There are no city guards in most towns, and crime and justice are handled by the people themselves, with predictable results. The strong succeed and the weak do not. Your average citizen here farms, traps, hunts, and has built his own house. There is a terrible streak of independence that exists among the people here, a pride in being able to take care of oneself."

Delun thought of the elder at Galan, who had chafed against their requests. At the time, Delun hadn't understood. The monks were here to help. Now he saw the other side—a man who believed his town could get along just fine without help, even if it came from someone as strong as a monk.

"Is that why you have so many monks training here? I'm surprised, both by the number and by their quality."

Guanyu gave a small nod of acknowledgment. "I

believe that the monasteries are here to protect the empire, to improve the lives of the people. We need to be strong to do so, and we need to maintain justice with an iron fist."

Delun couldn't help but be impressed. Guanyu seemed exactly the type of leader they needed more of. "I agree. As you know, I'm here to track down rumors of this Golden Leaf. Do you know anything?"

The abbot shook his head. "All I've heard are rumors. We've investigated, but if they exist and they are here, they are very well hidden. Personally, I suspect whoever is running them is a cunning foe. Their moves are subtle, based more in propaganda and lies than in violence. They seek to turn the people, and the empire itself, away from the monasteries."

Delun nodded thoughtfully. He'd wondered if perhaps that had something to do with the less than warm welcome he'd received in Kulat. Perhaps that reaction was due to the Golden Leaf. Guanyu certainly seemed to have his work cut out for him here. "Do you think they had something to do with Galan? Perhaps they staged the destruction, or had help?"

The abbot stared sharply at him. "You mean Lei?"

"Yes."

"You ran into him?"

"Kang and I attempted attacking him together." Delun didn't care to discuss the results.

Guanyu shook his head. "He's always stronger than we think he is." Focusing on the discussion at hand, he said, "Of course, it's a possibility, but personally, I doubt it. Lei is a thorn in my side I can't remove, but I do believe that all he wants is to be left alone. I have a hard time believing he would do such a thing."

"The power was incredible in Galan, and the only surviving witness retreated into the mountains."

The abbot considered it. "I *would* like to pin the blame on Lei, but I'm not convinced. He's lived in those mountains for decades now, and he's never done anything like this. I could be wrong, but until there's evidence, I can't say."

Delun accepted the abbot's opinion. Kang had believed much the same, and Delun would be foolish to not respect their views.

Together, the two monks climbed up onto the walls of the monastery, overlooking the town. Delun felt strangely exposed, and he had a memory of the arrow almost killing him a few nights back.

"Do you believe in the purpose of the monasteries, Delun?" the abbot asked.

Delun was momentarily surprised by the question. "With my whole heart."

The abbot smiled. "As do I. You asked me what my cause was earlier and I skirted the question. However, seeing you and Kang, and talking to you now, I feel confident in telling you the full truth." He extended his hands, taking in all of the town around them. "This is my cause. Here, I'm trying to build a new way forward."

Delun glanced at the abbot, wondering exactly what he was getting at.

"Here in Kulat," the abbot continued, not even noticing Delun's wary glance, "I'm going to show the empire how peaceful and prosperous a town can be when the monasteries are in complete control."

15

Bai and Lei left the quiet village behind them, following a trail that led higher into the mountains. After several days in the village, Bai's lungs were getting used to the altitude. The hike seemed far less strenuous than she expected. After a few days of a warm, comfortable bed and incredible meals, she felt stronger than ever before.

During her first days in the village she had suffered from recurring headaches. Those who checked on her suggested drinking plenty of water, and that seemed to help. So long as she didn't move around too much, she felt decent.

Today's adventure would challenge her newfound health. With every step up the trail, she imagined the pain building behind her forehead. Fortunately, when they stopped in a clearing next to a small mountain lake, Bai felt as good as ever. She'd actually found the walk invigorating. The height and the cool air combined to lift her spirits.

Lei hadn't said much on the walk. He hadn't spoken much to her since the first day she'd woken up in his village. He'd spoken briefly with her when he learned she planned on staying, asking her if she desired training. She hadn't been certain, but she'd said yes anyway. In response, he'd told her to rest and acclimatize for the next few days.

Since then, most of Bai's company had been a group of local women. When they learned of Bai's skill as a seamstress, they put her to work, and Bai found she enjoyed the distraction and the company. Both took her mind off of weightier matters.

Mending clothes and creating new robes allowed her mind to settle into familiar patterns. She'd been the same as long as she could remember. When work was put in front of her, she gradually lost her awareness of her surroundings, melting into the task. Some of the women gently chided her for not paying enough attention to the conversation, but Bai suspected they saw that she wanted to lose herself in the work.

Too many questions swirled endlessly in her mind. Lei's silence hadn't helped. He'd spoken to her about training, confirmed that he believed she was gifted, and said no more. Some moments, she wanted to believe him. Others, she wondered if he was a fool.

Then this morning he showed up and asked her to train, right then. Her first reaction was to deny him, mostly out of spite. But this was her way forward, and Hien's words stuck in her memory. She didn't understand Lei's silences or his methods, but at the same time, she couldn't shake the feeling there was *something* behind his actions, some greater purpose or plan she didn't recognize.

Lei had them take positions about five paces away from one another. He looked relaxed, his feet a little wider than hip width apart, his hands clasped behind his back. He had a hint of a smile on his face. "You don't believe me."

She shook her head. "Women don't possess the gift. Everyone knows that."

"And yet here you are."

"I want answers."

"You possess the gift."

She glared at him, but his smile never faltered. He seemed to relish being obtuse.

"Do you truly believe that half of all people don't even have the chance of being born gifted?"

Bai's brow furrowed. She hadn't ever questioned the knowledge. Doing so would be no different than wondering every evening if the sun would rise the next day. Some things in life simply were. "Why are there no women in the monasteries, then?"

Lei's grin grew a little, as though she'd finally asked a worthy question. "Tradition is a difficult master to disobey. You know how most gifted children are discovered?"

Bai opened her mouth to answer, only to realize she didn't know.

"It turns out, it's very hard to discover when a person is gifted. Personally, I suspect that there are hundreds, if not thousands, of gifted wandering the streets who don't realize their power.

"In most cases, power responds to power. A monk, paying attention, might feel the faintest flicker of energy in a young boy as he passes. It's often not much, and easy to miss. Like you, the monasteries believe only men can have the power. Why would a monk even look for women with the gift if he's convinced only men can have it?"

Bai turned that over in her mind. She didn't believe Lei, but his voice conveyed his sincerity. Even if she didn't believe, she knew he did.

"So, you can feel my power?" She tried to keep a mocking tone out of her voice and failed.

Lei nodded, and she started.

"You lie."

"No. Standing close to you, like this, is incredible. Your power is unmistakable to any with the gift. It reacts to my own."

Bai shook her head furiously. Of all the deceits she'd experienced, this was the worst. She was a village seamstress. Nothing more.

"Do you feel refreshed, standing next to me?"

Bai looked over at Lei. She did, but what did that have to do with anything?

"Stand here. Pay attention to how you feel."

She agreed, reluctantly, and Lei turned and walked away. He approached the shore of the lake and walked around it for a while. Bai had expected him to leave and come back a few minutes later. Instead, he put a considerable amount of space between them, and waited off in the distance. She felt awkward, standing here alone.

Bai ignored her anger at this game and examined herself. As Lei walked away, Bai felt the muscles in her legs begin to complain. She wasn't surprised. She was still a little sore from the escape with Hien, and while the walk this morning hadn't been more than a mile or two, much of the trail was steep.

Bai sat down on a rock, waiting for Lei to return.

Eventually, he started walking back, not in any rush. As he stepped close to her, she felt life return to her limbs. She stood up, her anger returning, then realized exactly what had just happened.

"You see?"

She refused to acknowledge his point.

"This is one reason why I didn't want to train you earlier," Lei said. "I can say more when we progress in our training, but bodies can only handle so much energy. When you came to us, you felt nearly drained, your life in danger in more ways than one. Rest and food have helped you recover, but I didn't want to attempt even basic training without you building your strength back up."

Bai nodded along, absorbing the words but not quite listening. She had gone her entire life believing she was a certain person, and now Lei stood here, telling her she was someone else. Her own skin suddenly felt foreign to her, like she shouldn't belong.

"Do you believe now?" Lei asked.

Bai shook her head. "I don't know."

Lei gave a short, sharp laugh. "At least you're honest."

With that, the two of them began training in earnest. Bai wasn't sure if she believed Lei's story, but she was willing to try, at least. She could follow his instructions. If nothing else, if she failed it would prove he was wrong.

They began with meditations and simple combat forms. Lei taught her how to throw a punch and how to block. He taught her how to kick and to blend one move into another. He was a patient but exacting teacher. Eventually, he taught her the first two-handed sign, which he described as one of the easiest ways to focus energy.

Together, they went through the sign over and over, Lei describing not just the physical process, but the mental ones as well. Bai had never assumed that training to be a monk was easy, but she'd never guessed just how hard it was either.

Try as she might, though, she couldn't get the technique to work. She did everything Lei requested, but nothing happened. As the day wore on, she could tell that even the normally unflappable Lei was beginning to get frustrated. Clearly, he had expected something more from her. But she'd been right all along. She wasn't anything more than a local village seamstress.

As the sun fell toward the mountain peaks, Lei had them take a break from their training. He studied Bai for a few long moments, as if trying to solve an impossible riddle. Finally, with a small shrug, his grin from the morning returned. "Care to spar?"

Bai didn't think she'd heard him correctly. "What?"

"Would you like to spar? It seems as good a way as any to finish out the day."

Bai agreed. They'd trained in the martial forms of the monasteries all day, and although she didn't think she could even hold a candle to Lei, she was curious to see what she could do.

They took fighting stances across from one another. Once settled, Lei came in, testing her guard with a few quick jabs.

None of them landed, but Bai didn't think Lei had tried very hard. He came in again with another combination, this time landing a soft kick to her left thigh. She shook the attack off, trying to land a few punches of her own. Even as she moved in, she could feel how wild they were. In practice, Lei had drilled into her the importance of balance and controlling the body. Now, as soon as the situation became real, all her practice vanished.

She retreated a few paces and relaxed. Lei had trained her well, even if it was only for a day. He came in again, and Bai slipped into the same state she did when she sewed. The world fell away, leaving only her and Lei. She saw the combination as it came in, dodged the first two jabs and cleanly blocked the kick. Her own fists snaked out, her balance better this time.

Bai missed, but Lei smiled. "Better."

He came in again, this time faster. Bai almost blocked him, but a quick jab found the side of her face. It hadn't been hard, and she'd been slapped before, but she'd never been punched in the face. Instead of cowering, though, she became determined. She would land one punch before the day ended.

When Lei approached the next time, Bai felt that something was off. Her world seemed more vivid, the sounds louder. Lei stepped in, jabbing with his right hand. She defended easily enough, then felt the power in his left hand, held low. By the time she realized he had gathered an energy attack, it was too late. She felt the force as it jumped out of his hand, aimed straight at her chest.

She felt the blow land.

Then nothing.

Lei slowed down in front of her. She had time to study the expression on his face, caught somewhere between curiosity and concern. His guard was down, his expectations obvious. His torso was exposed, not far from her leading leg.

Just as he had taught her, she lifted the leg, chambered the kick, and snapped out at him. She saw the shock in his eyes as he tumbled backward, rolling to a stop several paces back. The world sped up again.

He coughed, and she was at his side immediately.

"Lei! I'm so sorry!"

He blinked a few times, then laughed out loud. Shaking himself off, he got to his feet. He studied her carefully. "Perhaps we should call that a good day of training."

She saw that he was trying to hide his pain, but she had managed to hurt him. "I'm sorry."

He waved her concern away. "I've been hit worse."

"What happened?"

Lei shook his head. "I'm not sure. I have some ideas, but I need to think on this."

She was disappointed in the answer, but didn't want to push him after what she had done.

And what had she done? How had she knocked this man over with such ease?

After a full day of training, she was left with more questions than answers.

They came down to the village and stood for a moment in the village square. Lei turned to her. "We'll train again tomorrow. Make sure you eat a large meal and get some sleep. Your body will need both."

She nodded and was about to return to her rooms when she saw an older man in the square. Their eyes met, and Bai felt a deep-seated sensation of recognition. But her memory, as it too often was these days, was blank. More telling, though, was the man's reaction. When he saw her, his eyes widened in pure terror. He walked quickly away, never even glancing back her way. He moved with a definite limp, and Bai saw bandages on his legs and one arm.

Lei had noticed the exchange. He frowned. "Do you two know each other?"

Bai shook her head. "He seems familiar, but I don't recognize him."

Lei watched her closely. He didn't speak for a few moments. "He's a monk from Kulat. And I've never seen him so scared in my life."

16

Delun and Kang had become inseparable since Delun's arrival in Kulat. Delun suspected their relationship wasn't entirely by choice. Though Guanyu never spoke of the decision to Delun, since his arrival at the monastery Delun hadn't been able to go into Kulat alone. Kang's company was always offered under the guise of companionship, and Delun didn't care to offend his hosts, yet. Kang's presence raised an interesting question, though: was Kang supposed to protect Delun, or was he intentionally hindering the investigation?

Delun couldn't answer the question with any certainty. He didn't necessarily mind the company of the larger man, but Kang stuck out in town. Even if Delun could have convinced Kang to leave the walls without his robes, his shaven head, tall stature, and judgmental stare were enough to announce himself everywhere. With Kang nearby, Delun never had to worry about being threatened, but blending in with a crowd was also out of the question.

Because of the constant companionship, Delun hadn't been able to investigate as thoroughly as he would have liked. Some tasks required discretion, and Delun was certain Kang didn't even know the meaning of the word. Kang understood strength. On Delun's second day in town he had asked some polite questions of a shopkeeper, and when the man didn't answer the questions to Kang's satisfaction, Kang had almost thrown the poor man through a wall.

Delun became more aware of the feelings of the people in town as well. There wasn't a doubt in his mind they hated the monks. In fact, Delun often felt that when he entered town he was lighting a fuse to a barrel of black powder, waiting for it to explode in his face.

He would have preferred working alone. He could pass as a traveler and obtain more information through conversation than Kang and his fists could get in months. After years of this work, he had learned how to guide a conversation, how to get information without alarming suspects. Delun had pressed gently against his hosts, insisting he didn't need protection, but Kang couldn't be swayed, increasing Delun's certainty the monk acted on orders.

In short, Delun's investigation had stalled, and he blamed the interference of the Kulat monastery. The dilemma put him in an interesting place. He could either deceive the monastery or demand they leave him alone.

Neither option appealed to him. The idea of lying to a monk didn't sit well with him, but he didn't want to weaken potential alliances because of his demands. Unless his circumstances changed soon, though, he would need to do one or the other.

As night fell, Delun left his guest room and walked toward the monastery gates, interested in exploring Kulat by night. In his investigations earlier in the day he had picked up one interesting piece of information.

He was being followed.

Whoever the task had fallen to, they were an expert. Delun was certain it was a woman, but beyond that, he hadn't managed to force her to reveal herself. She was always in the shadows, an anonymous face in the crowd, like a ghost haunting his every step.

Tonight, he hoped to trap her.

As he neared the gate, Kang appeared by his side, trying and failing to look nonchalant. "Leaving?"

Just as he had expected. For all his complaining about Kang's presence, he would need the monk's assistance tonight. Delun didn't think he could trap the spy alone. At least, not without causing more damage than he wanted.

"I am. We were followed today, and I'd like to meet our stalker."

Kang's eyes sparkled with excitement. Delun knew how much the man enjoyed action. It made him a poor monk in many ways, but that desire to fight wasn't without its uses, he supposed.

Together, the two of them left the gate and walked into the darkened streets of Kulat. Delun took them to the night market. He purchased some grilled vegetables and ate with delight. The kitchen in Kulat's monastery lacked either experience in cooking or a desire for flavor, in Delun's opinion. The fresh food put a smile on his face. Now, no matter what the rest of the evening held, he could call the night a success.

Kang towered over Delun, refusing to partake. He claimed, a few days ago after Delun had asked, that the only food he needed came from the wilds or the monastery's kitchen. Delun hadn't argued the point. Let the man believe what he would. Delun would enjoy the wonderful bounty the land and people who worked in it provided.

Kang stared from one end of the market to the other, making it delightfully obvious that he was searching for the one who followed them. Delun watched with interest, not bothering to hide his amusement. The shadow had been with them within a hundred paces of the monastery's walls. Even now she crouched, the barest outline of a shadow on a rooftop nearby.

Kang looked down at Delun.

"We are not being followed," he said.

Delun forced himself not to smile. "Keep an eye out. I am certain they will try to find us tonight. When they do, we'll surprise them."

Contented by the light meal, Delun stood up. He led the way out of the night market. The whole market seemed to breathe a deep sigh of relief as they left, and Delun wondered how much longer it would be before something snapped the tension in this town. The more time he spent here, the more clear it was the differences between the monastery and the city would lead to violence.

In this, Delun's assessment of the town differed significantly from Guanyu's. The abbot, like too many monks, didn't see the threat the common people represented. Guanyu didn't care if the people were discontented. In his worldview, the people would come around in time. The peace of the region and the strength of the monks would win converts in time.

Delun held no such misconceptions. Sure, he and his brothers were much stronger than any individual citizen, but they were greatly outnumbered. Monks tended to overestimate their strength, forgetting that a dagger in the dark, a poisoned cup, or an arrow killed a monk just as dead as a regular citizen. Delun supported Guanyu's plan, but he believed the abbot was reckless in his disregard of the people.

He led Kang into a small alley. "I'm certain we're being followed. Together, we can catch our shadow. Wait here for the next five minutes, then follow my energy. If I'm attacked, come help."

Kang nodded his understanding. Delun was about to step out of the alley when he had a thought. He paused and stared at Kang.

"We need them alive, Kang."

Kang looked doubtful, but he gave a sharp nod of acknowledgment. It didn't inspire confidence, but Delun didn't think he'd get more from the man.

Delun made sure the man stood deep in the shadows, then returned to the street. Though it was nothing but a gut feeling, he suspected the spy was after him. With luck, she would discount Kang and get caught between the two monks. As far as plans went, it wasn't his most clever, but he didn't trust Kang to follow anything more than the simplest instructions.

With the streets nearly deserted, Delun decided caution was wise. He made some signs with his left hand, casting a shield around him. If the tail had hostile intentions, the shield would go a long way toward keeping Delun safe. Memories of his close call on the mountain still haunted him.

He turned another corner, seeing the shadow leap between roofs in the distance. That confirmed his intuition that he was the person of interest.

Delun paused, pretending to look around. He only stopped for a moment, but it was enough.

He heard the thunk of an arrow as it deflected off his shield.

Delun looked up, seeing the archer already drawing back another arrow. The woman's second shot was true, but it still deflected harmlessly off his shield.

Delun sent a small wave of energy at the assassin, but the woman saw his hands move and retreated before the blast hit. Delun frowned. There was no doubt the woman knew she was attacking monks, but her actions seemed calm and calculated, not uncertain or panicked. She'd moved as soon as he aimed his hand at her, sliding around and protecting herself.

This woman knew what she was doing.

Delun wished he was privy to her purpose. He scanned the rooftops, looking for any hint of the woman. He dropped his shield and took cover behind a corner, worried that he would lose focus and his shield at an inopportune moment. A few deep breaths later, he formed the sign for the shield and released it again, hoping the woman would reappear before it was too late. He stepped back into the street.

Delun felt his shield waver as his focus slipped. These techniques weren't meant to be held so long. Even weaker techniques, held for more than a handful of seconds at a time, could drain a monk. The shield he held wasn't weak, and he felt his focus deteriorating.

Was this what she wanted? For him to exhaust himself? He could run, but she had the high ground with a bow, and he wanted to capture her.

Something sparking flew from a rooftop to his right. Delun barely had time to focus on it before it struck his shield. The arrow didn't penetrate, but Delun noticed something different about the arrow just before his world was engulfed by flame.

A fire arrow. Delun swore and focused. The fire wouldn't last long. There was nothing on his shield to burn except the oil from the arrow. But if the shield faded now the burning oil would drop on him. To make matters worse, he was temporarily blinded by the flames. Who knew what awaited him when the fire faded?

For the first time in his life, Delun wondered if he had met a citizen capable of killing a monk.

Sweat poured down his face, not from the fire but from exertion. His muscles trembled as the power flowed through him. He wasn't sure how much longer he could hold the shield.

Then he felt another power, enormous.

Kang.

The other monk had come, sensing Delun's distress. The last of the fire burned away and Delun dropped his shield. He stumbled over to the side of the road, seeking cover from an errant arrow.

He felt Kang's attack and saw the roof of a building tear away from a focused blast. Delun's eyes went wide as the building slowly crumbled. From his perspective, he saw a figure, blacker than the night, leap from the collapsing roof to its neighbor. He wondered if Kang saw the woman from his position further down the street.

Apparently, he didn't. He walked toward Delun, not paying any more attention to the buildings. Around them, the street came to life, the noise of the collapsing building and the light of the fire waking up the neighbors.

Delun saw the attack as it happened. The assassin, persistent, popped up from a roof and released another arrow. Delun raised his hand and pushed what energy he had left at the space between Kang and the arrow speeding toward him. The attack wasn't much, but it was enough. It moved the arrow, throwing it off target, causing it to embed itself deeply in Kang's shoulder.

The large man roared, the arrow doing little more than angering him. He turned to the rooftops and unleashed a series of attacks designed to destroy everything. Roofs shattered and walls caved in as Kang threw attack after attack at the buildings near where the arrow had come from.

Delun watched in horror as one building collapsed just as a candle flickered to life inside. As soon as the light had appeared, it was gone. How many people lived in those buildings?

It happened too quickly for Delun to react. Kang had torn down three buildings before Delun found the strength to stand and put his arms around the other man. Kang fought against him, rage in his eyes. If not for the tremendous amount of energy he'd already expended, Delun wouldn't have had a chance. Delun could barely reach around the man to hold him.

Kang was looking for someone to attack. Delun saw it written on his face. The man had lost control.

Delun looked around the street. People peeked out from their houses to see what had happened. Many were leaving the protection of their homes. Some carried knives and daggers. Some carried poles and torches. For the moment, they looked more confused than angry, but Delun didn't think that would last long. Soon, they would realize Kang had killed their neighbors. Would tonight be the match that lit the powder?

Delun didn't want to be around to find out. "Kang, we need to go."

Kang didn't react, his focus completely given to the search for the woman who had wounded him. Delun was watching too, but saw nothing. It would have been difficult for the assassin to escape Kang's rampage, but Delun suspected if anyone could, she might have. She came prepared to fight monks. Kang's unrestrained attacks wouldn't have caught her by complete surprise.

The people began to clump in groups, their stares hardening. Delun pushed harder against Kang. "We need to leave, now."

Kang still didn't react.

"Guanyu needs to know what happened here."

The sound of his master's name snapped Kang back to reality. He looked away from the collapsed buildings and nodded.

The two of them limped their way in the direction of the monastery.

Delun kept looking over his shoulder, fearing he would see the shadow behind them, an arrow already on the way to claim his life.

He didn't feel safe until he put the walls of the monastery between him and the city.

17

Bai paced a small patch of grass in the mountain village. After days of slow, quiet recovery, her life had recently picked up a new speed. Like a rock sliding down from high in the mountains, she now felt her life crashing out of control.

Lei sat in the heart of her chaos. First the protection from the monks, then the revelation that she had the same powers they did.

She didn't believe him. Though she couldn't explain the events of her training, there had to be another explanation, a story that made more sense. She was a seamstress, a woman from a run-down village at the edges of the empire. Her gifts were with needle and thread, not strength.

But that didn't explain what she had just experienced. Her recent memories played in her mind over and over. She wanted to believe that he had let her hit him, like a friend letting you win a game after losing several in a row.

Lei didn't seem to be that kind of man, though, and she had felt the difference. Looking down at her hands, she remembered how they had felt, tingling with energy. She had hit him, with a strength that defied her understanding.

But she was a seamstress.

She had never felt so lost.

And now there was the old man, pouring oil on the fires of her confusion. Lei had gone after him, the two of them retreating into the tavern that served as a common room for the village. Bai didn't have to stay outside, but that man had recognized her. A *monk from Kulat* had recognized her. Worse, when he did, he ran away.

Monks didn't run from seamstresses.

Bai felt dizzy and her legs threatened to collapse underneath her.

As much as she wanted to know what happened, Bai worried that she couldn't face the truth. She feared it would destroy her.

Instinctively, she reached for the bracelet, spinning it around her wrist, trying to feel her mother's presence.

Her mother.

Whose story had ended.

Thinking of her mother, the truth no longer seemed important. She should run. It wasn't too late.

She looked over to the small inn where she lived. With a few steps and a brief climb up a ladder, she could be back in her room, curled under the covers. But every time she took a step in that direction, she faltered.

Before she could talk herself out of it, Bai turned and marched into the tavern where the two men sat.

She spotted them easily, seated at a table in the corner, huddled together. She felt the weight of the bracelet on her wrist and almost turned around. The momentary courage that had driven her into the room vanished in an instant, doubt assailing her thoughts. But Lei caught her eye and waved her over. The older monk, still looking uneasy, shifted his weight away from her. Bai had never seen a terrified monk, and it did little to ease her worry.

She had come too far, though. She'd be embarrassed to turn around now.

Bai approached the table slowly, pulling up a chair next to Lei. For a few tense moments, no one spoke.

Lei handled introductions. "Bai, this is Yang. He's a monk down in Kulat, and a friend of the village."

Bai glanced uncertainly at Lei. Why would any monk be a friend of this village? It represented everything the monasteries opposed. But Lei offered no response. Apparently, that question was Yang's to answer or not.

Yang dipped his head in acknowledgment, and Bai could see the force of will that kept him in place.

She too had a hard time sitting still. Her feet tapped against the floor as she bounced her knee up and down. She glanced at the door, still so close. Her urge to run almost overpowered her sense of shame.

Then she thought of Lei's words from that afternoon. She wasn't suffering from nervous energy. Her own power was responding to that of the monks. Further evidence that Lei hadn't been lying to her.

"Focus on your breath," Lei suggested. "It's a refrain often heard at the monasteries, and for good reason. It's always with you, and if you can train your mind and body to respond to that focus, it'll serve you well in almost every situation."

The table was silent for a couple of minutes while Bai wrestled with Lei's advice. Eventually, Yang spoke. "I wouldn't believe it if I wasn't sitting right here. No matter what I saw."

Bai looked at the monk. While she struggled to focus on

her breath, she had no problem focusing on him. "Do you know what happened in Galan?"

He met her gaze. "I was there."

Bai lost the thin control she had been holding onto. She leaned forward over the table, feeling more aggressive than ever. "What happened? Why are you here now, instead of weeks ago?"

Yang's chair scraped against the wooden floor as he put distance between them. He looked like a frightened rabbit.

Lei grabbed her shoulder and gently pulled her back. She resisted for a moment, but then relented. Now that she was paying attention, she could feel the power flowing through their contact. She ignored that for the moment. The real answers she sought were sitting right in front of her.

"Yang says he was down in Galan, in the market square, when it happened," Lei said. "But, as you can see, he's been injured."

Yang shifted forward, still nervous. "I was. My first thought was to come here, but I decided against it. I suspected the monks would send their own to investigate, and I didn't want to be nearby when that came to pass. I found a place in the woods where I could rest, far enough away from the traveled paths that my likelihood of being discovered by another monk was slim. I had an opportunity to fake my death, and I couldn't pass it up."

The explanation only confused Bai further. But she saw he was just getting started.

"I'm glad I didn't come this way. I felt the battle, even as far away as I was. Had I been here, healing at the time, I certainly would have been found."

Lei made a small motion and Yang's voice faded. Lei looked at Bai. "I've only spoken with Yang for a few minutes, but I know the heart of the story he is about to tell. He knows what happened, but I do not believe you'll like the truth. A truth told can never be unheard." He left the question unspoken.

Bai fiddled with her bracelet. It wasn't too late to put this all behind her. But, she suspected, it would be if she heard Yang's tale. She imagined leaving this village and starting a new life somewhere far away. The pull of the dream almost convinced her to stand and leave.

But she was lying to herself. She could leave without knowing the truth, but she couldn't go back to who she had been. She had no mother to watch out for her, and if Lei was telling the truth, and she was gifted, there would be no place she could hide. Hien's words about constantly looking over her shoulder echoed in her thoughts.

She couldn't find the strength to speak, but she nodded.

"Why don't you start at the beginning?" Lei suggested.

Yang nodded. "There isn't much to tell. I was traveling with another monk named Zhou. He was a young man, very brash, very confident in his powers, like too many of the monks right now, I think. Strong, though. Our journey to Galan wasn't supposed to be anything special. We were to make ourselves seen, solve whatever problems were brought our way, and speak to a few of our suppliers about the monastery's needs for the summer months."

Yang scratched at his chin. "I've been a monk now for over three decades. In that time, the monasteries have seen tremendous change, and I fear that more is coming. Zhou was the type of monk who had been trained in response to some of these changes.

"I grew up learning that the monks were supposed to serve the empire. Zhou grew up believing we should run it. Unfortunately, when a group of people begins to lose power, they'll do everything they can to hold onto it that much tighter."

The older monk sighed. "Zhou wasn't a good man. I had hoped that on our trip I might get him to see more deeply, but in that, I failed terribly.

"We were in the market square that morning. I was talking to a fisherman, and it all happened so fast. A group of boys were playing ball, and an errant throw struck Zhou in the temple. I have no doubt it hurt, of course, but it was hardly the sort of injury worth noting."

Yang paused. "Zhou didn't see it that way. He turned on the boys, yelling at them, telling them that they had no sense of respect. He turned to the boy who had thrown the ball, picking him up and slamming him against a wall."

Yang's gaze turned to her. "And that is where you come in."

Bai was even more lost than before. She had the memories of the boys playing ball. That much of the story rang true, at least. But what did any of that have to do with her?

The monk continued. "All of this happened right in front of you. When Zhou attacked the boy, you yelled at him to stop."

Bai frowned. "I did?" She couldn't imagine herself yelling at a monk.

"You did. By this time, I had turned to watch what was happening, and I saw everything. You looked furious, and I assumed you were the parent of at least one of the children."

Yang's look was questioning, but she shook her head. She had known the boys, but shared no blood.

Yang shrugged. "Regardless, what happened next happened so fast, I'm still not sure I understand it exactly. Zhou attacked you with the third sign. He was a strong monk—several orders stronger than me. I feared his blast would kill you. In fact, I was certain of it."

Yang stopped his story and Bai realized she was almost leaning all the way over the table. The monk didn't look like he wanted to share the rest.

Lei gently encouraged him. "It's okay."

Yang swallowed and continued. "The power that flattened Galan, it came from you. I can't explain why, but when Zhou attacked, it unleashed something greater than I've ever felt before. I felt your power swelling and had just enough time to form a shield. Fortunately, I was already next to a building, which provided me some shelter."

Yang stared down at the table. "You screamed, like you were in indescribable agony. I've never heard so much pain in a person's voice."

Yang looked up, and Bai understood now why he held such terror in his eyes. Why he had run when he saw her again. He paused to let it sink in, then finished his story.

"Bai, you're the one who destroyed Galan."

18

When Delun left the monastery the next day, there was no sign of his mysterious would-be assassin. He suspected the woman had either been injured or killed. Kang's assault had been vicious. Surviving it would have been no small feat. He had to admit, though, some small part of him was disappointed to have lost his shadow.

In the work Delun performed, he had more chance than most to encounter people who wanted to destroy the monasteries. As a point of fact, seeking out such people and killing them formed the basis of most of his adult life. What he had learned was that when it came to insurrection, there were no shortage of leaders who talked loudly and charismatically. There were far fewer capable of doing anything meaningful.

He'd lost track of the number of times he'd come across a rebel promising revolution. They all blended together in his memories, people who were dissatisfied with the systems that ran their lives. They spoke loudly about change and power, but their words were empty. Most often, when Delun killed them, the movement fell apart in a matter of days. Without the mouthpiece stirring up trouble, most citizens went back to their daily existence, their dreams denied.

The Golden Leaf felt different. Like so many others, they stood opposed to the monastery. The similarities ended there. Unlike most movements, they didn't seem to have a public leader. As near as Delun could tell, he wasn't even certain they had many members. If they did, he would have discovered some in town.

If the attitude of the average Kulat citizen was any indicator, though, the arguments of the Golden Leaf had plenty of supporters. Delun thought of hidden currents underneath the waters. On the surface, the waters of Kulat seemed calm. There were no rallies, no demonstrations, no outright violence prior to last night. But under the surface, discontentment stirred, ready to suck the monks into the murky depths.

Delun left the monastery just long enough to confirm that he was no longer being followed. He didn't dare risk remaining in town for too long, especially in his robes. Not only was he left alone by his shadow, but by Kang as well. He wanted to seize the opportunity to unravel the mystery of the Golden Leaf, but felt caution was more warranted today. Too many questions could pull him into the hidden currents below, and if the Golden Leaf had more warriors like the woman, he wasn't prepared to face their wrath yet. He turned back to the monastery, his mind churning.

Last night had been instructive. He'd learned the Golden Leaf had access to warriors willing and possibly able to kill monks. He'd learned that they considered him enough of a threat to try and kill him, breaking their otherwise non-violent streak. Unfortunately, he'd learned little else.

He could almost feel the pattern underneath the chaos. The attack in Galan, the former monk, Lei, hiding in the mountains, and the ambush the night before. All of it was connected. There was no coincidence. But he couldn't see the thread that ran between the events.

He suspected he and Kang had played into the Golden Leaf's hands with the ambush. In the time since, the mood in the town had become even more intense. Seven people had died in Kang's attacks. Delun didn't know if that meant six innocents and one assassin, or seven innocents. No one in town had anything to offer the monks but angry glares, and Guanyu had placed a temporary ban on monks leaving the monastery grounds. Delun had to pull rank on the monk at the gate so he could leave.

If they had stood at the edge of a precipice before, now they dangled off the edge, hanging by their fingers.

Delun recognized he and Kang had been put in a situation where they were almost guaranteed to lose. If the assassin had gotten one of them, it would have been a victory for the Golden Leaf. As it was, even though they hadn't died, their retaliation acted as free propaganda for the Golden Leaf's aims. It had been damn clever.

Delun returned to the monastery courtyard and climbed the stairs leading up to the walls, looking over Kulat. For a town that felt as though it was on the edge of eruption, the streets sounded remarkably quiet. Repair work was being performed in the streets surrounding the monastery, and while citizens didn't come too close to the monastery walls, they didn't avoid this area of town completely.

He felt a presence approach. Turning slightly, he saw Guanyu come and stand next to him. "What thoughts run through your mind?"

Delun gestured out over the city. "The Golden Leaf, and

the danger of underestimating an enemy."

Guanyu scoffed. "Nonsense. They might be more organized than some, but against the monasteries, what chance do they have?"

Delun looked over at Guanyu, surprised to see a complete lack of any subtlety on his face. The abbot truly believed the monasteries were without weakness. Delun's faith was strong, but he also believed any system could fall. He bit back his reply, asking a question instead. "Have you considered lifting the ban on leaving the monastery?"

"That's why I'm here. Tomorrow morning, we are going to march out on the city in force."

Delun forced his face to remain neutral. If the fuse to the powder keg that was Kulat hadn't been lit already, Guanyu sounded determined to light it himself. Delun managed to keep his voice even, barely. "Are you certain that's wise? There are many out there who are angry at us."

"All the more reason for the display. The city needs to know we are here to protect it."

"Thank you for informing me."

The abbot's purpose complete, he nodded and left.

Delun wasn't sure he'd ever found himself in a situation where he both agreed and disagreed so strongly with an abbot. He admired Guanyu's vision and the manner in which he ran the monastery. But his pride created a blind spot in his thinking. This action was unwise.

He sighed. At least the display would give him an opportunity. With all the movement, he could wear traveling clothes and sneak out of the monastery. He needed to find the leader of the Golden Leaf before they could complete their plans, and he couldn't do it trapped behind these walls.

. . .

THE NEXT MORNING, Delun set aside the robes of a monk and put on pants and a tunic. A cloak covered him up, and he gathered in the courtyard with the rest of the monks. His clothing earned him a few glares. The monks at Kulat were proud of their monastery and their role in society. They viewed his choice as a betrayal of sorts.

He didn't think they were wrong. The white robes of a monk were ultimately only clothes. But they meant much more. When Delun wore his robes, he wanted to be a better person. He represented the monasteries, the beacons that had guided the empire for generations. They were all the armor he needed.

Delun ignored the stares. To protect his brothers he needed to separate himself. He'd come to peace with that long ago.

Fortunately, Kang stood near Guanyu at the head of the procession. The big man wouldn't be a problem today. Delun stood near the back of the column, waiting for the march to begin. Once they opened the gates, he'd slip away from the rear of the procession and make his way into the city. He would return to the monastery when his work was done.

The gates swung open, ponderous and heavy. Up front, Guanyu gave some speech to the monks about their duty to protect the town and the empire. Delun heard the words, but they didn't quite register. His mind was on the Golden Leaf. His eyes wandered over the monks, their faces set with stony determination. Though he didn't quite see eye to eye with Guanyu, the man had created a formidable group of monks. Delun respected his work.

The march began. The monks marched side by side, the column two wide and nearly thirty long. Even Delun admitted the sight of so many white-robed figures was impressive. It was a bold enemy that would face such a force. Even a lord's army would quake at the sight.

He reminded himself that the Golden Leaf wouldn't meet the monks on a field of battle. Their methods belonged to the shadows, to whispers passed between friends over drinks. All the brute force in the world wouldn't end such a movement.

Guanyu led them from the gate and turned left, running parallel to the monastery walls. Delun had heard that the abbot planned on leading the monks up the main street that ran through the heart of Kulat, then would circle back to the monastery on another street.

As soon as he stepped beyond the gate, Delun looked for an exit. There was a smaller side street, not far from the gate. Delun could cross the street and be there in a few seconds. He looked around, but no one paid him any attention. Behind him, the gates of the monastery began to close.

Delun split off from the column, crossing the street to the buildings across from the monastery wall. He was about to walk down the side street when movement caught his eye. He stopped, watching as the column marched farther away from him. Maybe three blocks away, a young man walked briskly.

Perhaps it was nothing, but something about that walk raised the hairs on the back of Delun's neck. It was perfectly normal for a person to move out of the way of an advancing monk. But this walk wasn't just an attempt to step aside. The man was trying to get away, to put distance between himself and the column.

Delun's eyes traveled over the column and the area, looking for something else out of place.

Then he saw the construction in the street. Barrels sat

unattended as the monks walked by, not sparing the work area the slightest glance.

But in-between the marching monks, Delun could see that the worksite was abandoned.

His body put the pieces together, and he stepped forward, about to yell out a warning, when the barrels exploded.

He didn't have enough warning to throw up a shield. The blast knocked him down, but at his distance, he was safer than most of the monks. Even as he fell back, he knew his only injury would be his pride.

Before the debris had even settled, Delun saw movement in the buildings opposite the monastery walls. Tiny streaks of darkness launched from the windows, and Delun heard new cries of pain.

Then Delun felt Kang's energy, massive and enraged. As if stuck in his nightmare a second time, Delun watched as Kang flung wave after wave of energy into the buildings. Some walls cratered in, others fell completely. Soon, Kang was joined by other monks who had survived.

Delun stood frozen. He wanted revenge for his brothers, but it seemed his brothers were more than capable of taking their own. Delun didn't see any more arrows, but the monks continued to fling their powers into the buildings, destroying what little remained of the walls.

Behind Kang, Guanyu gathered monks together. Delun could sense the shields forming, protecting the monks from more harm. The monks' attacks slowed and then stopped, the disaster over.

Then a single arrow darted out from the buildings. It was stopped by the shields, falling to the ground without coming close to a monk.

The monks' reaction, though, was devastating. Every

able-bodied monk attacked the area, crushing the building into fine dust. The assault lasted long after it should have ended, monks throwing out their attacks until they wearied themselves to the bone. It occurred to Delun that if he had planned the attack, he might have prepared another wave. In their exhausted state, the monks would have fallen like wheat before the scythe.

Nothing else came, however. An eerie quiet fell over the street, not because it was silent, but after the explosion and the destruction of the surrounding buildings, the moaning of men and the shuffling of feet could barely be heard.

Delun had never seen so much destruction. Only once before had he seen anything close, and that was in Jihan all those years ago. Back then, the victims weren't monks. They'd been citizens, caught in the wrong places at the wrong time.

Delun took a faltering step toward the monks, then stopped, his sense of separation from his brothers stronger than ever. They were helping one another to their feet, carrying the wounded back toward the gate. For all of Guanyu's flaws, he led the men well. The shields remained, one springing up as soon as the previous one fell. The wounded were cared for first, and Delun knew the dead would be moved next. He could help, but there was nothing he could do that couldn't be done by another.

The work he needed to do was deeper in Kulat. The ambush had to be the Golden Leaf. No other explanation made sense. When he found them, they would answer for their crimes.

Delun turned his back to the monastery, every thought turned to the hunt.

19

B ai walked in a nightmare. Clouds obscured the night sky, covering what little light the stars and moon offered with dense shadow. As she picked her way down the main trail toward Galan, all she could make out was different shades of darkness. Rocks stabbed at her feet and roots reached out to trip her.

She was lost in a world of thought, the real world a dull reflection of the terrors she imagined in vivid detail. She heard the soft voices behind her but couldn't make out what they said. Even sound was muffled by the thoughts that crushed her spirit as she descended the mountain.

Yang's story had shattered her. She refused to believe. The monk had seen something, but not what he had described. This was yet another trick, some new hideous way of exerting power over others.

Bai couldn't live with not knowing any longer. She needed answers. She needed certainty, something firm she could hold onto as the world collapsed around her.

Lei and Yang accompanied her. Yang reported that the townspeople had stopped watching the pass, and life had returned to something resembling normal in Galan. Daiyu lent Bai a cloak with a deep hood so she could cover her face. Lei's wife had also given her a dagger to hide in the cloak. She had said it was unwise to travel without some protection. Bai had accepted it without question, not sure what she would do with it. Together, Bai and the two monks made their way down the trail.

Galan soon came into view, darker shadows against a barely lighter background. Bai shivered when she saw it. From a distance, her town looked dead. A small handful of torches flickered against the oppressive darkness, but she didn't see anyone on the streets, nor did she see many lights in the houses.

Lei caught up to her. "How are you?"

She ignored his question. "Can you feel that?"

"Feel what?"

"That sense of wrongness. It's... darker here." She struggled to find the right words.

She thought Lei would dismiss her ideas, but he didn't.

"The energy that the monks use, the energy that you use, is connected to life," he said. "There have been claims that when a tragedy occurs that takes many lives, monks feel it. Most don't, but there is speculation that the more sensitive among us are capable of feeling the echoes of the loss of life."

"Can you?"

Lei shook his head and Bei thought she saw just a hint of sadness in his eyes. "I think I'm grateful I cannot." She got the sense he wasn't referring to Galan, but to something deeper in his past.

They lapsed into silence then, but for the first time, Bai had stopped thinking about Galan. She thought of Lei instead, curious what series of events had brought this man to hide in the mountains away from the monasteries and the empire.

Then they entered the town and her thoughts turned once again to the past. They hadn't gone more than a few paces past the first houses when she needed to stop. Her new allies stopped and watched, concern evident on their faces.

They couldn't understand. Galan had been her home. She knew these streets intimately. She knew every single person that lived here. But it wasn't home anymore. There was no welcome here, no sense of belonging. She'd been sliced out of the only community she'd ever known.

Bai put one foot in front of the other, forcing herself forward. A path had been cleared to the market, but little else. The town hadn't yet started to rebuild. She wondered when they would.

Her legs weakened as they entered the square itself. Lei and Yang moved with purpose, traveling around the square and examining clues Bai couldn't even guess at. She couldn't bring herself to move. This place held hundreds of memories for her, but still, it didn't have the one memory she wanted more than any other.

Eventually, Lei came to her. "Anything?"

She shook her head.

Lei considered something for a moment, then asked, "You said you woke up here, with no memory?"

She nodded mutely.

"Could you show me exactly where you woke up?"

Bai thought the question strange, but it was enough to get her moving. She walked toward the space where she remembered waking up. Those first few moments after waking were still so clear in her mind. Why couldn't she remember the rest?

She neared the area and checked to make sure she was right. Confident, she pointed. "I woke up here." Her voice came out hoarse.

Lei sighed. His shoulders slumped, and when he looked at her, she almost couldn't take his pity.

"What?" she asked.

In response, he pointed at the ground beneath her feet. She looked at it, not understanding what he was trying to show her.

"Look at the grass. See how there is a patch undisturbed here, and how once you get a few feet away, the ground has been cleared?"

Bai looked slowly around, a creeping dread settling in her stomach. She saw what he meant. The place she had pointed out looked unremarkable. But it was surrounded by ground that had been stripped of grass and more. Now that he mentioned it, she remembered waking up, the grass poking at her like sharp needles.

"This was the epicenter of the blast," Lei said, his voice soft and damning.

And she had woken up right in the center of it.

Her imagination quickly came up with other scenarios. She had been placed there after. She had crawled there before passing out.

But she knew, deep in her bones, there was only one explanation.

She collapsed to her knees, a soundless scream tearing through her throat.

One thought stood above all others.

She had killed her mother.

BAI LOST track of time and her surroundings. They

remained in the square for a while longer, but Bai had the answer she was looking for. Eventually, Lei pulled her to her feet and led her away.

She followed, like a dog after its master. Her mind was empty. Whenever a thought attempted to plant itself, the memory of her mother's arm, sticking out of the rubble, washed the thought away.

After they were well out of town, Lei guided Bai to an outcropping of rocks they could sit on. Yang walked a little further up the trail and took his rest apart from them.

Lei didn't offer words of consolation. Words were too shallow. Bai believed he understood. He simply sat next to her, his presence all the comfort he offered.

Bai felt the dagger in her pocket and pulled it out, removing it from the thin sheath that protected it. The blade looked sharp and somehow bright, even though there was no light for it to reflect.

She brought the dagger close to her eyes, studying it. She'd carried small knives before, but never as a weapon.

This dagger left no room for doubt as to its purpose. Its edge was razor sharp, and it was too large for any household task. This was steel meant for killing.

Bai imagined drawing the blade across her throat. She didn't know much about violence, and wasn't exactly sure how to kill herself. But the throat should do. She would just have to make sure she cut deep enough.

Perhaps Lei would do it for her. He certainly knew how to kill. Though he'd never said as much, she was as certain of that as she was that she had killed her own mother.

She couldn't allow her life, or her death, to weigh down any more people, though. She was guilty, which meant this was her responsibility.

For a long time she stared at the blade, feeling her life balanced on its edge.

To her side, Lei sat, unmoving. She knew if she made the decision, he wouldn't try to stop her. She'd never felt more grateful for another person in her life.

When Lei spoke, it was softly, so as not to startle her. "When I was a very young man, I killed a girl."

The line snapped Bai out of her reverie. She looked over at him.

"I had been discovered by the monasteries. While there, I discovered I was unique. I can use weapons to focus my strength. It's a dangerous skill, and the technique is forbidden. I wasn't much for rules, though, and eventually I used it in a sparring match. A young girl from a nearby village was watching, and she died."

Lei paused. "I should have been executed, but my brother was also training to become a monk. He saved my life."

Lei stopped, and for a minute, Bai thought he was done. But then she saw the way his eyes watered.

"My brother saved me in more ways than one. But that's a different story. It took me years to recover. I started drinking. Eventually, my brother managed to convince me to change, saving my life again.

"I'm not sure of many things in this life, Bai, but I do know this: no matter what, we should always keep pushing forward."

He took a deep breath, now finished.

Bai could sense the depth of emotion behind those words, terse sentences masking a bottomless well of emotion. She considered his words.

"Why go on?" Bai asked. "I destroyed my home. I killed people, including my mother."

"You did, and I can't give you your purpose. That's a question only you can answer. But you can't change anything once you're dead."

Bai stared at the dagger. She felt herself slip out of time. She saw the wisdom in Lei's words, even if she didn't believe them. Ending it all would be easiest. Lei might disagree, but he would let her make her own choice.

She studied Lei, wondering if the answer lay in him. His peace radiated off him, calming her even as she considered the most dramatic action she'd ever taken. And that peace had come from a turbulent past. Could she someday be like him?

Lei was a man capable of great violence and tremendous strength. She couldn't even imagine what man stood calmly against the monks. Suddenly, something about Lei seemed incongruous, like a weed among a beautifully cultivated garden. "Why are you hiding?" she asked.

"I'm not," he replied. "The monasteries know who I am and where I live. I live in the mountains beyond the reach of the empire because I want to be free, and there is no freedom for me within the empire. Those who have come to live with me are usually the same. Hien is wanted for no less than a dozen crimes that carry the penalty of death."

Bai wondered at that. Hien had never been anything but kind to her.

She understood so little. Giving up would be easier, but it would disappoint both Lei and Hien. As she thought of them, she couldn't bring herself to do it. She couldn't disappoint them.

She was sheathing the dagger before she even realized she had made the decision. She stood up, her gaze fixed on Lei as he remained sitting on the rock. He met her gaze evenly.

"I won't take my life, on one condition."

Lei gave her an inscrutable little grin. "And that is?"

"You train me."

Lei almost responded, but Bai held up her hand.

"I want you to train me so I can make sure that I never use that power again."

20

D elun looked down at his cup, staring at the beer within.

He hated beer.

In the monasteries, the only beverages consumed were water and tea. If one's entire philosophy revolved around becoming as strong as possible, alcohol had little place in daily life. When he was younger, Delun had been curious, but whenever he took a sip, he was reminded of how disgusting beer was. It was bitter, foamy, and left a sour taste in his mouth.

He didn't understand why anyone enjoyed it.

He suspected if he voiced his complaints to the man sitting across from him, though, he would only receive a blank stare.

The man was a trader. Given the quality of clothes he wore and the healthy belly he possessed, Delun assumed that trade had been bustling lately. Despite the tension across the empire, the land was relatively peaceful. Traders like this one, who had enough money to hire escorts of mercenaries, would rarely be attacked by bandits on the road.

To hear him tell it, though, the world was a very different place.

The man was deep into his cups. He'd joined Delun at his table without an invite, probably because Delun was the only other patron of the inn. Delun considered leaving, but the man had launched right into the problems of the day. Delun's interest had been piqued. As a consequence, he sat here, sipping on his beer while the man rambled on. For several minutes now all he had spoken of was how dangerous the roads had become.

"It all comes back to the monasteries, doesn't it?" he asked, the question clearly rhetorical.

Without even a pause, he continued. "It was a brilliant idea when it was conceived. The monasteries would help keep order. No one with half a mind would challenge their authority. Towns could raise militias or city watches if they chose, and lords raised their armies, but the monks were always the backbone.

"But no one asked what would happen if the monks shirked their duties. Nobody likes to admit it, but right now, we need the monasteries. Even with all their problems, their very threat keeps trouble at bay. But I'm not sure for how much longer."

The drunk trader was an interesting man, Delun decided. His tone made it clear he despised the monasteries, yet he saw their value all the same. Such balanced thought seemed rare these days.

He didn't seem like a man with the connections Delun was looking for, but better to leave no stone unturned. "You don't think we need to get rid of the monasteries?"

For a moment, Delun worried the man wasn't as drunk

as he appeared. His eyes grew sharp, but the focus quickly disappeared. The man waved the idea dismissively away.

"No. Perhaps someday, but people born with the gift need someplace to train, and the empire isn't ready to assume the monasteries' responsibilities. I do think that something needs to change, though. It feels to me the empire is a tree branch. The branch is bending, and I worry that it will soon break. The monasteries are like children on the branch, jumping up and down while the rest of us are trying to stay balanced."

Delun smiled at the image. From the trader's own grin, Delun guessed he'd drawn the same comparison at other inns before. He had the look of a man proud of himself.

"Kulat is a perfect example," the man continued. "Out here, near the edges of the empire, the monasteries are even more important. Lord Xun is what, a fortnight away at best? The monastery here should be a beacon of justice. Instead, the monks have turned to more and more violent means. It can't last."

"Do you think the people will turn on them?"

The trader shrugged. "All I know is that once my wagons are loaded, I'm going to leave Kulat as quickly as possible, and I don't plan on coming back anytime soon. If you're wise, I'd suggest you do the same."

Delun ignored his frustration. He'd been trying to find someone connected with the Golden Leaf for days now, but his inquiries had yielded nothing. By now, he should have turned up something. The Golden Leaf couldn't be this hard to find, especially after the attack they had organized against the monastery.

Delun had certainly learned enough. Most of the attackers had been townspeople. A few spoke of friends being hired as archers, and he had even managed to track down one of the young men who had fired a bow at Delun's brothers. The young man didn't know enough, though. He'd met a hooded figure in a dark tavern and had asked no questions. Delun burned with the desire to exact vengeance for his brothers, but his cover was too important.

He knew the Golden Leaf approached people. They didn't allow themselves to be found. He was becoming increasingly certain the actual Golden Leaf wasn't more than a handful of people at most. That small handful had set the powder—no one knew about that.

Before Delun could ask more questions of the trader, the door to the common room burst open. An older boy came in, his eyes wide with terror.

"You need to get out of here, now! The monks are marching!"

Delun and the trader cursed in unison. Delun had wondered how Guanyu would react to the ambush. The abbot would never let the attack go unpunished.

But Delun didn't think marching into the city was the right idea. It portended a storm from which there would be no shelter.

By the time Delun got to his feet, the trader had already gulped down his beer and run out of the room. Delun couldn't help but notice the trader hadn't paid his bill.

He left enough money for them both on the table and stepped outside. The loud chaos of the streets was disorienting after the quiet of the inn's common room. People shouted to one another and ran in every direction. After a few seconds of being out in the street, Delun realized he still had no idea what was happening. He wasn't even entirely sure which direction the monks were coming from.

Delun took a deep breath. The panic of the people was infectious. The urge to run infused his muscles, but he fought the impulse. Running would do no good, not until he knew exactly what was happening. A small crate sat near the entrance to the inn. Delun stood on it, looking down both directions of the street.

The inn he had chosen sat on the main street that ran through the town. It wasn't quite in the city center, but close. He saw, off in the distance, in the direction of the monastery, a cluster of white-robed individuals. Now that he was focused, he felt their power, too.

His options were limited. Curiosity warred with his desire for independence. If the monks found him, whatever slim cover he'd been able to create would be blown. They'd request his return, at best. Guanyu might demand it.

But he wanted to know what Guanyu planned. If he had an advantage, it was that it would be difficult for the monks to sense his strength. The power the monks were radiating was intense. In the center of that, only the most sensitive would pick him out.

Delun settled on the inn's rooftop. It was easy to access, with a table set up for patrons to enjoy sunny weather. There were also a number of ways down if something disastrous came to pass.

From his elevated position, Delun could see the unfolding drama more clearly. The monks were in a three-column formation. Delun recognized it immediately and swore under his breath.

In recent years, the monasteries had started developing techniques for working as a large group. In one sense, it was surprising that the monasteries had taken so long to do so. But fighting as a group had never been part of their role in society. At most, they traveled the country in pairs.

The Battle of Jihan had changed that. Pairs of monks hadn't been enough to handle the energies of that day.

Abbots had started to ask what they could do if such an event came to pass again.

The formation Delun saw marching down the street was one of their answers.

The two outer columns of monks acted as a shield wall. They weren't close enough for Delun to sense individually yet, but he knew what he would feel as they approached. Every second or third monk would be holding a shield that overlapped with the surrounding ones. When they tired, they would give a signal to their partners, who would take over. The result was a virtually impenetrable defense that could last for some time.

The center line was concerned with offense. The outer columns of monks were spread out wide, giving the monks in the inner column plenty of directions to attack. Protected by the shield, they could attack at will, taking the time to form whatever strikes they wanted. Delun had practiced in such formations and they were a considerable advance over the past ways of fighting.

It didn't bode well for the people of Kulat. Perhaps Guanyu was only trying to protect his monks, but Delun's gut told him otherwise. Why the inner column if they were only protecting themselves? That third column told Delun that even if the monks weren't out for a fight, they were certainly prepared for one. Dread left a sour taste in his throat.

Below him, a crowd was gathering. Delun watched another young man rallying people to him. He anchored the feelings of the townspeople, getting them to stand against the monks. Delun's eyes narrowed. Was that man a member of the Golden Leaf? It seemed likely. Delun memorized the face, and was about to head downstairs when he felt a wave of energy pass below him.

His eyes widened as they traveled back to the monks, now only two blocks away from the protesting group. The monk at the head of the column was now easily recognizable.

Kang.

And he had just attacked the citizens.

The attack hadn't been much more than a warning. Delun was certain of that, knowing Kang's strength as well as he did. His suspicion was confirmed a second later.

"Clear a path!" Kang's voice boomed over the street.

Inspired by the youth near the front of their group, men and women stood against the advancing monks. A few rocks arced over the group, bouncing harmlessly off the shields the citizens couldn't see or feel. The boys who had thrown the rocks ran away, passing out of sight quickly.

Delun wasn't sure what to do. The two groups met about a block from the inn. He considered attacking the ringleader of the protesters, but quickly dismissed the idea when he saw the anger on the faces of the people gathered below. If their ringleader went down, chaos would ensue.

Could he get between the groups and tell them to stand down? He didn't think so. The protesters didn't know who he was, and he was an outsider to the monks.

Delun clenched his fists, hating the feeling of impotence building within. There had to be something he could do. But this felt like a nightmare that couldn't be stopped.

The young man who had gathered the people stepped in front of his followers, walking all the way up to the shield. When his outstretched hand touched it, he stopped. "Return to your monastery!" he yelled. "We want nothing to do with you!"

Kang never hesitated. He extended his hand and the

youth was blown backward and tossed into his followers, who struggled to catch him.

It was just the spark the people needed. They surged forward, reason forgotten as a mob mentality crashed over them. Above, Delun watched, frozen. Any choice he made would be wrong.

Rocks flew toward the monks, useless. They hit the shield and slid off the side, one or two endangering the protesters themselves.

The group crashed against the shields, pushing their way against the invisible force. Delun watched as some of the monks tired against the pressure. Eventually they would have to drop their shields so others could replace them.

Delun wondered for a moment if the protesters might make progress. More people, emboldened by the trailblazers, were coming in from different parts of the city.

He got his answer soon enough. Kang gave an order Delun couldn't hear from the chaos, and waves of energy crashed into protesters. Delun's vision blurred as he lost all hope.

The men and women in front buckled like rag dolls. Given the energies involved, Delun had little doubt their organs had collapsed from the pressure.

Kang ordered more attacks, and for a moment, there was a fragile equilibrium. The protesters kept pressing against the monks' attacks, even as those in front paid for the advance with their lives. Then the protesters realized their friends in front weren't just injured. Anger turned to panic, washing over the protestors like a wave. The advance turned into a haphazard retreat, everyone running to get as far away from the monks as possible.

The retreat was just as bloody as the advance. Kang and the monks didn't relent in their attacks, even as they aimed at the backs of the very citizens they were supposed to protect.

From his perch, Delun could see everything, but could do nothing. His body refused to respond to his commands.

As quickly as it had started the event was over, the monks proceeding down the street as though nothing had happened, stepping over the bodies as though they were just debris.

Delun watched them walk past. Somehow, he knew he had just witnessed the beginning of a new era in the empire.

As the monks left, people started slowly returning to the street, mourning their lost ones.

21

T he clearing above the village had become something of a second home for Bai over the past few days. Spring faded into summer, and the cool mountain air and soft scents of blooming wildflowers calmed her racing mind. When she trained with Lei, she found some small measure of peace.

Lei seemed to understand, giving her all the time and training she asked for without question. He willingly woke early in the morning and trained with her late into the afternoon. Left to herself, Bai would have trained until the sun fell and only the moon illuminated the clearing, but Lei always left in time for supper with Daiyu. Even his kindness had limits.

She hadn't announced her decision yet, but she planned to leave his village soon. As soon as she was certain she could contain her power, she would slip off into the night. She would find some small village, far away, and try to find work. In time, she was confident she could make her way in the world. Lei's training had given her that much, at least.

Lei wanted more for her. She could see it in every action

he took. He didn't foresee any specific future for her, but he wanted her to make use of her strength.

He didn't see that she couldn't. While he had found a way to move past the mistakes of his past, he didn't understand there was no moving past what she had done. No matter how many times he told her it wasn't her fault, that there was no way she could have controlled her first reaction to the gift, his words rang hollow. The fact remained that if she hadn't been there, Galan's market square would still be standing.

Her mother would still be alive.

She had made a truce, of sorts, with her sorrow. So long as she kept herself busy, she could almost feel like a normal person. But as soon as she rested it returned, like a boulder tied to her throat, pulling her deeper into despair.

A couple of times a day her thoughts turned to ending her own life. If she really wanted to control her power, the solution was in her hands. Yet she could never do it.

She had thought a lot about her inability to end her life, forcing herself to confront truths she'd rather not.

At first, she told herself that she believed what Lei had told her outside of Galan, that she still had something to live for. She could find purpose and move on with her life the way he had with his. She wanted to believe him, desperately. She held onto his words as though she was dangling from the side of a cliff and they were the ledge supporting her weight. But she knew, deep in her heart, she was lying to herself.

There was only one reason she hadn't killed herself yet.

She was a coward.

The thought of dying terrified her. Even though it would solve all of her problems, when she looked at the dagger Daiyu had given her, that terror stilled her hand.

"You're not terribly focused this morning," Lei said.

Bai cracked open an eye. Across from her, Lei sat casually in the grass of the clearing. She'd been so lost in thought she hadn't even noticed him move from his meditative position. They were supposed to be meditating together, but one thought had led to another. She didn't have any idea how long ago her master had given up his own meditation.

"What, exactly, distracted you?" he asked.

"Thoughts of killing myself."

Lei didn't show the surprise Bai expected. His face remained at peace, but his gaze did focus on her. After a few moments, he leaned forward. "I will only make this offer once. If you ask me, right now, I will do it for you." He grabbed his sword, propped up on a rock next to him. "It will be quick and painless, and you will know no more suffering."

Bai's eyes widened, and she leaned away from him. She'd thought about asking him, but had never dared. He didn't deserve to carry the burden of her death. She looked at his sword. The blade was still sheathed, but she could see the well-worn leather of the hilt. It was a sword that had seen plenty of use.

It would never be easier. All she had to do was say the word.

Moments ticked by, one after the other.

She couldn't.

"No, thank you." She bowed toward him.

Lei stood up. "Good. Get up."

Accustomed to obeying commands, she was on her feet before consciously realizing it.

She had never heard the steel in Lei's voice before. "You've made a choice. Stop questioning it and accept it. You want to live, no matter what you believe." His argument was simple and direct.

"But..." Her words trailed off as Lei summoned a weak attack in his right hand. They'd been training together often enough, she had come to recognize the movement. He attacked her without warning.

She had become accustomed to the sensation of being flooded with power. She felt his energy slam against her. But against her, it didn't carry the destructive force it should. Her body soaked in the energy, the power infusing every part of her with more life.

Lei snapped a quick roundhouse kick at her, but thanks to his own energy, he moved sluggishly, his body a lumbering oaf to her sharpened senses. Before the kick could even reach her, she stepped inside his guard and gave him the gentlest of shoves.

Controlling her strength presented a constant challenge. Had Lei been on both feet, the shove might have only made him stumble back a pace or two. In mid-kick, though, it sent him to the ground. As she'd come to expect, though he was surprised, he rolled smoothly on his back and onto his feet again. As he did, her perception of time returned to normal.

"Can you change the past?" Lei asked, his hand summoning another attack.

"No."

"Then you need to let it go. All that matters... is now!" Lei attacked again, this time the energy stronger.

Despite all her training, she still couldn't form even a weak shield. She had no choice but to stand there and absorb his attack, his power making her feel as though her skin was on fire. The power had to go someplace, but she'd never formed anything beyond the weakest attack.

She jumped at Lei, surprised when a single leap carried

her all the way to him. She landed roughly and sprawled out on the grass. When she came to her feet, she saw the grin on Lei's face. Suddenly angry at him, she punched at him. She could still feel the power coursing through her body.

For a moment, her punch slowed. Her perception was sharp enough to see that Lei held a shield in one hand. He'd been expecting the reaction.

But the shield didn't stop her. Her fist slowed for a moment, then sped up as it absorbed the shield as well. Fortunately for them both, Lei was quick enough to lean away from the punch. The strength of the missed blow spun Bai around.

"Release it!" Lei commanded.

Again, her instinctive obedience took over. She made the first sign of the attack, snapping her right wrist into place. Aiming up at the sky, she felt the energy flow through her and out her hand, blasting into the sky above. It was the only energy attack she could perform, and could only control it enough to treat it as an emergency release.

The feeling of power subsided, as did Bai's emotions.

Lei didn't often show many reactions, but a sheen of sweat covered his forehead, and the heat of battle seemed to have gotten to him. He laughed and shook his head. "Amazing."

Bai felt suddenly guilty. That last punch, had it landed, could have hurt him. "I'm sorry."

"For what?"

"I don't have enough control. I could have hurt you. I—"

"Bai!" he interrupted her.

"What?"

"I'm fine. It's in the past. Let it go."

She wasn't sure she could, but she decided not to press the matter.

Lei led them to a tree on the edge of the clearing. It was a younger tree, no more than three times Bai's size, with a trunk not quite as wide as she was. Compared to some of the old giants that grew nearby, it was almost nothing at all.

"If you go to some monasteries," Lei began, "you'll find that they hold onto one particular belief. They believe that all their power comes from within. That's the reason why the monks train as hard as they do. Through a lifetime of working both mind and body, they believe they will get stronger."

Bai gave Lei a suspicious glance. Her own experience proved that belief false. She could feel some power that came from within her, but in their trainings together, it was only when she absorbed Lei's power that she could perform amazing feats. "Really?"

He nodded. "Some monks have suspected the truth for some time. But the traditional ways have usually worked well enough, so no one ever thinks to question too deeply. Do you believe I am as strong as I am because of my muscles?"

She stared at him. Lei wasn't weak, but she'd seen much stronger men even in Galan. She shook her head.

"Of course not. Life is the source of all strength, and it is our connection to that life that allows us to use it. That was my brother's final lesson for me." Lei looked lost in thought for a moment.

"The most important thing you can learn," he said, "is how to connect to that energy. We know your body can do it, but you must learn to control your connection. I think you are ready."

Lei had her take a basic fighting stance, her feet slightly

wider than the width of her hips. Then she closed her eyes, focusing on his voice.

"Good. Now, you can feel my energy, right?"

"Yes." After the time together and the training, she couldn't help but feel his energy. It was like a beacon compared to anything else. She was continually amazed by his strength, knowing she hadn't seen any of his true power yet.

"Can you feel the rest of the energy around you? It will feel similar, but not quite the same."

Bai tried to focus, but couldn't feel anything besides Lei.

"Relax," he suggested. "Deep breaths."

Feeling somewhat foolish, she took his suggestion.

Still nothing. She shook her head.

Without a hint of frustration in his voice, he kept guiding her. "Reach a hand out and place it against the tree. Can you feel it?"

For a second, she didn't feel anything but the rough bark against her hand. But then, at the edges of her awareness, there was something else. As Lei had said, it felt similar to both his power and hers, but different. She lacked the words to contain her experience.

As if the tree had been a key, the entire world suddenly unlocked before her. The entire clearing hummed with life, an undercurrent of power as deep as a bottomless well. She suddenly felt incredibly small. All life was connected, and she was nothing but the tiniest part of something indescribably vast.

Lei's voice broke gently into her awareness. "Good."

His voice brought her attention over to him. Even his strength, among all this energy, was almost completely meaningless.

"Now," he coached, "imagine drawing some of this energy into yourself."

She took a deep breath and tried. To her surprise, she felt herself welling up with energy. Before long, she knew she needed to release it. Her body could only handle so much. Just as she had been trained, she formed the sign of the first attack.

"Wait," Lei commanded. "Let's try something new. Imagine the energy drawing into your fist."

She did, feeling her arm buzzing with power.

"Now punch the tree, as hard as you can."

Bai opened her eyes in surprise. She could still feel the power surrounding her, could feel her fist practically shaking with unspent energy.

But she had trusted Lei this far.

Bai swung at the center of the tree, as hard as she could.

Her fist slammed through the heart of the tree, causing wood to explode in every direction. The tree tipped over, crashing to the ground as the remainder of the trunk cracked loudly. Bai looked at her hand, expecting to see a bloody mess. Instead, she saw that her hand was unharmed, without so much as even a splinter inside. She shook her head in wonder.

Lei stepped up next to her, a look of awe on his face. He looked at where the tree had stood, then turned and grinned at Bai.

"Well, that went better than I expected."

22

Delun approached the hall of healing, feeling like a fraud. Two guards stood at the door, bleary-eyed men from the city watch who had no doubt volunteered for the additional duty. The guards recognized him, giving him a short bow of appreciation as he passed them.

When he stepped into the hall, his steps slowed. The air had a different quality here. Beyond the walls, in Kulat, the air felt thick with the tension of the past few days. In here, he breathed easier, his purpose clear and simple. The halls were packed with people, many of them volunteers like himself. Now that the initial chaos had died down, all that remained was the practiced and unhurried efficiency of those who knew what needed to be done.

Delun found a healer. The man was practically an elder, but still moved with a vigor that men half his age would have envied. His silver hair hadn't slowed his mind or his step one bit. "How can I best be of service today?"

The healer looked around the hall. Delun's gaze followed. Men and women lay scattered wherever there was room. As crowded as the building was today, three days ago had been much worse. Those with injuries quickly mended were already back at home, and those with the most grievous of injuries had already died. The patients that remained lived somewhere in-between, with wounds that still required consistent attention.

Delun had stopped attempting to give name to the mix of emotions he felt as he saw what his brothers had done. He'd silently threatened to avenge the innocent himself. He'd shed tears alone in his room as he remembered the devastation that had occurred right in front of him. After days of dashing from one emotional extreme to the other, all that was left was hollow emptiness, carved out by disbelief.

As his eyes wandered over the hall he saw that two of the beds that had been occupied were now empty. Knowing how shattered those particular patients had been, Delun could easily guess the end of their story.

The healer's voice broke his reverie. "There's not much more to be done. In another day, our staff will be able to handle the wounded without volunteers. Feel free to speak with those whom you have befriended, and offer what comfort you can. Many here have become attached to you."

Delun nodded and stepped forward, stopping when the healer laid a gentle hand on his arm. "And thank you for the service you've given these last few days. We've all appreciated your perseverance and spirit. You will always be welcome here, either as visitor or patient."

Delun gave the healer a deep bow and the man returned to his work. Would the healer feel the same if he knew Delun was a monk? Or would the gratitude turn to hate in a heartbeat? Delun suspected he knew the answer, but hoped he never had to find out for sure.

He wandered from bed to bed, speaking softly with one patient after another. One man thought he would be able to return home again soon, his eyes twinkling as he spoke about his young daughter waiting for him. An older woman, unconscious, wheezed with difficulty as she slept. The healers believed she wouldn't survive. Delun knelt down next to her and held her hand, feeling the wrinkles as he gently ran his thumb over the back of her hand.

It didn't take long for him to finish his rounds, and with nothing more useful to contribute, Delun was forced to think about leaving the peaceful walls of the hall.

After delaying for a few more minutes, he finally stepped out into Kulat. The bright midday sun caused him to blink rapidly as he came out of the dim hall. Though summer was just beginning, the day already felt hot and sticky. Looking left and right, Delun decided to visit the birds.

His thoughts wandered as he ambled down the street. They'd been harder to control lately, and at times, sudden awareness would stab into Delun, and he'd realize that he'd walked for blocks without paying the slightest attention to his surroundings. His training was deeply embedded in his routines, but he'd been far too distracted as of late.

Some part of him knew he should care more. Even though he wore unremarkable clothes and stayed at an inn, he was still a monk investigating a serious threat to the monasteries. The Golden Leaf had marked him before, and very well could again.

But even that threat against his life felt petty now. For the first time in his life, he doubted. Ever since he'd been young, he'd believed in the monasteries. He'd killed for the monasteries. He still would. His conscience didn't bother him on that point.

Guanyu's actions, though, were another matter. Above all else, Delun believed the monasteries existed to serve the people. Sometimes, that service meant taking control. The monasteries could provide guidance that lifted the people up, sometimes unwillingly.

Delun had killed. He had tortured men without blinking. He'd done both on this trip alone. He didn't delude himself over his actions. He had taken fathers away from children, brother away from brother. What he did was horrible, but it served a greater good. The monasteries protected so many; it was worth the suffering of a few to ensure that protection.

That philosophy had steadied Delun's hand for many years.

But Delun never attacked the innocent. Everyone he fought was involved in a plot to destroy or harm the monasteries. He never could have imagined doing what Guanyu had.

In short, he found Guanyu's orders despicable, but didn't know how he should respond. Ultimately, their goals were similar, if not identical. Delun didn't like what Guanyu did, but he knew plenty of monks who felt that way about his own actions as well. Delun believed he should do something, but the idea of working against a monastery, even a misguided one, was anathema to him.

Delun stopped walking and looked around, noticing his surroundings for the first time since leaving the hall of healing. He had no idea where he was. It wasn't the first time he'd gotten himself lost in the past few days.

He followed the sound of voices until he came out on a major street. A sweeping glance told him where he was, and he looked for anyone following him. He didn't notice anyone, but that didn't surprise him. A tail gave themselves away as one moved from one place to another. Standing still, any of the people in the street could be following him and he'd have little idea. He needed to stop losing focus. He turned on his heel and resumed his journey.

The last few days had been spent doing what good he could. He helped in the healing house and made halfhearted efforts to infiltrate the Golden Leaf. Part of that investigation led him to the local messenger. He searched for any messages labeled "Truth," as the tall man in the alley had spoken about so long ago, but no matter how many times he visited, he saw nothing amiss. Once, he considered revealing his identity and interrogating the owner of the shop, but after the Massacre of Kulat, as it was being called by the locals, he found that his heart wasn't in it. He didn't want to blow his cover.

He found the shop with little effort and hid the true purpose of his visit by writing a short message back to Taio. It said little, as there was little to say. He'd already informed Taio of the massacre. Part of him hoped to receive new orders, but he suspected none would come. The problem was his to solve.

"Two Bridges?" the clerk asked, now used to Delun's routine.

"Yes."

"You're a long way from home."

It was the first time the clerk had said anything beyond matters of business, but Delun wasn't feeling conversational. He simply nodded. That was how he felt, too.

He looked for any messages that had "Truth" or anything else out of the ordinary, but saw nothing. It had been a slim hope. Without more aggressive investigation, Delun didn't think the shop would provide any leads. But he was running out of ideas.

He stepped outside the shop, not sure what else to do for

the day. Lacking purpose, he decided to wander the streets of Kulat.

For all his efforts, Delun couldn't stir up any other leads, either. From the hushed conversations inside the inn, there was little doubt as to the public's attitude regarding the monasteries. But at the same time, he hadn't heard more than a whisper about the Golden Leaf. But the group had to be active. Kulat had become a hotbed of anti-monastic thought, and that didn't happen just by chance.

His abject failure proved one thing to him absolutely, though. The Golden Leaf was small, perhaps no more than a close-knit group of friends. A few words spoken to a crowd here, some gold paid to triads there, and it wouldn't be hard to create the impression of a much larger conspiracy. Nothing had happened yet, as far as Delun could tell, that truly required the resources of more than a few people. The black powder was expensive, but all that told him was that the Golden Leaf had access to money. Actually setting the trap and lighting it wouldn't take many people to organize. Finding men good with a bow and willing to shoot at a monk didn't seem like a particularly challenging task in Kulat.

Delun also believed the rise of the Golden Leaf here wasn't a coincidence. Guanyu's policies had created the ideal conditions for resentment to grow. It served as another reminder that this type of monastery created more problems than it solved.

He spent an hour wandering the streets, stopping at one restaurant he'd come to enjoy for their food. Kulat's monastery had served poor meals, and one advantage to living on his own was the opportunity to enjoy a good meal. He ate with pleasure, watching the other patrons.

Monks shouldn't separate themselves as much as they

did. Delun recognized the importance of solitude for training. Minds and bodies didn't develop without time and effort. Having the time and space to engage in the difficult monastic training was important. But it bred a certain attitude, a detachment and aloofness from the rest of society. That was dangerous. Delun had never worried about it quite as much as he did now.

Being among the people eased the problem. Hate could only stem from ignorance. It was difficult to detest someone you knew, someone you had spent time with. As he looked around the room at the people eating, he couldn't imagine turning his strength against them.

With a soft sigh, he stood up after his meal and began the journey back to his inn. Another day had passed and the noose around the neck of Kulat seemed to grow tighter. He had accomplished nothing of note. A mug of beer at the inn sounded suddenly appealing, more than one ever had before. He'd have one, then retire for the evening. Perhaps tomorrow he would have better luck.

At the inn, Delun wondered at his beer. What would Taio say if he saw his prize monk drinking with the commoners? When he'd been a little younger, Delun had told himself he needed to drink to blend in on some of his assignments. Now that he was older and slightly less sensitive to criticism, he acknowledged that although he detested the taste, he enjoyed the feeling of relaxation it provided.

Finishing his drink, Delun stood up. He took the stairs two at a time, glancing behind him to ensure no one paid too much attention to him. No one did. He went to his room, a small affair that was far less than he could afford, thanks to the money Taio had given him. But old habits died hard, and he didn't see the need for more space than he could use.

He opened the door and stepped in, ready for a long night of rest. He barely noticed when the shadow detached itself from one corner of the room and slid after him.

At any other time, he might have been ready. If he hadn't been distracted by thoughts he couldn't control, and if he hadn't stopped for a beer, his reaction might have been quick enough. Few people got the drop on Delun.

All he could do was stand there, shocked, as the shadow grew in his vision, a hand coming up and down, aimed straight at his temple. He was so surprised, he didn't even think to duck.

Delun collapsed, unconscious before he even hit the floor.

23

Bai felt the power fill every part of her body from the tips of her fingers to the center of her chest. Like a water skin, filled beyond capacity, she wasn't sure if she could hold any more.

She wanted to hate it.

This was the power that had killed her mother and had taken more than a dozen innocent lives.

But she felt alive. More than ever before.

Her body, or at least her senses, were changing. Colors seemed sharper, her skin became more sensitive, and sounds, even those at a distance, were clearer. When she and Lei finished their training at night and she released the deep wells of energy she had collected, she felt empty and dull.

Had that been the way she had lived her entire life?

Bai formed the first sign, released the excess energy into the skies above. She still felt powerful, but in control. That last attack from Lei had been stronger than anything she'd absorbed before.

Bai wanted to hate the techniques she was learning.

But she couldn't.

All she could do was hate herself for loving this power.

When she had started this training, she told herself it was so she would never hurt people again.

She had learned enough to keep others safe days ago. Now, if the strength and connection that flowed through her reacted to another, she could channel that energy away, fling it up into the sky if nothing else.

But Bai remained in the village, accepting Lei's continued guidance. He taught her more about the powers she possessed. His skills were not like hers. His were the skills of the monastery, honed to an edge few others had ever achieved. Her abilities were something different. Something Lei didn't think the monasteries had ever seen.

"Once more, please." She stood, balanced on the balls of her feet, ready for the fight.

Lei's look was incredulous. "We've been training for hours. I do have other tasks besides training you."

"One more time. Harder."

He shook his head. "If I go much harder, a mistake would kill you."

She didn't respond, her look answer enough.

After their time together, she thought she understood Lei. He hid up in the mountains, supposedly unattached to the cares of the world. Bai didn't believe him. He sheltered rebels and was well aware of everything happening throughout the empire.

She didn't believe Lei was a hermit. She believed he was biding his time. He was waiting, even if he wasn't sure what he was waiting for. No one trained as hard as he did without some reason, conscious or otherwise.

She couldn't have asked for a better teacher. He couldn't train her in his techniques because they didn't work for her.

He could make a single sign with his hand and blow a centuries-old tree clean in half. She could summon the same power from the world around her, but at best she'd knock a few leaves from the tree. She couldn't manifest the power externally, the way so many monks did, but she had other skills.

Lei guided her discovery. Some of what he knew was useful, especially the ways in which he could manipulate internal energies. That seemed to be where their abilities aligned best.

Like her, he was aware she had learned everything she had set out to learn initially. But he kept training her, driven by some of the same curiosity. What was she capable of?

So he stood up from his rest, despite the fact they had sparred all morning. "Very well, then. I'll give you everything I've got short of using a weapon."

Bai nodded, excitement pounding in her heart.

Just then, she felt another presence. It was nowhere near as strong as Lei's, but the fact that she could sense it meant it could only be the one person she didn't want to see.

Yang climbed up into the clearing, a broad smile on his face. "I figured I would come say my farewells before departing."

Lei gave the monk a knowing grin. "And you wanted to see what all the fuss was about?"

Yang looked like a child caught in the act. "Perhaps," he answered with a sly grin.

"You're in luck, then. Bai and I were going to have one last training session for the day." Lei put added emphasis on the word "last."

With that, Lei focused his energy. Bai felt an attack forming in his left hand and a shield with his right.

Their matches had become something of a deep

strategic game. They'd sparred often enough now that both knew what the other could do. Bai knew Lei's attack wouldn't harm her much, just as the shield would only slow her down for a second. But Lei knew the same, and had found some creative ways to use his powers against her.

Bai summoned more energy into herself, a practice that was now almost as easy as breathing. Before Lei could take the offensive, she leaped forward, angling from side to side so Lei couldn't get an easy attack off.

Lei waited until Bai was ten paces away, then released his attack. He hadn't aimed at her torso, but at her feet.

The trick was old. Bai's body easily absorbed most of the strength of attacks, but sometimes a little nudge to the feet was enough to get her to fall. She'd tripped often enough to learn from her mistakes.

Bai leaped into the air, still amazed she could jump such distances with ease. She moved her power to her feet to cushion the landing.

Lei didn't dodge as she expected him to. Instead, he swiped his shield around, catching her feet with that. She absorbed the energy, but not before the shield imparted its momentum. Bai's world spun as she flipped uncontrollably in midair.

She didn't panic. Time moved differently for her, and she'd gotten intimately familiar with what her body could do over the last week. She saw the rocky ground coming up to meet her as her head plummeted down. With a thought, her energy moved to her right hand and arm.

Bai reached out, stopping her descent. She cartwheeled over the outstretched arm, using the momentum from her leap and Lei's strike to carry her feet over her head and back to the ground. She landed softly, then darted toward Lei.

Of course, Lei had expected her to do something of the

sort. He'd seen her agility too many times by now to be surprised. He had a stronger, second attack queued, and Bai hadn't thought to weave as she approached.

Lei attacked, and Bai felt the energy stab from his hand in her direction. She was too close to dodge and was forced to take the blast full on.

For a few seconds, the world slowed to a crawl. Her skin felt as though it was peeling away from her, pinpricks of light and energy tearing away at her flesh as it tried to escape.

She was beside him before she realized it, her speed even greater than she realized. With this power, she didn't dare punch at him. Given her speed and strength at the moment, she was certain she would kill him. Instead, she jumped, putting the energy in her legs.

She had never put so much into a jump. The trees surrounding the clearing had to be thirty feet high, and for the briefest of moments she looked out above them, on the small valley below that held Lei's village and the greater valley in the distance, the home she could never return to.

Then she was falling, losing control as she dropped. She tried to summon more energy, but she wasn't grounded. All she could draw was a trickle of power. She needed far more if she was going to survive the landing.

Lei must have sensed the same. Before she even had time to utter a cry of terror, he attacked her again, this wave of energy gentle compared to the others he had used.

She felt the energy flow into her once again, and she directed it down to her legs. She landed on the stone, deep gouges driven into the rock with a tremendous crack. The impact on her barely registered.

Bai stood and checked herself. She seemed unharmed, as near as she could tell.

Lei studied her, his face not giving much emotion away. He gave her a small nod. "Impressive."

Behind him, Bai saw Yang's mouth hanging open. After a few seconds, he came to his senses and joined them. "I've never seen anything like that in my life, and I've lived a long time."

Bai wasn't quite sure what to say to the older man. Ever since he had told her what occurred in Galan, they hadn't seen much of each other. She knew he was in town, but she spent her time training or resting in her room. She didn't visit the inn's common room often.

She didn't dislike the man, but he was a reminder of a past she would rather forget.

Lei filled the silence. "Her abilities are unique as far as I know. You can see for yourself the powers she can summon, but she has no external control. Internally, though, I've never met her like. You sense how she can shift power within herself?"

Yang nodded. He seemed too awestruck to speak.

Eventually, the rebel monk looked out over the valley. When he spoke again, his voice was lower, filled with concern. "I fear she is a harbinger of things to come, Lei. The monasteries aren't developing fast enough. Not for this." He paused. "Bai, do you know just how dangerous those skills are?"

She clenched her fists. How could she not? It was her power that had killed so many. Only after a moment did she realize that wasn't what he spoke of.

Lei shook his head. "She's not invincible. Without external abilities, she's more vulnerable to arrows and swords than monks who can form shields."

He had drilled this into her constantly. Power was not the same as invincibility.

Yang's retort was quick. "That's not what I speak of, Lei. You can't tell me you haven't realized that you're creating a monk killer."

The phrase stopped Bai's heart. In all her excitement, she'd never once realized the true power behind her abilities. Against her, the combat skills the monks possessed would be almost useless. She could already go toe-to-toe with Lei most times they sparred now, and that was only after a bit of training.

Yang turned so he faced her directly. "What do you plan on doing with these powers?"

It wasn't that she hadn't thought of the question before. She spent most of the time in her room wondering about exactly that question. The problem was, she had no answer. Some part of her still wanted to run and hide. But that instinct, so long developed in her, was beginning to fade. She recognized it now as advice from a mother who hadn't possessed the ability to defend herself or her child from the harsh world.

But Bai could defend herself. She could even protect others, or bring judgment. The thought alone was intoxicating and heady. More than once she had imagined what she could do to Wen, if they were ever to meet again. The onetime jailer would regret his treatment of her.

Yang thought for another moment. "If you wish, I could make use of your skills. I help lead a small group known as the Golden Leaf. We are dedicated to building a new future for monasteries and the empire."

Bai looked from Yang to Lei, then back to Yang. She'd suspected something was different about Yang. Obviously, she suspected most monks wouldn't be welcome in Lei's village. She'd never heard of the Golden Leaf, but she had heard plenty of talk about overthrowing the monasteries down in Galan.

"What would you have me do?"

Yang smiled. "I don't know. But a woman with your abilities could make a tremendous change."

"You want me to kill monks."

"I would hope not. You may be able to protect us from them, though. Some in my group believe violence is required for change. I do not agree, personally. But the matter is far from settled. You would be a great help, though."

Bai had no ready answer. She detested the monks, but had never considered the possibility of fighting against them. "I'm not sure, but thank you for the offer."

Yang nodded. "I won't pressure you. I do believe change is coming, but the choice is yours alone to make. Just know, the offer is always open, if you're interested. Lei trusts you, so I do, too." He handed her a slip of paper. "If you're ever interested, use this to contact me."

Bai bowed, grateful for the trust.

Together, the three of them began making their way down the mountain toward the village. They were saying their farewells when a young man came running up to them. Panting for breath, he said, "There's a man on the trail below who says he wants to talk to Bai."

Both Lei and Yang glanced at her. She shook her head, as uncertain as they.

"Who is it?" Lei asked.

The boy gulped. "He announced himself as Lord Xun's questioner, sir. He says he's come for answers."

24

Delun returned to consciousness unwillingly. His head pounded, his mouth was dry, and he knew, as soon as he woke up, that he was in for a rough day.

He was tied tightly to a chair, with thin ropes around his wrists, torso, and ankles. Even more concerning, his hands were tied to the arm of the chair he sat on. The ropes weren't perfect, of course. Given enough time, he'd be able to at least free his hands.

Given the circumstances, though, he didn't think that was likely.

A thin rope was tied loosely around his neck. It led up to the ceiling, where a water pail hung above him. His eyes narrowed in curiosity, until he saw a second thin rope, taut with the weight of the pail. He followed the weight-bearing rope until it ended underneath the leg of the other chair in the room, currently occupied by the most dangerous woman Delun had ever met.

His gut told him this was the same woman who had ambushed him in the streets, an act that felt like a lifetime ago. Her current trap seemed even more complete. If her weight shifted too much, the bucket would drop and either snap his neck or choke him to death. Neither option sounded pleasant.

A fine trap, indeed. He would have been more impressed had he not been the victim. Few people could prevent a monk from saving himself, but this woman seemed to have the knack for it.

She watched as he took in the room.

"You've figured out that if my weight shifts from this chair, you're dead?"

He nodded.

"Good."

He expected more questions, but she sat there silently, staring at him.

For a few seconds, he kept silent, too. Two could play at that game. But he realized he was acting like a fool. This woman obviously knew who he was, and had tried to kill him earlier. This time, she hadn't. "Why am I still alive?"

"Why have you been visiting the halls of healing, and why are you no longer at the monastery?"

Delun wished for some water. His throat was parched and his voice cracked, but the woman across from him didn't seem terribly interested in quenching his thirst. She wanted answers.

He worked on the problem. This woman was the best connection to the Golden Leaf he had found. Someone confident in their position might make a mistake, might let something slip they didn't mean to. He needed to direct the conversation, get her to open up.

Before he could reply, she interrupted his line of thought. "Stop whatever you're thinking. You're alive because I'm curious. If you don't answer my questions immediately, or I think you're lying, I'll stand up and we'll both be done here."

He nodded, impressed despite his circumstances. "I originally left the monastery because they were interfering with my mission. I was always accompanied..."

"What was your mission?" the woman interrupted.

"To find and destroy the Golden Leaf."

The woman scoffed, but motioned for Delun to continue.

"I felt I could do better if I wasn't always accompanied. Guanyu's monks are particularly difficult to work with. That's why I left the monastery. As for the halls of healing, I wanted to help how I could."

The woman's face hardened. "I don't believe you."

"I don't particularly care. I wanted to help."

"You were looking to infiltrate the Golden Leaf."

"I wasn't. At least, not there. I'm still trying, of course, but visiting the halls of healing had nothing to do with my mission. I had no ulterior motive other than to ease my conscience."

The woman studied him. "What are you trying to accomplish here?"

He shrugged. "I don't know anymore. Since Guanyu sent his monks into town the second time, I haven't been sure. I've continued my mission, as best I can, but I've made no progress. You're the closest I've come."

Her eyes reminded him of a large cat he'd seen one time in the mountains closer to Two Bridges. They seemed relaxed, but they held a deep awareness of her surroundings. There was no doubt about it. This woman was a predator. Still, his curiosity couldn't be contained.

"I've answered your questions honestly, now answer mine. Why didn't you kill me?"

She seemed more amenable to his question this time. "Because I've spoken with the healers, and I've been following you for days. You are different, and I wanted to know how different before I killed you."

He looked around the room. "At considerable risk."

"Unlike monks, I don't kill just anyone."

He nodded, acknowledging her point. "So, what happens now?"

"I haven't decided yet."

"May I ask you a few questions, while you decide?"

She narrowed her eyes, but then leaned back. Delun eyed the rope underneath her nervously. "Sure."

"Are you a member of the Golden Leaf?"

She scratched at her cheek. "I suppose you could say that."

"Is the Golden Leaf responsible for Galan?"

"No."

He'd hoped for a different answer, but he believed her.

"Are you responsible for the explosions outside the monastery?"

"Some of us are, yes. Not all agreed."

"Are there monks among your members?"

She smiled at that. "Yes."

A few weeks ago that answer would have sent him into a rage. He could still feel a spark of something, but it wasn't the righteous anger he'd once felt. Not after what he'd seen.

"What are the goals of the Golden Leaf?"

"To build a new monastic system."

Delun blinked. If he'd harbored any doubt about the woman before, it was gone now. He had been prepared for a spiel about destroying the monasteries. He hadn't expected talk of a reformation instead. "What do you mean?"

"The system is broken. Monks like Guanyu and Kang can destroy lives with impunity, and that power, no matter how well intentioned, eventually changes a person. The Golden Leaf isn't foolish enough to believe that the monasteries aren't needed. But they do need to be controlled."

"The monasteries don't need control. They need leaders worthy of the task."

"Such leaders are rare. Would you sit idly by, waiting for one?"

Delun shook his head slightly. He didn't have time for this. "Are you going to kill me or not?"

The woman answered his question with a question. "Who do you believe needs to be stopped more—Guanyu or the Golden Leaf?"

In his days of wondering, Delun had never considered the choice in such black and white terms. The Golden Leaf had killed monks, but Guanyu had killed innocents. In this struggle, no one could claim to be justified.

Guanyu's actions reverberated further, though. As word of the massacre spread, more discontent would grow throughout the empire. The abbot might bring about the Golden Leaf's stated goals sooner than they did. The murder of a handful of monks paled in comparison to the fire Guanyu played with.

Had his loyalties switched so suddenly?

He thought back to Jihan, and the first monk who had changed his life. Guanyu desecrated that man's memory.

In his travels, Delun had met plenty of incompetent monks, but he had never met a monk as committed as Guanyu. The man truly believed his methods would work, that citizens would embrace his leadership. For as much as he claimed to be a student of history, he didn't seem to have learned any of its lessons.

But still, could he turn against his brothers? The shame seemed too great for him to bear.

"I'm sorry," he said. "But I cannot side with you. Guanyu needs to be removed, but I won't condone the killing of my brothers."

She nodded. "I can respect that. Would it change your mind if I told you that Guanyu has put the city under monastic law, and that Lord Xun is marching one of his armies here to fight the monks?"

Delun's eyes went wide. If true, all his worst fears would be realized at once. Kulat could very well be the spark that set off the entire region, or even worse, the entire empire. Delun had spent his entire life fighting against just such an event. He couldn't sit idly by.

"What would you ask of me?" The question wasn't as difficult to ask as he'd expected.

"Can you remove Guanyu as head of the monastery?"

"No. I have autonomy, which is far more than most monks have, but my authority doesn't extend that far. Although…" His voice trailed off.

His orders were open-ended. He'd certainly be punished, but perhaps he could remove Guanyu. He imagined the scenario, shaking his head as he did. The abbot wouldn't accept Delun's authority. The monks supported him, too. Kang had come to Kulat specifically to serve under the man. Delun had no one's loyalty.

"There's nothing I can do on my own," he concluded.

"What if I introduced you to others?"

"Where?"

"In the mountains above Galan."

Understanding suddenly clicked into place. He remembered one arrow narrowly missing him, then another only stopped by his shield. "You were the one we were chasing!"

She frowned in confusion, then made the connection herself. "I wondered if that was you. But yes, Lei might have other ideas, and there might be members of the Golden Leaf there."

"Lei isn't part of the Golden leaf?"

The woman shook her head. "He'd rather stay out of the affairs of the empire. But he welcomes all into his village." She smiled as she remembered who she was talking to. "For the most part."

Delun was starting to understand so many pieces, and yet the whole still eluded him. Lord Xun's involvement changed everything. He considered options for a few minutes, and she let him think in silence. No other options presented themselves, though. He sighed. "Very well, I will come with you."

The woman went to work dismantling the trap she'd tied him in. Then she drew a knife and cut through his bonds. He flexed his fingers, grateful for the release.

She looked out the window of Delun's room. "More monks have patrolled the streets lately. They've been traveling in groups of four. The good news is, there aren't too many, and the city is large. So long as we're careful, we shouldn't run into them."

"You mean to leave now?"

"No reason to wait. Xun's men won't arrive for a fortnight yet, but once they do, it's going to be much harder to reverse the course of events. We need a solution before they arrive."

Delun reluctantly agreed. They left the room together, heading down to the common room and out the inn. The streets were dark and empty, and Delun realized he didn't even know his companion's name. He asked.

"Hien," she replied.

Delun gave his own name, not sure what else to do. Introductions were short. He had more questions for her, but held them for a better time. Right now, Hien moved with purpose through the city.

He followed her twisting and turning route, surprised when he came out at the main gate of Kulat. He was surprised again when the gate was closed and attended by monks.

Hien barely missed a step. In moments, they were back on the side streets.

"Where are we going?" Delun asked.

"There are plenty of ways out of the city," Hien replied.

He supposed that was true. Kulat wasn't walled. The gates protected the roads, but simply leaving the city was an easy matter on foot. They would only have to avoid any patrols the monks might have placed.

Delun followed Hien, fascinated by this woman who didn't seem perturbed by anything. She had escaped his grasp several times, almost assassinated him, and now he followed her. Life was strange, sometimes beyond belief.

Soon they found themselves at the edge of town, looking out over an empty field. The nearest roads were visible, but barely. In the dark, at this distance, it was unlikely they'd be spotted. Again, Hien led the way.

They walked through the field for a time, then cut over toward the road. They'd passed the gate. Now they needed to head for the road so they could make good time toward Galan and then the mountains beyond. Hien led them to some stables not far out of town, meeting with a man she clearly knew. Within minutes they had horses being prepared.

They had just saddled their horses when Delun sensed a presence on the road behind them. He cursed as the sensations accelerated towards him.

Hien looked over.

"We've been discovered," he said.

25

A casual glance at Lei revealed little about his attitude. His face remained serene, and he looked as though meeting a questioner from a lord of the empire was a routine matter. But Bai had been with him enough to recognize the signs of distress.

His weight, normally perfectly balanced, shifted back and forth. His hand would occasionally drift down to his sword, just brushing the hilt as if to make sure it was still there. Though he said little, Bai got the sense he was prepared for a fight.

Bai felt panicked enough for both of them. What she knew about questioners was little more than rumor, but those rumors were terrifying enough. If even half the stories were true, the questioners weren't people she wanted to cross paths with. Part torturer, part detective, and part executioner, they reported only to the lord.

Lei had offered her protection, but how far did it extend? A word from a questioner could summon an army to his doorstep. Surely he wouldn't take that risk for her?

Yang had disappeared immediately after the messenger

delivered his news. Bai suspected the monk would take an alternate path out of the village. His decision seemed wise.

After only a moment's hesitation, Bai remained close to Lei. The questioner had asked for her by name. That meant he had already been down to the village, had heard the stories they told about her. Stories that were closer to the truth than she wished. Lei couldn't protect her from him. He shouldn't have to.

She decided then that she would sacrifice herself for this village if needed. They had shown her nothing but kindness, and they didn't deserve whatever future a questioner might visit upon them.

She hoped they could find a different way.

As she and Lei walked down the path toward the village, she recognized a new emotion.

Curiosity.

After growing up hearing nothing but nightmarish stories of questioners, she wondered what was true and what was myth. She felt nervous, but the fear she expected to feel wasn't present. The questioner couldn't harm her unless she chose.

Bai rubbed absentmindedly at her bracelet, wondering at the change within her. A month ago, her legs would have melted and she would have huddled in fear.

No more.

When the questioner's head appeared on the trail, followed by the rest of his body, Bai felt a pang of disappointment. The man was of average height, and although his eyes were quick and sharp, nothing about him looked particularly dangerous. Bai couldn't feel his presence, either, so he wasn't gifted.

As far as nightmares went, Bai had seen worse.

As the questioner neared, Bai realized she'd been wrong

on one count. The man was as cold as they came, and he definitely seemed dangerous now that she faced him eye to eye. In the corner of her vision, she saw Lei tense the slightest amount. He felt it, too. The man's appearance didn't seem outwardly threatening, but something about him made the hairs on the back of her neck stand up.

He offered a short bow to Lei. "Master Lei, it is a pleasure to meet you in person after all this time. I've heard so very much about you."

If Lei was surprised the questioner knew his name, he didn't show it.

The questioner's gaze turned to Bai. "And from your description, I must assume that you are Bai."

She nodded, seeing no point in lying.

"Perhaps we could move to your common room and have some of your local tea?" the questioner suggested, with the air of a man who already knew everything about the village.

Lei smiled and shook his head. "I apologize for my lack of hospitality, but I suspect you will be leaving our village soon enough. The empire is not welcome here. I made that clear to Xun decades ago."

Bai fought to keep her face calm. No one spoke to a questioner with such disrespect. She tensed, ready for a fight to break out at any moment.

The questioner laughed. "How refreshing, Master Lei. It has been years since anyone has met me with calm assurance. Of course, given your strength it is no terrible surprise.

"Then let me ask my questions. Are you the one who destroyed Galan's square? The locals all blame the woman, but they don't know who you are. Lord Xun has allowed you to live in relative obscurity, but not if you harm his subjects."

Lei met the questioner's gaze calmly. "I did not."

Bai was surprised that the questioner took Lei at his word. "If not you, then you certainly know what happened."

Lei nodded. "I do."

The questioner waited in expectant silence.

"The story is not mine to tell." Lei glanced over at Bai.

Bai realized Lei's intent. If she wanted to continue to hide up in the village, she could refuse to speak to the questioner. He wouldn't turn her over.

The temptation pulled at her heart, but her conscience argued against it. She would never be welcomed in Galan again, but they at least deserved to know the truth.

Bai took a small step forward. Even that small step felt like one of the largest she'd ever taken. "It was my gift that caused the destruction."

The questioner looked at her with a surprised expression. Bai imagined not many people confessed freely to crimes before the questioning actually began.

Slowly, but with more confidence as she went on, Bai told him everything that she had learned. She spoke about her gift, and related the story Yang had told her. How she had stood up to a monk, and the reaction to that monk which had leveled part of her town.

The questioner listened with interest, never interrupting her story. When she finished, he stood silent for a few moments. "That is one of the more difficult stories I've ever been asked to accept," he confessed.

Bai didn't respond. She found that telling the truth, telling the story from beginning to end, had made her feel lighter. At the moment, she didn't particularly care how the questioner felt about it.

The questioner let out a sigh. "I believe you, though." He turned his gaze to Lei. "You confirm her story?"

"I wasn't there," Lei admitted, "but I have also investigated, and I believe she speaks the truth. Since she has been here, I have been training her, teaching her to control her power."

The questioner's gaze turned sharp. "Lord Xun will not like to hear that you've taken on an apprentice."

"Would you rather she wander the streets, unable to control her gift?"

The questioner's answer was calm, as though he held no personal stake in what he said. "I'd prefer if you were both dead. I would sleep much better at night."

Bai tensed again for a fight, but Lei was more relaxed than before. What did he sense that she didn't?

The questioner turned his back to them. He looked out over the trail he'd just hiked, gazing at the valley below. When he turned around, he looked at the village and the people going about their lives. No small number of eyes were on them. "Is there someplace more private we can speak?"

Lei studied the man for a moment, then nodded. He followed a trail out of the village, one Bai had never hiked before. Together, the three of them climbed above the village, stopping on a rocky point that provided a majestic view of the land below.

The questioner looked down. "A magnificent view. I can see why you selected this location for your village." He looked back to Lei. "Also a good place to kill a questioner."

Lei's grin held a hint of menace. "The thought had occurred to me."

"I suppose it goes without saying that I send messages to Lord Xun daily, and that he knows I planned to visit here today. Killing me only delays your problems."

"Let's hope it doesn't come to that, then," Lei responded.

The questioner turned back to the view below, drinking it in. "Have you heard of the latest events?"

"No," Lei answered. "News has been slow to reach us lately."

"The monastery in Kulat has had difficulties with the citizens. Apparently, a group known as the Golden Leaf blew up a few monks with black powder. In response, the abbot sent his men into the town square and massacred a group of citizens."

Bai couldn't believe her ears. She had never been a fan of the monasteries, but this… this was too much. How could the monks go so far?

"We know you've got connections to the Golden Leaf, Lei. We know the assassin lives here."

Bai started at that. After a few moments, she understood. Hien.

When she had left the village, it had been to set that black powder.

Bai tried to reconcile the two women in her head. Hien was certainly a warrior, but she had rescued Bai. That didn't seem like the action of an assassin. Bai wondered how much more was happening she didn't know about.

"I offer shelter to those who wish it," Lei responded.

"Are you telling me you had no idea what Hien was up to?" the questioner challenged. Bai was still surprised at how well-informed the man seemed to be.

"I knew she was working with the Golden Leaf. I did not know she planned such violence."

Bai studied Lei. She wanted to believe him, but did she? She wasn't sure anymore. She hated doubting the man that had shown her such kindness. But it was hard to separate truth from lies.

The questioner turned on his heels, staring at Lei and Bai.

"Lord Xun has always had a respect for you that I never quite understood, Master Lei. I presume you two have crossed paths in the past, but knowing your history, I'm surprised he feels so strongly about you. He's left you alone because you've left the empire alone. But if you continue be involved with the Golden Leaf, his hand will be forced. Do you understand?"

Lei's voice was hard. "I do."

The questioner's voice softened. "Galan was the spark that has lit this region on fire. The people blamed the monks, and as far as we can tell, the Golden Leaf fanned those flames until it exploded into a full-fledged rebellion. It's caused the monks to take drastic steps, and they've gone too far. I just received word that they've locked down Kulat. In response, Lord Xun is marching troops toward Kulat. The monks have been too ambitious as of late, and he needs to react strongly before this gets more out of hand."

"He's going to start a war," Lei interrupted.

"I fear the war has already started," the questioner replied. "Now it's up to us to end it before it spreads."

Lei looked like he was about to retort, but stopped when another thought crossed his mind. "What do you mean?"

The questioner looked at the two of them. "I risked my life to come here because I believe that you are a man of honor, Master Lei. But she is the person that began this chain of events." He pointed at Bai. "I see a way to end this all. If she comes down and confesses publicly, we might be able to turn the anger of the populace away from the monks. Right now, the Golden Leaf is telling everyone the monks were responsible for Galan as well. But if she confesses, perhaps tensions will cool enough for Xun to take more reasonable actions against the monastery in Kulat."

"And what happens to me?" Bai asked.

"After you confess, you'll be executed. Quickly."

Lei stepped forward. "It might have been her gift, but it wasn't her fault. If not for the actions of the monks, it wouldn't have happened."

The questioner held up his hand in a gesture of surrender. "I'm not here to tell you it's fair. It's close enough to the truth, and it can save many lives. Her life could be the sacrifice we need to end this now."

"I won't let you take her," Lei growled.

The questioner laughed. "I'd never try. As much as I'd love to test my skills against the most dangerous man the empire has ever met, I'd be a fool to think I could win, especially with your apprentice right here. No, I won't force anything. I'll simply make an offer to both of you.

"Bai, if you turn yourself in within the next three days, you can stop the violence that is about to happen. You can save Galan, Kulat, and this village here. If you do not, I'll be forced to report to Xun that Lei is hiding the person responsible for the deed right here in the village. After that, I do not know what will happen, but I would rather those events not come to pass."

With that, the questioner took one last look at the valley below. "It really is a gorgeous view."

He turned and started scampering down the trail. Lei and Bai watched him go.

Before he passed out of sight, he gave them one last look.

"We can meet at the large boulders about twenty minutes out of town. I shall wait there every sundown for three days. I hope to see you soon, Bai."

26

Delun and Hien made quick time. They left the stables as soon as Delun sensed the other monks. As they rode away, Delun felt the power of the monks behind him fade.

He hoped that he had seen the last of the monks for a while. If they were trying to hold the city, Guanyu wouldn't spare any to chase a lone monk. They began their ride in silence, which he also appreciated. He needed time to think, and after they had run their horses for a time without evidence of pursuit, they finally slowed down.

The scenery surrounding them was spectacular. Off to their left, the mountains that marked the edge of the empire rose to incredible heights. Snow-capped peaks glistened in the early morning sunlight. On their right, an old forest stretched for almost a hundred miles. The road to Galan straddled the boundary of the forest. The trees here were younger and smaller, but still cast ample shade upon the road.

He noticed little of the view, though. His mind was distracted with thoughts of his loyalties, a milieu from which no answers emerged. Hien had killed monks. The monks had killed civilians. He didn't wish to be associated with either action. And yet he found himself with Hien instead of the monasteries he had given his whole life to protect.

His logic held. The actions Guanyu and his monks had taken were a step too far, even for Delun. The consequences could reverberate through the empire. Hien gave him the best chance of actually doing something to stop them. Once Guanyu was reined in, perhaps Delun would have more information on the Golden Leaf. Maybe enough to shut them down.

None of the logic made the twisting feeling in his gut subside, though.

His thoughts came to a screeching halt when he felt monks behind them. Before, Delun had guessed there were one or two. Now, he suspected there were at least four. They were eating up the distance, too. They had to be mounted. He told Hien, who cursed. For the second time that day, they kicked their horses into a gallop. He hoped the animals weren't too exhausted from their previous run.

Delun was a passable rider. He was no expert, but considered himself better than most monks, who rarely rode. Delun had always wanted to be ready for just such a situation. He was glad for the training now.

They made good time, but the monks were gaining. Either they had better horses, or were better riders. Delun didn't care for either option. When he told Hien, she slowed her horse. "Stand and fight, or escape through the woods?"

Delun's choice came without a second's hesitation. "Through the woods."

Hien nodded, directing her horse off the road and

deeper into the woods. "We'll ride as far as we can, then abandon the horses if we need to."

Delun agreed, and they were off. He leaned forward as far as he could in the saddle, keeping his head low to avoid overhanging branches. Horse and rider disappeared into the forest.

Hien found a game trail, a narrow track running through the wood. She turned her horse to it, and Delun followed. Hien, by far the superior rider, could move faster, but she kept herself in sight, waiting for him as necessary.

Delun lost track of time and direction between the trees. The paths cut left and right, sometimes without reason, and as they penetrated deeper into the forest, Delun lost track of the sun. Shadows played out in all directions, and one grouping of trees looked much the same as any other. He kept his eyes on Hien in front of him and his sense on the monks behind him.

He felt the energy being focused and barely had enough time to make a turn as an attack slammed through the woods behind him. Branches snapped and trees groaned as the attack passed through.

The monks in Kulat were strong. He'd seen evidence of that in their training, but that attack confirmed his suspicion. Most monks couldn't have summoned that much power, especially at the distances still separating them. It didn't have the feel of Kang's energy, which meant there were other monks of considerable skill.

More attacks followed the first. At this distance, they couldn't do much more than frighten Delun's horse, but even that was enough to slow him down and allow them to catch him. One attack brushed against them, but the distance was too great, and Delun managed to keep the horse on course.

The monks were closing the distance, despite Hien's and Delun's efforts. Delun wondered how much he had underestimated the monks.

Tree branches snapped at him as he galloped past. Some bent, some broke, and others tore through his robes and flesh. He couldn't keep focused on both riding and avoiding attacks.

He didn't want to fight the monks, but he was running out of options. Distracted by the monks behind him, he almost ran headfirst into Hien, who had brought her horse to a halt.

"We can move faster on foot," she said. "The woods are becoming too thick."

Delun didn't argue. They slid off their horses and ran.

In the monastery, Delun had run frequently. Like all other aspects of physicality, he believed in being ready for any occasion, even if that meant pushing himself to his limits on occasion. So he took to his feet lightly, following Hien's blistering pace without a problem.

For a moment, he stared in amazement as he watched Hien. She moved as fast as any monk he had ever met, as fast as *anyone* he'd ever met. In his entire life, he'd never met anyone like her. She was a remarkable woman.

More attacks blasted near them, but none found their target. So far, the woods had provided enough cover, but Delun didn't know how long it would last. Behind them, he could hear the shouts of the monks.

"You can hide," he gasped to Hien as they ran. "They can only track me and my power."

She shook her head. "I'm not leaving you behind. You might be the best chance at stopping this madness."

Delun almost laughed when he realized she didn't

understand. "I'm not suggesting you leave me behind. I'm suggesting you ambush them."

She glanced back at him. "You want to fight?"

"No other choice. With my strength, they'll track me too easily."

She thought for a second, then nodded. She looked around and darted off into the brush, disappearing after only a moment. Delun was a little surprised. He'd expected that she'd agree, but thought that maybe they would discuss it a bit more. Now he felt truly like bait, caught in a trap.

As he felt the powers behind him, he realized he wasn't wrong. The monks had separated and were trying to encircle him. He wished he had a way to warn Hien, but that time had come and gone. She was on her own.

Without warning, one of the monks suddenly vanished from his awareness. Hien had found one. The loss of pursuit elated him, but the knowledge of what that victory had cost left him feeling hollow.

Delun focused on a pair of monks, their progress slowed by the sudden loss of their brother. Before they could react, Delun was on them, attacking with his own signs.

For a few seconds, waves of energy blasted back and forth, Delun abandoning the idea of forming shields in exchange for using trees as cover. He signed and released as fast as he could, driving the two monks back with the ferocity of his assault.

They defended themselves well against his onslaught. Attacks cracked against trees, ripped branches from trunks, and sent leaves flying everywhere. Delun relied less on sight and more on feel to find his targets.

He thought he might be able to drive them off. Strong as they were, they'd never faced a series of attacks from someone so dedicated to surviving. And he was still the strongest in the forest.

His optimism lasted until one of the monks had the good sense to cast a powerful shield around both him and his brother.

In the battle of energies, sometimes all that was necessary to change the course of the battle was a second to catch one's breath. Delun had hoped to prevent that, but he'd been stymied. The monk put everything into his shield, preventing Delun from breaking through easily. Safely inside the shield, the other monk gathered his energy.

Delun knew at that moment he was in trouble. The shield dropped as powerful energy struck at him. Caught off-guard, the first one hit him in the shoulder, punching him back and sending him rolling. He felt his shoulder dislocate from the blast. The second one passed harmlessly over his head.

Now the two monks worked in unison, and he was down an arm. He'd hoped to destroy their teamwork, but his success had only been temporary. Now one held the shield ready to cast while the other attacked.

To make matters worse, there was still the problem of the third monk, now coming up behind him. The third monk's arrival would spell his doom.

Where was Hien?

As soon as he had the thought, an arrow streaked by him, taking one of the pair of monks in the chest. The monk looked down in surprise as dark blood spread over his robes. He looked to his friend in disbelief.

His friend shared the same look. He'd been holding the shield in expectation of Delun's attack. But there was no sensing an arrow. Just in time, the monk realized the danger he was in, throwing up his shield as another arrow came at him.

Delun saw the look of rage pass over the monk's face. It was the look of a man pushed too far. In a normal man, the look was frightening. In a monk, it made Delun's knees quake.

Delun's terror was well-founded. The monk gave a throat-ripping scream, focusing all his energy into a single attack.

The monk made it to the third sign, and Delun swore as he felt the energy gather. The monk was holding nothing back, and rage amplified his already considerable energy. Delun signed a shield as the monk released his energy.

Hien chose a poor time to launch another arrow at the monk. It was caught by the wave of energy and flung back, moving even faster than when launched. Delun threw up his shield, covering himself just as the attack struck.

Delun grunted from the effort, but in the end, he was stronger than the other monk. No matter how the other monk might struggle, he couldn't get past Delun's defenses.

In a moment, the monk dropped to the ground, his breathing heavy. He'd spent everything.

Delun had seen that before, too. If the monk didn't get help soon, he would die. Too much energy had been released. The body and mind could only handle so much.

"Delun."

He turned around to see Hien for the first time since they'd separated. She looked pale and unwell. When he looked at her, he quickly saw why. The last arrow she launched had been sent back at her, and it was embedded deeply in her side. She had fallen down beside him, curled around the arrow. It didn't look like it had struck any major organs, but blood loss and infection would be equally dangerous.

Delun stepped toward her when he realized there was still a monk nearby. He stopped and turned, focused on the last surviving monk. The monk never even came close enough to see. Instead, he ran the other way. No doubt, the monk would tell Guanyu what happened. Delun would be labeled a traitor to the monasteries. Delun considered chasing the monk, but decided against it. What good would it do? He didn't want to kill the monk, and Hien needed attention. Guanyu would brand him a traitor no matter his actions.

Should he even save her?

She had killed his brothers.

But she was the only one who would vouch for him to Lei to prevent the murder of others.

As he knelt down next to her, he realized that wasn't the entire truth, though.

When he looked at Hien, all he could think was that he wanted her to live.

27

An unusual sense of peace settled over Bai as she walked down the path from Lei's village to Galan. Her courage surprised her. Though she walked to her death, her heart barely beat faster no matter how close they came to the meeting spot.

She noticed other changes as well. Walking down a mountain was never as difficult as walking up one, but there was a spring in her step she'd never had before, a slight bounce that was new to her. She could feel the energy coursing through her body. Granted, she let most of it return back to nature, its potential untapped, but she felt connected to everything in a way she never had before.

Beside her, Lei walked in silence. She could almost feel his thoughts, his face was so unguarded. They had argued plenty in the past few days. They still didn't agree, but at long last he had consented to accompany her. Despite her courage, she didn't care to make the journey alone.

"Are you sure you won't reconsider?" Lei asked.

Bai smiled. He'd lasted nearly half a mile this time before his control broke.

"What else is there to say, Lei? You know my mind."

They walked for a few seconds in silence before Lei came up with a new approach. "It feels like surrender."

"Sometimes surrender is better than fighting."

She wondered how much she meant that. The old Bai would have believed the statement with her whole heart. Now, she was less sure. She didn't want to turn herself in, but she also didn't see a better path. There was enough blood on her hands already. If she refused, it wasn't just her life that was in danger, but the lives of those who had nothing to do with her fight.

Once she had considered ending her own life. Now the questioner could do it for her.

"I don't like it," Lei said. "There's always another way. We just haven't figured it out yet."

Bai shook her head. "I'll gladly listen to any suggestion, but we've already taken all the time we had to think."

Lei acknowledged the point. It was the evening of the third day. They'd debated options endlessly, but the results remained the same. Bai had made her peace with it. Lei hadn't.

She knew all his arguments by heart. He believed she was vital to the monasteries, that she would unlock doors that had been closed for centuries. Her life was more valuable than she believed.

Bai appreciated the thought, but didn't agree. She couldn't be the only one with her gifts. Others just hadn't been discovered yet. Perhaps it would be years, but the time would come. She wasn't that special.

They reached the boulders the questioner had suggested, finding them unoccupied. Lei settled onto the rocks, but his posture still reminded her of a giant cat. He might look relaxed, but he would have his sword out in a moment if needed.

"There's still time," he muttered.

His insistence began to grate on her nerves. They'd spent three days searching for a better way, but every idea resulted in the deaths of others. Lei knew it as well as she did. "Please stop, Lei. This is hard enough as it is."

He grimaced and bowed his head quickly in apology. "I'm sorry."

"Don't be," she said. "It means more than you know that you care. But if you care, I need your support, now more than ever."

The sun had fallen behind the mountains, but the sky was still light. Bai had always enjoyed this time of day, when the colors were muted but the world hadn't yet slipped into night.

As the light faded, Bai began to worry. They had agreed to meet the questioner here, out of town, but there was no sign of the man. What would it mean if he didn't show? Would her willingness to sacrifice herself amount to nothing?

And yet the time continued to pass and still no sign of him. Bai glanced over at Lei, who clearly wondered the same. "He didn't seem the type of man to miss a meeting," Lei observed.

Bai bit her lip. She couldn't think of what else to do besides sit and wait. The questioner could appear at any moment, and she needed to be here when he did.

Soon the sky was perfectly dark, and the stars twinkled brightly overhead. Bai's worry increased. Had they shown up too late?

"What should we do?" she asked.

"I don't know," Lei responded. "If this is still your desired course of action, I recommend we wait for a few more hours. Then we can make the hike back to the village as the sun rises."

Bai nodded and dared to hope. What if the questioner had decided on another course of action? Perhaps she could be free.

At least an hour passed and Bai felt the tension growing inside her. Before long, she was standing and pacing, waiting for anything to happen. Lei watched her for a few minutes before standing himself. "There's no reason we can't at least train a bit while we're here."

Bai looked around. "Are you certain that's wise, this close to town?"

"We don't need to spar."

Lei had them stand ten paces apart from one another. "Close your eyes."

Once he was sure she had, he said, "Now, focus on me. Can you sense the way I move energy around my body?"

Bai took a deep breath, trying to find the place of mental calm from which she could perform the tasks Lei asked of her. She relaxed the tension in her body, allowing her muscles to soften. As soon as her breath was easy, she felt Lei's presence.

It was more than that, though. She felt his presence acutely. Before, she had noticed him like a pressure near the back of her head. Now she could picture him, the energy coursing through him, right in front of her. He was a beacon of light in the darkness. She could feel the way energy traveled between him and the ground he walked on.

"I can feel you," she said.

"Good. Now, where is my energy focused?"

She saw the energy shift inside him. "In your legs."

The amount of the shift wasn't great. Unlike her, Lei had

trouble directing his energies internally. She found it a simple matter to direct her energy to any part of her body. Lei fought for weak results.

They continued. Lei formed the different attacks and shields and asked her to identify them, not by sight, but by feel. She didn't find the task particularly challenging, but it required all her attention. She lost track of time, abandoning herself in the practice.

Bai felt the presence first. It was faint, but had the feel of a fire off in the distance. Though it only felt like a small spark to her, she imagined it was a raging inferno up close. "Do you feel that?"

"No."

Bai opened her eyes, breaking her concentration, the memory an afterimage on her sight. "Someone is coming, someone strong."

Lei frowned, lines of concern etched on his face. "You're sure?"

She nodded.

"How many?"

"Just one."

"That doesn't make any sense," Lei whispered. Bai wasn't sure if he had intended to be heard or not.

"What direction?" he asked.

She pointed to Galan. "Past town, I think."

"That's a long way away to sense someone. Let's check it out." He stepped forward, only stopping when Bai didn't follow. "What's wrong?"

"I can't leave this rock."

Lei looked like he was about to argue, but when he saw her face, he stopped. "I'm sorry, I forgot." He looked toward Galan and Bai could see the curiosity and concern on his face. "Let's see if your gift can uncover more."

They ran through the previous practice again. They calmed their breaths and focused their minds. Bai used Lei as a jumping off point, focusing first on his energy.

It didn't take her long to feel the other monk. His fire blazed bright, even at this distance.

But he wasn't alone. The large fire was being pursued by other flickering flames, like moths drawn toward light. She counted six, she thought.

She was so focused, she felt when they began attacking one another. Her eyes opened wide as her heart raced. Monks were fighting. Had Yang been found?

But Yang wasn't that strong. From her limited experience, few were. The monk being chased was closer to Lei's strength than those of the monks who chased him.

Lei's eyes were open, too. "I felt the attack."

Bai nodded mutely.

She thought she had a sense of the distance between them now. She stood about a twenty-minute walk from Galan. The lead monk had just entered town on the other side.

Bai felt some of her worst fears become real.

Galan had become the site of a battle between monks.

28

If Hien hadn't been so stubborn, Delun would have picked her up. Despite her protests, he was certain that he could move faster carrying her than helping her support her own weight.

But Hien was nothing if not proud, and she had expressly forbidden his attempts to pick her up. In the end, it was faster to lend his arm than to fight her. She'd even helped him pop his shoulder back into place, as though she was the healer and he the patient.

As they neared the outskirts of Galan, the wisdom of Hien's insistence made itself clear. He could feel the six monks behind him gaining quickly on their horses. He would need his strength.

As he had feared, the monastery had sent more warriors after them. Guanyu had no plans to let him escape.

Delun wished his journey hadn't turned out this way. He wished they could have kept their horses and not had to walk half the distance to Galan. He wished Hien hadn't been pierced with her own arrow. More than anything, he wished he didn't have to choose between the monasteries and the empire.

He didn't want it to be too late.

But perhaps it already was.

Monks who had pursued him out of Kulat were dead. There was no avoiding that truth.

Guanyu wouldn't listen to a word he said, now.

He'd fought against his brothers, and while he hadn't killed one yet, he'd stood by while they died. If this fight continued, he'd have to choose, and that decision would mean the death of his brothers, possibly at his hands.

His stomach twisted at the idea. In all his years, he'd never considered he'd have to fight monks. How did he choose between the empire and the monasteries, his two homes?

He could feel the choice barreling toward him like an angry boar. He could only avoid it for so long before he had to plant his feet on one side or the other.

That moment felt closer than ever as Galan came into view. He glanced over at Hien, who somehow remained on her feet. If she'd looked bad a day ago, she looked like walking death now. Her skin was pale and her steps uneven. Despite their best efforts at bandaging the wound, it continued to leak. She refused to rest, refused to let Delun lead their pursuers astray. Whatever chased them, they faced together.

Delun found her noble but foolish.

The sight of Galan gave them a boost of energy. They were close, the end of their journey finally in sight.

But the monks were close, too, and gaining every moment. Given how far away Delun had sensed them, they were strong.

"When we get to Galan, we need to find a place for you to hide," Delun said.

"I'm not going to hide." Hien's response was filled with icy determination.

"Then you're going to die, and I still need you to get me to Lei, to get him to believe me."

Hien didn't have any quick retort to that.

Delun didn't have a plan. He knew Hien needed to stay alive. He knew he needed to stay alive, and to stay free. Ideally, both could be accomplished without violence, but Delun had no idea how. The monks would keep following him. His strength prevented him from hiding.

He finally gave in to fate. Guanyu's actions couldn't be tolerated and were the more immediate threat. That logic had led him this far. He needed to follow it. He would fight, but he didn't need to kill. That was a line he still refused to cross.

"If you stay hidden, then I can fight them freely."

"Can you take on six?" Hien eyed him warily. She knew the argument raging inside him.

Had they been average monks, trained anywhere besides Kulat, Delun might have said yes. But here, he was less certain. Thanks to Hien's refusal of assistance, he wasn't as exhausted as he might have been. Against any one of the powers following him, he was clearly superior, but against six, and especially six who would work together, he was less certain.

Delun pushed his worries aside. His decision was made. In answer to Hien's question, he replied, "I'm not sure, but I'll have a better chance if I don't have to defend you."

She growled at him. "I don't need your protection, monk."

"You can barely walk."

"But I can still fight."

Delun shook his head. There was no point arguing with Hien. The woman was as strong and stubborn as any warrior he'd ever met, and to tell the truth, he appreciated the attitude.

They made it to the outskirts of Galan before the monks came into view. Delun figured they didn't have more than a minute or two before the fighting began. Unceremoniously, he dumped Hien into a dark corner between two small huts. "Find a place to fight if you can, but don't get too close to me. They'll be able to track me no matter where I am."

She looked as though she was about to tell him she knew that, but held her tongue. Delun nodded, wishing there was something more he could say to her. After a heartbeat of silence, he disappeared into the night.

He kept to the outskirts of town, using the houses as cover. After a few moments, though, he realized how foolish that was. The houses all had people in them, and if a fight did break out between the monks, the people inside would be the first ones to suffer. He thought of Kang's attack within Kulat.

Delun wondered if it was too late to reason with the monks. Though the likelihood was low, he wasn't sure that he would rest easy unless he tried. He stepped out from the cover of the houses, approaching the monks.

He didn't even have time to wave a hand in greeting before an attack shot his way.

Surprised, Delun didn't have time to even sign a shield. He dove to the side, the invisible wave of energy crashing against the wall of the house he'd just stepped out from. The wall, made only of wood, cracked and collapsed. Terrified screams rose from inside the house, peaceful slumbers destroyed by sudden devastation.

Delun rolled to his feet, distracted by the screams. His first instinct was to help.

His compassion almost killed him.

Another blast flew from the hands of a second monk, this one catching Delun squarely. He tumbled and crashed backward, feeling fortunate the attack wasn't as strong as the first. Still, he struggled to draw breath as the monks dismounted, a bruise already forming against his ribs.

He pushed himself to his feet, half-rolling, half-falling as another blast took his feet from under him. All he needed was a moment, but the monks didn't plan on gifting him one.

Desperate, he released an unfocused blast in their direction. If nothing else, perhaps it would throw them off balance for a precious second. His effort was wasted, though. One of the monks had already thrown up a shield in front of the others, protecting them from Delun's weak attack.

Delun made it to his knees when he knew he was going to die. He felt several attacks gathering, any one of them strong enough to finish him. His fingers made the gesture for a shield, but he knew it would be too little, too late. His heart plummeted as he realized he was about to be killed by his brothers, the very people he had spent his entire life defending. None of them possessed the hesitation about fighting Delun he felt about fighting them.

Before the first attack was released, an arrow suddenly appeared through the neck of one of the monks. The remaining monks pivoted to face the new threat, leaving them exposed to Delun.

Hien had given him the moment he needed. In one hand he finished his shield while his other danced through the signs of the attack. He stopped on the third.

One monk sent an attack in the direction the arrow had come from. The blast blew through the walls of a house, and all Delun could do was hope that the people had had enough time to get away, and that Hien had been able to stumble away. She was smart enough to move after shooting, but was she able enough?

Another monk felt Delun's growing energy and turned to meet the threat. Delun held his attack, wanting to get in close and make his energy count. Against five, he couldn't afford to waste any of his strength. The monk attacked and Delun released the shield.

He'd underestimated the strength of the monk's attack. His shield held, but Delun almost lost his balance. The monk saw the opportunity and formed another hasty attack.

Delun got his feet under him in time to sidestep the next attack. For the moment, the monk had left himself defenseless. Delun reached out his hand and released his own attack, sending the monk cartwheeling through the air. He hoped he hadn't killed the man.

Only four remained, but they weren't fazed by the losses they'd suffered. One of the monks cast a shield that surrounded the rest. Just in time, too, as an arrow bounced harmlessly off the reformed shield. Hien had survived the first attack, then. He had no idea how she was pulling a bowstring with the injuries she'd suffered.

He had his own problems to worry about, though. The momentum shifted back in the direction of the monks. Delun needed to focus an impressive attack to break the shield, and he didn't think he had the time. Two attacks reached out for him, crashing into his shield. A third brought down yet another house. Either they were fine with wantonly destroying the properties, or they actually knew where Hien was.

Delun wasn't sure how best to react. He sent an attack at one of the monks, but the shield intercepted it without problem. Two attacks responded, forcing Delun to run once again. Unless he took cover behind the houses, there wasn't much more he could do. He simply couldn't match the coordinated power of the remaining monks.

Several events happened at once. The first was Hien. Delun finally spotted her, stumbling from cover to cover between the houses. Unfortunately, he wasn't the only one to notice her. One of the other monks did as well, hitting her with a prepared attack before Delun had a chance to react. She went tumbling into the street.

Delun measured the distance between them, then decided it didn't much matter. He formed the signs for a shield, sprinting toward Hien.

As he did, Delun felt a surge of power behind him, stronger than anything he'd ever felt. He glanced back, his legs still churning toward Hien, just in time to see a face he'd never forget.

Lei stood outside the village, his sword drawn and alive with energy. Delun's eyes went wide as the sword snapped down, opening a sharp slice in the ground as a tremendous crescent of energy sliced at the four monks. The attack shattered the shield, the force of the attack sending the monk whose shield it had been to the ground.

Lei followed it up with another attack, this one from his hand. It blasted a monk backward with tremendous force.

Delun turned back to the task at hand. The monk aiming at Hien had been distracted, but from the look in his eyes, Delun knew he meant to finish the weakest of targets before he turned to fight Lei.

The delay gave Delun enough time to get between the monk and Hien. He threw up his shield just as the monk released an attack, the blast powerful enough to send him crashing backward on his side. Delun landed with enough speed to roll twice before coming to a stop.

Delun looked at the monks. The other three were completely focused on Lei, and the fourth could tell he'd been abandoned by the group. Groaning, Delun formed the signs for a shield to surround both him and Hien. Before the monk could attack again, Delun crawled next to Hien and released the shield.

Despite the beating he had taken, Delun still felt as though he had plenty of energy to draw from. He hadn't done nearly as much fighting as he'd like. His shield was strong enough to handle the monk's next attack. Through the confluence of their energies, Delun could feel the monk's hesitation.

The monk wanted to fight Lei. After a moment, he turned his attention to the new intruder, leaving Delun alone.

Delun couldn't have hoped for more. Lei could handle the monks, and Delun could sit here, protect Hien, and not have to fight against his brothers. If any of the monks turned toward him, he'd be ready, but from the glimpses of battle that he saw and felt, Lei had their full attention.

He knelt down over Hien, who had fallen unconscious. Although he could feel her breath, she looked as pale as a ghost.

He looked back at the battle. If she died from this, his brothers would pay.

29

B ai had never felt a battle between monks before. Such battles were rare in these times. The only one she knew about was the Battle of Jihan, over twenty years ago. But Galan, the town she'd once called home, now crackled with energy. A group of monks was attacking another. To her recently developed senses, it felt as though six mice had attacked a large cat. Individually, none of the mice stood a chance, but together, they might just beat it.

If Lei hadn't intervened.

She'd become more used to his strength over the last few weeks. But she'd never realized how much his strength dwarfed that of the other monks. Her sense of him almost blinded her to the others.

Attacks whipped from his blade, driving the other monks away like dead leaves before a howling wind. She caught a glimpse of his face and saw a new side to him. The gentle peace he radiated up in the mountains faded and she saw the steel of the man underneath. For all his power, each of his cuts was precise and exacting, control almost beyond imagination.

She'd been changed by Lei, too. Part of her screamed in fear, shouted at her to hide from the tempest of power raging in front of her. Her own body hummed with the ambient energy.

But the old Bai was dying, if she wasn't already dead. She felt the energy from Lei's attacks and the monks' defenses filling her limbs with fire. Her body absorbed the power like a sponge, and she thought she could take on the whole world if she wanted.

Bai stepped forward, her fists clenching in anticipation. Yang had called her a monk killer. She'd feared them her entire life.

No more.

Out of the corner of her eye, she saw two figures. One was prone and the other crouched over the first. Her eyes narrowed as she made the two of them out.

She didn't recognize the man kneeling over the prone figure, but the sight of the second person stopped her in her tracks.

Hien.

Bai sensed the energy radiating off the kneeling man. He was the strong one, the one who had fought the other monks.

But he was also a monk, too close to Hien to be safe.

Her only thought was to save Hien. She darted toward the pair, the power in her legs allowing her to cross the distance in only a couple of seconds. The monk sensed her coming, but wasn't prepared for her speed. He started to stand, twisting out of the way as she drove her knee at him. Thanks to his twist, the blow was only a glancing one, but it lifted him off the ground and sent him tumbling away.

The monk came to his feet quickly, confusion writ large on his face. "Who are you?"

Bai felt power concentrating behind the man's back, where he hid one of his hands. She fought down the grin on her face. She stood tall and walked toward him.

When she was about ten paces away, he swung his hand in front of him, the focused power aimed directly at her chest. Bai funneled strength into her legs, jumping as he released the attack.

The power passed harmlessly beneath her. Moving some of her strength into her hand, she swung as she fell toward him.

The wide-eyed look of shock on his face almost made up for the fact that he fell away from her punch before she could connect. The monk stumbled backward, but Bai couldn't take advantage of his lack of balance. Her missed punch threw her off, causing her to crash to the ground as she landed.

The monk recovered before Bai did. In a moment, he was on top of her, hands wrapped around her throat, his weight bearing down on her. She couldn't force air through her throat and panic took over. She kicked uselessly, her legs unable to reach the monk sitting high on her chest.

Then she felt the power flowing through the monk's hands, his sweet, life-giving energy. She didn't think, but *pulled*, some deep instinct in her taking over. The man's strength poured into her.

His grip around her throat loosened, his eyes widening as he slowly pulled his hands away and stared at them in disbelief.

Bai took a deep, heaving breath, the air tasting sweet.

Now she had strength to spare. The monk's wide-eyed gaze traveled from his hands to her, just in time for her to shove him with all her might.

Again, the monk was lifted off the ground, then tossed

backward like a rag doll, tumbling end over end. He came to a rest and stood up, more quickly than Bai had hoped. She came to her feet as well. She'd surprised him, several times, but she hadn't done much damage.

She glanced back at Hien. The woman still lay prone where Bai had first seen her. Bai didn't need to defeat the monk, she just needed to give herself enough time to get Hien away from the battle.

A particularly strong surge of power outside of town distracted the monk for a moment. Bai sprinted forward, pulling in as much power as she could. Here, it was almost too easy. The monk made a sign and a shield grew between them. Bai hit it at nearly full speed. She felt the power as she ran into it, but it did nothing but slow her for a moment. She pushed through the shield, absorbing most of its strength. With a throaty cry she punched at the monk.

The monk's other hand came up, releasing an attack right in front of her strike. The attack met her fist, two tremendous powers colliding. Bai thought she saw the air bend and warp between them before it snapped like a string pulled too tight. She flew backward, spinning slowly through the air. The world twisted around her, but she breathed deeply, feeling the energy still within her. She landed on one foot and skipped backward until she found her balance.

The monk didn't fare so well. He'd been slammed into a wall and was slow to get up. When he did, his eyes focused on Bai. They stood there, facing one another. Bai breathed deeply, feeling the power building within her again. She was surrounded by it, embraced by it.

The monk turned and ran deeper into Galan.

Bai was caught flat-footed, fully expecting their fight to continue. Hien was safe.

But Bai wasn't done. She didn't know what the monk would attempt, but Bai didn't want him running free through her town. More than that, she felt the strength flowing through her limbs. She was fighting a monk, and she wasn't scared.

The freedom intoxicated her, made her head spin. She wouldn't hide in corners, or quietly suffer the abuse of others.

They couldn't hurt her anymore. They wouldn't hurt anyone.

She took off after the monk. She could feel his energy moving away from her, but after running into corner after corner, Bai gave up simple pursuit. She looked up and smiled, that feeling of freedom infusing her very thoughts.

Bai leaped onto the rooftops, landing as gently as a bird. Then she took off, jumping from rooftop to rooftop, every motion somehow instinctual.

In only a few seconds she had caught up to the other monk. A vicious grin painted on her face, she jumped down at him.

She didn't think he was surprised anymore. Now she saw only fear in his eyes, the same fear she imagined so many had seen in her over the years. She saw the terror of someone who knew that their safety was nothing more than an illusion. All the monk's power and training meant nothing.

Bai didn't come down swinging, as she had before. Lei taught her that control was the essence of strength, and she had calmed down enough to remember her lessons. She landed softly in front of the monk, stopping him cold.

He attacked with his monastic techniques, but being this close to him, she could draw on his strength. His moves seemed lethargic, and she dodged around them with ease, landing what felt like three light punches in return.

The blows rocked the monk back. He kept his feet, but barely.

Staggering, the monk formed another attack. Bai stepped forward, extending her left hand. She wrapped her hand around the monk's as he unleashed his energy, feeling the wave of strength fill her limbs. She punched him in the face. Not hard, but his eyes rolled back in his head as he collapsed to the ground.

Bai looked down at the fallen monk. He had been strong. She had sensed his strength relative to the others, relative to Lei. And he lay at her feet. She held her hand in front of her, turning it back and forth and staring at it in fascination. She made a fist and studied her knuckles. The skin was unbroken and smooth. She felt no pain.

The meeting of powers outside the town snapped her from her reverie. She left the monk behind, leaping up to the rooftops again. This time, her feet moved easily, her footing more certain with experience. She crossed the distance in a few seconds, dropping down to the battleground and throwing herself into the fight.

Lei didn't need the help. He'd sparred against her with more strength than he was using against the monks. She wondered at that for a moment, but understood quickly enough. He didn't want to kill any of the monks. Holding back his power was possibly even harder than fighting at full strength.

She stepped into the middle of the fight, standing tall as she absorbed the energies being flung about. It took the monks a few moments to realize she was even there. But then she darted between them, sending fists and elbows into exposed torsos and faces. She kept her strikes light, but when she hit the monks, they staggered under her attacks.

After only a few seconds, the fight had gone out of the monks. Against Lei they had stood, their shields largely protecting them from harm. They had no answer for Bai's fists, though. They stumbled away, bruised and bloody, eyes full of confusion.

Bai wanted to laugh and to spit at them. Her body still quivered with energy. Throughout the fights, she had filled herself as much as she dared. With a yell that came from deep in her chest, she made the first sign of the attack and released some of the power into the sky.

She was breathing hard, sweat pouring down her forehead. She hadn't noticed before.

Lei came to stand beside her. She felt his gaze studying her, but her own thoughts were on the monks retreating. She had been a part of that. Lei had helped, of course, but she had broken their lines and sent them away.

She wanted to chase the fleeing monks, to finish what they had started. Under her watch, the monks wouldn't threaten innocents any longer. No one would. Lei interrupted her thoughts.

"Where's Delun?" Lei asked.

"Delun?"

"The monk you fought."

She jabbed her thumb behind her, pointing back toward the center of town. "Somewhere back there. He won't be moving for a while."

"He is a monk of considerable strength."

Bai grinned viciously. "Not enough, it seems."

She knew Lei was studying her closely. In the corner of her vision, she saw his eyes narrow. But his question about Delun had reminded her of Hien. Bai turned away from Lei and jogged toward where Hien lay. For the first time, Bai saw Hien's injuries. The warrior had been shot through the abdomen, and from the amount of blood in her bandages, the wound was serious.

Lei joined her a moment later. "We need to get her up to the village. She can be cared for there."

Bai had been thinking the same. Pulling energy from Lei, she picked the woman up and cradled the injured warrior in her arms. Lei gave her a questioning glance, but Bai ignored it. She could make the climb. Hien's life depended on it.

Lei looked out over Galan. Quiet had fallen over the town and people slowly started to trickle out of their houses. "There's going to be a steep price to pay for what happened here today."

Bai agreed. But it was the monks who had to pay.

They began the journey toward Lei's village. Off in the distance, to the south, there was a flash of lightning and a deep rumble of thunder.

A storm was brewing, and it was heading their way.

30

Delun woke to the sounds of a crowd gathered around him. He opened his eyes and squinted against the harsh early morning sunlight full on his face. The group of people milling around were close enough to disturb his enforced slumber, but too far away to cast any shade on him.

He blinked away the tears that trickled from his eyes and sat up, immediately regretting the decision. He felt the exhaustion in his body that was the familiar effect of fighting with his powers, but his pain went deeper than that.

That girl had destroyed him. He could feel bruising on his chest, and now that he was sitting up, his head was pounding in torturous rhythm with his heart.

Questions about the girl threatened to overwhelm him, but he pushed them aside for the moment. He had more important and immediate matters. The first was dealing with the people of the town. Hiding his pain as much as possible, he worked his way to standing, suffering through every movement. He wasn't sure he'd ever been beaten so badly, even in his early days of training. As he stood, the townspeople took a step back.

Delun looked around. It felt as though the crowd was holding its breath, waiting for disaster to strike.

None of them offered to help.

No one offered water, or pointed him to a healer.

Curiosity kept them near, but he would find no succor here.

"How many?" he croaked.

No one answered.

"How many died last night?"

An older man stepped forward with the attitude of a defiant criminal condemned to death. He didn't bow, nor show any other sign of respect. "Eight."

Of all the punches he'd taken recently, that one hurt the worst. He sighed and tried to breathe deeply. Memories rose, unbidden, from deep in the well of childhood he'd tried to bury. In all these years, had so little changed? Had he made so little difference?

Grunting with the effort, Delun got down onto his knees and bowed to the assembly. "I'm sorry."

An apology wasn't enough. Nothing was enough. But an apology was all he could offer. At least for now.

Delun stood up and the crowd shuffled another step back. He wondered if they were even aware of their reactions to him.

He considered remaining in Galan. He wasn't an expert in healing, but he had some skill. He could help.

But they didn't want him here. They wouldn't say no to him, of course. No one would. But it would be better for them all if he left. The town would bury their own. Lord Xun still had an army on the way and Guanyu had a rogue monastery that condemned itself more every day. Remaining in town, no matter how noble an idea, was only hiding from his real problems.

Delun gave another short bow and turned away, finding the road out of town with little difficulty. He felt the stares stabbing daggers into his back as he left. He was probably lucky they hadn't tried to kill him while he was unconscious. The fear of monks still proved useful sometimes.

He couldn't stop thinking about the woman. If not for the bruises covering his body, he might not have believed any of it. Nothing she did should have been possible. It went against everything he knew.

Yet, it happened. He didn't doubt his experience. How could he?

Delun felt like a trapdoor had opened up beneath him. For years he had walked on solid, predictable ground. Now, suddenly, the illusion had been revealed, and he stood over a bottomless abyss. He had felt like this once before, when everything he thought he knew turned out to be a lie.

He was young then, only a handful of years old. He had been in Jihan, the capital of the empire, for the harvest festival. It was held at the end of every growing season to celebrate the end of harvest. In Jihan, the celebration brought in people from all over the empire, Delun and his father among them.

A fight had broken out between monks. At the time, Delun and his father hadn't known that. No one had. All they knew was that buildings began to collapse and the ground itself seemed to tremble. There was a panic. Delun only remembered a few vivid moments forever etched in his memory. He clutched tightly at his father's hand as they ran, then he glimpsed a wall of a building tipping over toward them. His father didn't even see the wall. Only Delun, looking up at his father, watched it come down.

A monk had appeared, seemingly from nowhere. The

wall crashed down all around the three of them. Delun, awestruck by the sight, had no idea how the wall missed them. Now, he knew the monk had cast a shield over the three of them, protecting them from the debris. But at the time, Delun saw the monk as a miracle.

That was also the day when Delun had discovered his own power. He had yelled in terror, and thanks to the proximity of the monk, his own strength was greater than usual. Both his father and the monk had felt the unfocused blast of energy.

There wasn't much more to the story. From the monk's perspective, nothing altogether special had happened in those moments. He'd saved a family and discovered a boy who possessed the gift. But Delun's life changed forever. He'd always been somewhat afraid of the monks. Most of the boys he played with were. Once he was identified, he was brought into the monasteries.

His path had been set that day. He'd seen the heroic abilities of the monks firsthand, and that one experience overshadowed all others. The monks existed to serve the empire, and they did it well. His whole life was proof enough for him.

He'd been fortunate to train with several monks he still respected. His worldview had deepened, but he'd never lost that fundamental belief, that certainty in his gut that the monks were heroes. It justified all the actions he'd taken in his life, acting as his own guiding star, illuminating his way through the years.

He wasn't blind. He knew his own actions were horrible, and he recognized too many monks spent too much time inside their walls. But he'd always believed.

Until now.

Certainty remained elusive. He was still a monk, and a

proud one. Despite Kulat, there were monks all over the empire saving lives the same way his had been saved. He'd always fight for the monasteries.

But now it seemed he would fight against them as well.

The more time passed, the more certain he was this could only end in conflict. Even if they somehow stopped Kulat from becoming a pitched battle, the seeds of discontent would be fertilized all over the empire. Finding and preventing those seeds from sprouting into something worse had been most of his life's work.

His thoughts and steady stride carried him up the mountain, the only destination left to him. This time, he followed the main trail leading out of Galan. It was little more than a wide footpath, but it was considerably more pleasant than his first nighttime ascent of the mountain.

The sun was kissing the horizon by the time he made it near the summit. He sensed their presences before he saw them. They came over the lip of the summit and walked down toward him. He'd never seen two people walk so nonchalantly toward a monk, especially a monk of his strength. But they had earned that right. Each of them had defeated him. He had no illusions about his chances of victory.

They met several hundred paces below the summit, safely away from the village. Delun stopped thirty paces from them. He hadn't summoned any of his strength, but neither had they. For several seconds they stood there, silently judging one another.

Delun had spared some thought for this moment. He needed them, far more than they needed him. He could imagine what he should do. But he wasn't sure if his pride would bend as it needed to.

Moving stiffly, he came down to one knee, then to both.

He kneeled for a few moments, then bowed his face to the dirt. His cheeks flushed red with shame. A monk never bowed. Taio, if he saw, would be aghast.

But perhaps that was part of their problem. If a monk was a servant to the empire, he should bow, not be bowed to.

Still, those moments were some of the hardest of his life. He held the bow, trying to hide the brightness in his cheeks. Neither Lei nor the woman spoke.

Finally, Delun could take no more. He came to his feet. Lei looked at him. "Why are you here?"

Delun took a deep breath. "I need your help to bring down a monastery."

31

Bai watched as Lei led Delun to the tea house. The monk certainly seemed sincere. She had thought, for a moment, he might actually die of shame after bowing to her and Lei. His face was still flushed minutes later, as though shame haunted his steps.

She found trust to be elusive, though. People often broke their word. They would say anything to get what they wanted, only to retreat from their statements once their goal was obtained. How many times had she accepted less money than agreed on for the work she'd done? She'd lost track of the count long ago. Her mother had taught her to accept it as part of life.

Delun could be waiting for Lei to drop his guard, to ambush him when the time was right. Bai almost followed them to the common room, just to keep an eye on the monk. She'd been invited to join them but had declined. Her head was too full of the fight from the night before, and the absence of the questioner before that. She didn't need to hear about the monk's mad plan, if he was telling the truth. It still could be a trap.

With one long last look, Bai turned away. If anyone here could protect themselves, it was Lei. He gave the appearance of outward calm and relaxation, but Bai had seen the way his eyes constantly scanned his surroundings. She wasn't sure it was even possible to surprise the man.

Instead, Bai walked toward Hien's house. Bai had missed the woman desperately when she'd been gone, and now she was returned, gravely injured. As she approached the house, she ran into Daiyu coming down the ladder. No doubt, the woman who helped run this village had been caring for Hien.

Bai had long since realized her initial impressions of Daiyu had been incorrect. If anything, the two of them had more in common than either was comfortable admitting. Daiyu wanted to live in peace, and being married to Lei meant removing her family from the affairs of the world.

"How is she?" Bai asked.

"She should live. The arrow missed the vital organs. She lost plenty of blood, but the wound is clean. Given enough rest, she should recover." The tone of Daiyu's voice suggested that enough rest was anything but given with Hien.

Bai looked up at the empty balcony. No doubt, Ling was at Hien's side, as she had been since Bai had carried Hien up to the village. Her gaze traveled back down to Daiyu. "Thank you for taking care of her. For caring for all of us."

Daiyu gave a curt nod. She didn't care for acknowledgment. Every time Bai tried to thank her, Daiyu looked uncomfortable, as though she wanted to be somewhere else. The other woman looked over Bai's shoulder toward the building that served as the inn and tavern. "They are in there?"

Bai nodded. The whole town knew of Delun's approach.

Daiyu's eyes hardened, reminding Bai of when she'd first met the woman. She knew now the cause. Daiyu was content with her life up in the mountains. She loved Lei and loved the people who formed their small community. She didn't mind outsiders, but she had told Bai directly that she had no interest in seeing Lei get involved with the affairs of the world below. Bai, when she'd first arrived, threatened the order Daiyu had established. Now Delun did the same. Bai was grateful not to be on the receiving end of that glare again.

She opened her mouth to ask a question, then stopped. She knew how Daiyu felt, but she wondered if the woman had any idea where Lei's thoughts were. Despite possibly offending her, Bai asked. "What do you think Lei will do?"

Daiyu's shoulders slumped, revealing the fear she lived with. "I don't know. Those of you who have this gift, you always believe that it comes with some sort of responsibility. Lei will be torn, again. He believes it's wrong for him to ignore what's happening below. He also knows that if he acts, he will be forfeiting the peace he's worked so hard to obtain."

"You think he'll fight?"

"I worry that he will, yes."

The thought gave Bai a sense of hope she hadn't felt before. Now that she had faced other monks she understood just how strong Lei was. Having him fighting against the monks at Kulat would change everything.

Bai tried to hide her feelings from Daiyu, but the woman was too observant. "You hope he will fight?"

"I grew up in Galan. I spent most of my life fearing the monks at Kulat. My town might have abandoned me, but it is still the closest I have to a home. I don't want others to suffer the way I did."

Daiyu stepped toward Bai and clasped her hands. Bai almost jumped back in surprise. She couldn't remember ever being touched by Daiyu. Her hands were warm but firm. "Lei sometimes feels the same, and it tears him up inside. It has for years. My hope is that someday, both of you will understand there is nothing wrong with a quiet, peaceful life. It is just as honorable as any other."

Daiyu let go of Bai's hands and walked off toward the inn, sorrow hanging off her like a heavy cloak. Bai watched her leave, unsure if there was anything she could say. Eventually, she turned and climbed the ladder that led to Hien's room.

As Bai expected, Ling was at Hien's bedside, reading and offering her presence. Bai bowed to her. At first glance, Hien appeared to be sleeping. "How is she?"

"Awake, and tired of people speaking about me like I'm not here," growled Hien.

Bai grinned. Hien's rough nature had grown on her. She appreciated never having to wonder where she stood with the woman. She was as straight and unforgiving as an arrow aimed at your heart.

Bai stepped deeper into the house and knelt down next to Hien. "How are you feeling?"

"Like I've been shot with my own arrow. It was a foolish shot, and now I'll never hear the end of it. The woman who shot herself with her own arrow. But I'll be fine." Hien's sharp eyes turned their gaze onto Bai. "What about you? I heard you and Lei got into a bit of a fight last night."

Bai nodded. "I went down to Galan to turn myself in."

Hien sat up straighter in her bed. "Why?"

For the next few minutes, Bai caught Hien up on the questioner's arrival and her decision. Hien listened carefully, but when Bai's story was done, she sagged back into her bed. "You're a fool, Bai. So is Lei, but I would have expected it from him."

The words stabbed at Bai. She thought Hien would approve.

Hien caught her expression. "It was noble enough, but foolish. Lei's village is always going to be in danger. I've been around enough to know it's not as secret as he likes to believe, but he won't listen to me. Eventually, someone is going to come here looking for trouble. Several already have, I suppose. But Lei has nothing to fear. He's strong enough to protect the village. He's more concerned about the number of deaths he would cause if he did."

Hien's hand snaked out from under the blankets and held Bai's. "I know you're still getting used to this, but you can do whatever you want now. I didn't free you from that cell just so you could walk back into one that's even worse."

"You think I should have fought the questioner?"

Hien shrugged. "I don't have any answers for you, Bai. All I know is that surrendering is never the answer. You know I've spent much of my life smuggling women and girls out of rough situations, right?"

Bai nodded. Hien had spoken briefly of it.

"You know the difference between a woman I can save and one I can't?"

Bai shook her head.

"I can only save the ones willing to fight to save themselves."

Bai wasn't sure how to respond, but Hien continued. "It was something I learned early on. A lot of people talk about doing something. They whisper and they plot and maybe they start, just a little. But that's where most people stop. To actually make a change, they need to do more, but few do." The warrior paused. "I don't think I need to tell you this, but you have more choices than you once did. Don't choose to surrender."

Bai felt her ire rise. She hadn't chosen surrender. She had been sacrificing herself for the village. Why didn't Hien see that?

She stood, and Bai saw Hien notice her distress. But Hien made no effort to comfort or soothe her. Instead, she asked, "What will you do now? Your questioner didn't make the meeting."

Bai paced the small room twice more before returning to kneel next to Hien. "You know I fought with the monks down below?"

Hien nodded. "To hear it told, it was quite the sight."

Bai hesitated. She'd been wondering this since the night before, and hoped Hien could help her. "It felt good to fight."

Across the bed, Ling's eyes flashed with disapproval. Hien laughed softly, grunting with the pain as she did. "Yes, it does, doesn't it?" Hien gazed at Bai for a moment, missing nothing. "That scares you, does it?"

Bai bowed her head, ashamed.

"There's nothing wrong with fighting," Hien said. "You must know *why* you fight, though."

Bai's brows furrowed. "Why I fight?"

Ling, glaring but silent, stood and left the two of them alone. Hien watched her go, a hint of pain in her eyes. Then she turned back to Bai. "Fighting to defend a village, or to protect those who can't protect themselves—those are good reasons to fight. Fighting to exert your will over others, or to intimidate... those are poor reasons. Violence is a tool, nothing else."

Bai digested the philosophy slowly.

"So, why will you fight?" Hien asked, assuming Bai's choice to fight was already made.

Bai thought of Hien and Daiyu, two women with completely different outlooks, yet both content with their choices. She thought of Lei, willing to fight off two monks as Hien brought a stranger into the village. She was jealous of all of them, who seemed to know what they wanted from life. She'd never even thought to ask herself the question.

Bai ran her fingers over her mother's bracelet. All her life, she'd been taught that the highest she could aspire to was to remain unnoticed. Even now, the thought of running away tempted her.

Invisibility was the dream of the weak.

Bai didn't believe there was a single right answer. But Lei, Hien, and Daiyu all had something in common. They had asked themselves what they wanted from life and had found an answer.

Meaning was the dream of the strong.

She lifted her finger from the bracelet. Her mother had spent her entire life hiding. She'd been miserable, and had died for nothing. If Bai could prevent one other person from growing up like her, or like her mother, life would have meaning.

She looked down at Hien. "I'm not sure exactly what I will do, but I know why I will do it." Her voice rang with conviction. "I promise you, Hien, I will never surrender again."

Hien gave her a weak smile. "Good. Now, if you don't mind, I could really use some rest."

Bai reached out and gave Hien's hand a squeeze. "Rest. You've done more than enough. Thank you."

Hien's eyes were closed by the time Bai stepped to the door. She stopped short when she saw Ling standing silently on the balcony. Their gazes met and Bai saw that the woman had been crying. "I hate that she believes so deeply," Ling said. "One day, she'll leave and not return."

"But you wouldn't love her if she didn't leave." Bai's leap was intuitive.

"I was one of the women she rescued, a long time ago."

Bai wasn't sure what to say to that.

Together, they looked out on the village. Finally, Bai smiled. "She does need to be on bed rest for at least a few weeks. By then the worst of this should have passed. So long as you don't let her fight her way out, she'll miss this storm."

Ling nodded. Bai knew the comfort wasn't enough, but it was all she could offer. She climbed down the ladder.

She still wasn't sure what she was going to do with her gift, but she knew she needed to join the meeting between Delun and Lei. More than most, those two would decide the course of the valley.

Bai didn't intend to be left out.

32

Delun followed Lei into the building that apparently served as part tavern, part common room for the village. When they stepped inside, conversations quieted and eyes fixed on them. Even Delun, used to being a stranger, felt more like an outsider than usual. They all saw Lei, though, so their expressions were more curious than concerned, even though Delun wore the white robes of a monk. Within a few moments, the conversations returned to normal, as though Delun wasn't even there.

Perhaps that, more than anything, was remarkable. They trusted Lei so much that he could come in here with a monk and cause nothing but a brief ripple of curiosity. Few men had that kind of respect from others. The monks certainly didn't.

Delun was certain Lei had earned the trust. Though the older man walked in front of Delun, exposing his back, Delun saw no openings for attack. Lei radiated a sense of calm, but Delun didn't think he had ever met a man who stood his hairs on end in quite the same way. Lei's hand never moved far from a dagger tucked into his belt. He had let Delun into his village, but he remained wary. If Delun summoned even a bit of his energy, he suspected he would be signing his own death sentence.

The two of them sat at an empty table and Lei ordered tea and beer. Delun raised an eyebrow.

Lei smiled cryptically in response. "I enjoy tea more than I once did, but beer is still my preferred beverage."

Delun shook his head. He had no doubt that at some point in time, Lei had lived in a monastery. And yet he didn't have many of the familiar mannerisms of a monk. Seeing Lei's ease, and seeing the respect of the locals, Delun didn't wonder if he was looking at the answer to the monasteries' problems.

He found the thought both intriguing and disturbing.

Their drinks arrived and Delun took a sip, his eyes widening slightly. "That's really good."

Lei's smile became genuine, and Delun thought he saw a hint of the true man underneath the mask of peace. "Thank you. One of our residents has a small plot of land about half a league away. It's apparently ideal for this plant, and our tea leaves come from him. He would be pleased to hear you enjoy it." Lei's pride in the villager was plainly evident. How often were the monks proud of those they supposedly served? Delun couldn't help but let his mind wander in that direction.

Delun took another sip. The first notes of the tea were grassy, but gave way to a pleasant sweetness. He'd traveled much of the empire and he couldn't remember having a better cup. Jihan, the capital that claimed to be the height of civilization, certainly didn't have anything of this quality. At least not that Delun had ever tried.

Delun set the cup down and watched Lei take a sip of beer. Even though the other man looked relaxed, Delun wasn't fooled. Lei was still ready to fight if Delun displayed even a hint of threat. It almost made Delun want to try, just because of the challenge.

The monk couldn't help himself. He took another sip of tea, then asked, "Who are you?"

Lei gently shook his head. "Who I am isn't very important. All that matters is I live here now, and I'm doing my best to live in peace."

It wasn't that the statement was a lie. Delun believed Lei wanted to believe what he said, but the monk couldn't accept the statement at face value. "And yet you're harboring a member of the Golden Leaf, an assassin who tried to kill me."

Lei grimaced. "I'm harboring Hien, a woman who sometimes makes choices I wish she wouldn't. But I owe her a debt."

"What do you want?"

"Mostly, to be left alone."

"You've been training the woman?" It was a guess, but Delun trusted his instincts.

Lei nodded. "Bai. Since you chased her up here, yes."

"Why?"

"I sensed some degree of her ability. I had a suspicion about what happened in Galan. Part of me wanted to make sure she learned control so that would never happen again. But as I discovered what she was capable of, I became driven by curiosity."

"Who is she?"

"A seamstress."

Delun shook his head. "*What* is she?"

Lei shrugged. "That I do not know. The next step? Her abilities are truly special."

With a start, Delun realized he had become relaxed. The

delicious tea, Lei's demeanor, and the atmosphere of the common room all eased his mind. Delun blinked and sat up straighter, remembering the events that had brought him here. Still, he found he enjoyed Lei's company. Talking with the man seemed so easy, their relative abilities making them at once familiar and strangers.

"She's the perfect enemy for the monasteries."

"The thought occurred to me. But what she does is up to her." Lei turned the conversation back to Delun. "What about you? I get the impression that your claim about wanting to bring down a monastery was more than a statement to give you access to the village."

The monk sipped at his tea. "You know Lord Xun is marching an army toward Kulat?"

Lei nodded.

"The two forces can't be allowed to fight. Not only would the battle itself be a disaster, but it could be the beginning of the end for the empire."

Lei leaned back in his chair. "The situation has become that dire?"

It was Delun's turn to nod. "The monasteries have isolated themselves for too long. We've turned inward, spending more of our time studying our own powers and less time involved in the empire. It's bred resentment on both sides. The monasteries feel attacked and the citizens feel as though they are no longer protected. I've spent years quelling minor insurrections, but this is beyond anything I've faced."

Lei looked around the room, his eyes pausing as the door opened. Delun, curious, turned around in his seat to see Bai enter. His heart sped up as he saw her, a reminder of how she'd beaten him once before. She saw them and approached. "May I join?"

Lei nodded and Delun followed suit. Bai sat down next to Lei.

"We were just discussing Delun's request," Lei said.

"Good," Bai said. "I want to hear what he has to say, too."

Lei looked at Delun expectantly.

The monk wasn't sure how he felt about Bai taking part in the conversation. It was Lei's help that he wanted. But he supposed there was no harm in her listening in.

"I need to remove Guanyu from power at his monastery," Delun started. "I'm not sure how deep his ideas have taken root, but he cannot remain the abbot of Kulat. He desires power, and his desires will destroy us all."

"He's a strong warrior," Lei said. "That much I know. He's mastered techniques that few have. Without a weapon, I think he and I would have a close battle on our hands. I've also heard rumors of the devotion he's inspired in his monks. Many of them have come to Kulat from other monasteries after hearing of him."

Some of Lei's information was new. Delun hadn't guessed Guanyu was so powerful. It made sense—a group of warrior monks would hardly follow a weakling, but he'd sensed no great power when standing next to the abbot. Delun acknowledged the points. "It may be a fight. But I know no other way. Do you?"

Lei shook his head.

"That's why I came here. You've seen my strength. But I'm no match for that entire monastery if it comes to a fight." Delun fixed his eyes on Lei. "But if you were to help, I'm certain I could prevent more bloodshed than necessary. I also believe you alone value monastic life as I do."

Delun wanted to say more. He wanted to persuade Lei of the necessity of the man's help, wanted to emphasize the importance of the next few days.

But Lei knew Delun's arguments already, and Lei didn't seem like the type of man who appreciated more words than were necessary. So Delun held his tongue, sipping at his tea to give himself something to do while he waited, his weight leaning forward.

Bai seemed equally curious. She looked back and forth between the two men, as though judging something for herself.

Lei took a deep breath, and Delun leaned in even closer.

"I will not help you."

Delun almost doubled over from the verbal punch. Without Lei, he'd have to hope not all the monks at Kulat were as traitorous as Guanyu. From what little he'd seen, Delun knew that was unlikely. Lei had essentially condemned him to death.

"Is there nothing I can say that will persuade you?"

Lei shook his head. "My heart wants to join your fight. But it is not my place. If I fight with you, I only bring more attention to myself and to my village. It also breaks a promise I made a long time ago."

Delun's voice rose. "You could save thousands of lives. Tens of thousands!"

Lei leaned back. "And there will always be another conflict. If the empire doesn't collapse now, there will be another event five years from now, or ten. I can't stop them all. But I can protect my village, and that I will do."

Delun felt anger building inside of him. Lei had the strength to do something, but he refused. The man was a coward and a disgrace.

He was about to say so when Bai bowed toward him. "I will help."

Her action took the wind right out of him. He looked

over at Lei, expecting him to protest, but the traitor just looked at her with curiosity in his eyes.

"You'll help?" Delun asked.

Bai nodded. "I've spent most of my life being afraid of the monks of Kulat. They've scared everyone in our village, often. But no more. I need to face my fear. I need to do something to help."

Delun almost dismissed her out of hand. She was a woman, and one who had discovered her ability only a few weeks ago.

He stopped himself. She had also beaten him handily in a fair fight. And he was stronger than most monks at Kulat.

There was another argument in her favor, too.

If she died while fighting against the monks at Kulat, then justice would be served. Either way, Delun accomplished something useful.

The thought passed in a moment. Delun smiled. "Very well, I accept."

They both looked at Lei, as though he might disagree and attempt to prevent them from working together.

Lei simply nodded, as if he'd seen this coming.

They finished their drinks and discussed tactics. They'd made their choices, and their fates were now bound tightly. Together, Bai and Delun would take on the monastery at Kulat.

33

Bai glanced over, still struggling to believe she walked down the trail side-by-side with a monk. And not just any monk, but a monk who traveled the empire crushing dissent. The two of them had spent the rest of the day in Lei's village, training together and attempting to understand their respective gifts and weaknesses. As they sparred under Lei's careful supervision, they learned more about each other.

Bai considered Delun to be a man with a deep well of passion, masked by layers upon layers of armor. He'd never spoken of the actual event, but something happened when he was young to create his devotion to the monasteries. He believed with his whole heart, but that fire was hidden underneath the placid mask of a monk.

His true self came to the surface when he fought, though. Bai had felt it before when they dueled in Galan, but she'd had him on the defensive then. In their sparring matches, when he was prepared, he flourished against her. In battle he was careful, but aggressive and committed.

Unlike Lei, he rarely feinted, relying instead on his years of training and experience to overwhelm opponents.

He'd gotten the better of her a few times. He'd used attacks to trip her up, used the environment against her. She beat him more often than not, but he learned quickly and never gave up.

In short, he was a monk you wanted on your side. As an enemy, he'd be fearsome indeed. Bai had been lucky to escape him as often as she had.

Now they walked down the trail in something resembling a companionable silence. They weren't friends, but necessity made them allies. She remained surprised that he seemed to hold her in a measure of respect.

Bai, for one, was grateful for the silence. Her head filled with thoughts and doubts chasing one another.

She still couldn't say exactly why she agreed to help Delun. The decision had felt right at the time, and it still did. But it was also foolish. She knew her strength, but who was she to attack an entire monastery?

She remembered her own fear, though. If she could protect another little girl or boy from that same terror, why shouldn't she?

In her heart, though, it wasn't about protecting others. That was a story she told Delun and Lei.

The truth was, she wanted to fight. After years of hiding and cowering and accepting the abuse, she wanted to kick, punch, and rage against those who had been part of the problem.

Knowing her true reasons made her feel as though she was going mad. It was the height of foolishness to fight a monk, and worse yet to be the one who instigated that fight.

But she wanted the fight.

Her thoughts slowed and focused when Galan came into

view. It was the first time she'd approached her old village this closely in the daylight since the incident. As much as she tried not to think of it as home, it was hard not to. This was the place where she had grown up, the place where she had lived with her mother.

The place she had destroyed.

Delun's thoughts seemed to mirror her own. "You're sure?"

"If he's around, there's almost no doubt he's in town."

"I could do it alone."

She shook her head. "Thank you, but no."

Delun didn't respond.

She didn't want to go into Galan, but she wouldn't hide from what needed to be done.

They were noticed even before they reached the outskirts of the village. Two men watched the road, no doubt due to all the recent excitement. One man ran back into town while the other stood in the center of the road, holding what appeared to be an old, rusted spear.

Bai found the scene foolish but did not laugh. No doubt the man would be quaking in fear. Delun's robes announced who he was as clear as day, and Bai was no stranger, but the man still stood his ground. That took courage.

Delun was about to step forward and deal with the sentry, but Bai laid a hand gently on his shoulder. "That won't be necessary."

She led the way, pulling some power from Delun. Hopefully he wouldn't mind. Her senses sharpened, and she saw the way the man shuffled back as she approached. She smiled at him, trying to put him at ease. The idea might have been well-intentioned, but it didn't work.

Bai saw the man's weight shift, his center of gravity moving back as he prepared to lunge with his spear. To her heightened senses, the movement was easy to spot. She stepped to the side as the spear jabbed at her, then caught it in one hand. She gripped the shaft tightly as he tried to pull away.

Bai watched the man struggle. Holding the spear was barely a challenge, but the man looked like he fought with his whole body. She focused some of her energy into her hand and squeezed, snapping the spear. The man fell backward as his anchor gave way.

She looked down at him. "I'm not here to hurt you—"

He didn't give her time to finish the sentence, scrambling away and sprinting back into town.

Bai and Delun watched him go.

Delun grunted. "That could have gone better."

Bai shot him a withering glare, but it did nothing to disturb the monk's composure.

They continued into town. Bai kept drawing a trickle of energy, ensuring she would be difficult to surprise. Behind her, she felt Delun begin preparations for a shield. It felt like the second sign, but she wasn't experienced enough to be certain. Regardless, he seemed ready to protect her. The gesture offered her some slim comfort.

When she'd imagined this moment, she'd imagined some sort of conflict. She had prepared for the townspeople to attack her, or yell at her, or confront her in some way.

As she walked through Galan, though, she was greeted with nothing but silent glares. She saw people looking out their windows, or staring at her from the small hidden spaces between houses. The most daring fixed her with angry looks as they passed on the opposite side of the street.

Everyone looked angry at her, but Bai didn't feel that emotion. She felt their fear. No doubt, rumors about her had spread after her escape from the cells weeks ago. Rumors that were perhaps closer to the truth than Bai had once imagined. For all the hate in their eyes, Bai felt only pity in return.

She had been one of them, not that long ago.

After walking for a few minutes, she had to turn to Delun. She wondered if he felt the same when he traveled through towns in his white robes. "Is it always like this?"

"Sometimes."

A slowly rising wave of sorrow filled Bai's heart, cresting as they walked past the destroyed market square. Weeks had passed and still no one had tried to rebuild. Bai asked Delun to stop. She wasn't sure when or if she would ever be in Galan again. She found her old house. At first, she had intended to leave the bracelet behind, proving to herself she had moved on from her childhood.

Now the action seemed foolish. She had moved on, and the bracelet was all that remained besides her mother's memories. She bowed to the house and to the spirit of her mother. The woman hadn't been perfect, but Bai believed she had done her best. She thanked her mother for all she had done.

Eventually, she returned to Delun. "How do we find the questioner?"

Delun gave a grim smile. "If he's here, he'll find us."

The two of them continued, and before long, Delun's prophecy came true. A single man stood in the middle of the street. Even if she hadn't recognized him from before, Bai would have known him. There was no fear in his stance, no turning away.

He gave them a slight bow as they approached. "Bai. Master Delun. It is a pleasure."

Bai almost asked how he had found them, but then

stopped. They were in Galan. No doubt everyone in town knew they were here. Word traveled fast in a small town.

Delun stepped forward before Bai could speak. "We need your assistance."

The man gave Delun a quizzical look, as though a request for help was the last thing he'd expected.

"If you are able," Delun continued, "we need you to stop or slow the advance of Lord Xun's troops."

The man laughed, then saw the expression on their faces. "You're serious?"

Delun nodded.

The questioner shook his head. "My responsibility is only to take Bai into custody. What you ask is beyond my duty."

Delun stepped forward with such menace that Bai actually stepped away from the two, her protective instincts overriding her reason for a moment. The questioner didn't so much as flinch.

"Your duty," Delun growled, "is toward the empire, the same as me. Bai and I are going to Kulat to stop the monastery. If you can slow the army, you can prevent war."

The questioner's eyes slowly looked back and forth between the two warriors. Bai had no problem imagining the calculations running through his mind. The questioner's gaze settled on Bai. "Your work is well-known, Master Delun. But this woman has the skill to assist you in this?"

Delun nodded. "More than most."

The questioner stood in silence for a few more moments. "I can try, but I'll have little authority with the military itself. My best effort would be to ride to Lord Xun personally and then send a messenger to the army, but I don't think that will be fast enough. I will do what I can, though."

Delun gave the questioner a respectful bow. "That is all any of us can do."

The questioner returned the bow and was about to turn away when Bai spoke up, curiosity overwhelming caution. "Why didn't you show up that night?"

The questioner smiled. "I was there."

Bai's questioning look caused his grin to grow even wider. "I was watching you and Lei, attempting to better judge your character. I wanted to know you better before apprehending you. My plan had been to show myself in time, but then events spiraled out of control. I don't regret my decision, though. I saw what you two did that night."

Bai shook her head in disbelief.

The questioner slipped away without another word, and Delun breathed a sigh of relief. Bai gave him a questioning glance.

"Not all men are so reasonable," Delun replied. "He gives us a chance at averting this tragedy, though."

Bai nodded. "On to Kulat?"

"Unless there's something more you need to do here."

Bai looked around. They were near the outskirts of town, approaching the area where she and Delun had fought. Although she still called Galan home, it didn't feel that way anymore. Now that she was here, it was just a town, a place she had once lived. A small part of her felt homeless, an empty feeling in the pit of her stomach that she wasn't sure she would fill anytime soon. "No," she said. "I'm done here."

She believed it, too. Until a door to a house opened in front of them and a familiar face stepped outside, the man as surprised to see her as she was him.

Bai couldn't believe the coincidence. Her stomach

clenched in knots as soon as she saw the man, but she forced herself to relax.

Wen stood in front of her.

The man who had been responsible for so much of her suffering. The man who had beaten her in the cells.

Bai barely felt the power surge through her, her instincts and anger taking over. She dashed toward him, grabbing him by his throat with one hand and slamming him up against the wall. His feet, just off the ground, kicked feebly at her.

She held her grip, impervious to his weak attempts at escape.

She wanted to yell at him, to beat him the way he had beat her. As she held him there, choking the life out of him, she looked for that hint of anger in his eyes.

Instead, she saw only fear.

Wen was a coward.

"Bai." Delun's voice behind her was gentle but firm.

The last of Bai's rage cooled. She released her grip, sending Wen collapsing to the dirt at her feet. She knelt down next to him. "If you ever treat anyone the way you treated me, I will return."

Then she stood back up, looking at the man who had once inspired terror in her. She shook her head.

"Now I'm done."

34

D elun rested in a deep squat as he gazed at the road in front of them. Behind him, Bai paced back and forth, covering the width of the road time and time again. She had run out of patience an hour ago.

Over their past days together, Delun had come to a realization: he enjoyed Bai's company. The woman had lived through some difficult experiences, her behaviors indicative of the person she used to be. More than once he had caught her startling at some small sound with the awareness of frightened prey. But she kept pressing forward, a trait Delun saw very little of in his life. In his experience, more people were governed by fear than by reason.

She had more reason than most to be afraid. When the monasteries learned of her gifts, she would be hunted across the entire empire. Lei's village wouldn't be able to shelter her for long.

She knew as much. She'd admitted it to him as they walked. Yet here she was, risking everything to help him.

"Are you sure?" she asked.

Delun gave a short, bitter laugh. "Not at all."

"Do you really think they'll be interested in peace?"

Delun shrugged. "From what I've seen, it seems unlikely, but we need to try."

That morning, Delun had found a messenger to deliver a letter to the monastery. It requested a meeting between him and Guanyu.

The reasoning was simple. If Delun could somehow convince Guanyu to step down, this disaster could be averted. If, as Delun thought more likely, Guanyu decided to attack him, at least the battle would happen outside the city.

Perhaps he was too much of an optimist, though. Some small part of him still believed it wouldn't come to a fight.

Perhaps he was just blind. He couldn't imagine a world in which monk willingly fought against monk.

He glanced over his shoulder again at Bai. She had handled herself well thus far, but he still worried about her. If Guanyu attacked Delun, the abbot would send some of his best and fiercest fighters. Despite her preternatural skills, she did not have the lifetime of training experience the monks did. How far could she trust her skills in a pitched battle? How far could he?

There were no easy answers to his questions, but at the moment, she was a tool willing to be used, and that was enough for him.

She sensed them coming before he did. "There's quite a few of them."

Delun couldn't feel them. "How many?"

"Six, maybe seven."

Delun narrowed his eyes. "That's fewer than I expected."

Delun had figured Guanyu would respond to his request with overwhelming force. Six or seven monks was no force to sneeze at, but was only a fraction of what Guanyu could afford.

Delun had fought off six already. He'd had help, of course, but Guanyu would have taken that into account.

Delun tried to put himself in Guanyu's shoes, adopting the abbot's mindset.

It occurred to him he might be viewing the problem incorrectly. He was considering this insurrection as the end, but Guanyu wouldn't. For the abbot, the uprising on the western edges of the empire was only the beginning. He didn't have that many monks to work with, and they'd already taken losses in previous encounters. Guanyu was playing a game much bigger than Delun.

Bai was about to retreat into the woods when Delun stopped her. "Hold on. Guanyu will want to protect his monks as much as possible. It might make him more defensive." Delun paused, his mind racing through the possibilities and how he could best exploit them. Their original plan had been for Bai to hide, only to defend Delun if the worst came to pass. "If things go bad, I want you to attack them instead of defending me."

Bai gave him a quizzical look.

"If they attack me," Delun explained, "I want you to attack the monks with everything you have. Your immunity to their attacks should send them off balance for at least a minute or two. If you can take one or two down, I believe the rest will retreat."

Bai looked doubtful.

Delun attempted to give her a comforting smile. "Trust me. It is our best chance."

Bai nodded and walked away, disappearing into the shadows of the woods. He hoped she trusted him. It was an incredible ask, to trust the man who had once hunted her.

Delun had chosen the location of the meeting carefully. The road between Galan and Kulat ran along the western edge of a great forest, and Delun had chosen a section where the forest swallowed the road, a place where Bai could easily hide. If she didn't pull power into herself she was difficult to sense, and Delun hoped the monks wouldn't be expecting her.

A few minutes later he sensed the group coming towards him. He confirmed Bai's estimate. He sensed seven people, and he recognized two of them. One was Guanyu. His energy was strong, but not as strong as the man who walked beside him. Kang.

Delun had expected that particular companion. Still, it didn't make him feel any better about the meeting's prospects. Although he believed he had a slight edge on Kang, the margin of difference between them was narrow enough that a fight could easily go either way. Regardless, fighting Kang would take almost all his attention. If it did come to a fight, Bai would be left with the other six, including the abbot. The odds hardly seemed fair.

Delun mentally shrugged. He had gotten used to long odds early in life. Whatever the challenge, he wouldn't go down without a fight.

Sensing the monks approaching, another question that had nagged Delun wormed its way to the front of his thoughts. How had Guanyu became the abbot of so many strong monks? From Delun's senses, Guanyu was perhaps the third or fourth most powerful in this group. Monks didn't necessarily base rank on strength, but Delun had a hard time imagining this particular group of monks following a weak fighter.

Delun thought of Lei's words in the village above. The rebel had indicated Guanyu was incredibly powerful, but Delun didn't sense it.

It made the hairs on the back of his neck stand up. Was he underestimating his opponents?

Delun shook his head to clear the thought. It was too late to change their course of action now.

A few more minutes of waiting brought the two sides together. The monks spread out in a line across from Delun, stopping about forty paces short of his position. Each looked relaxed, but all were clearly ready to fight. Fortunately, no one went so far as to form the signs for any attacks or shields.

Delun did his best to stand casually in front of them, as though he didn't have a care in the world. As though facing seven of the strongest warriors in the empire didn't make his knees quake and his stomach twist in knots.

He gave the tiniest of bows to the abbot. It was disrespectful, but in Delun's mind, Guanyu didn't deserve anything more. "Thank you for coming," Delun said.

The abbot waved his hand dismissively. "Get to the point, Delun. You're lucky I don't kill you where you stand."

Delun raised an eyebrow at that. It was all the reaction that he allowed himself. He wouldn't let Guanyu's verbal tactics dissuade him. "I asked you here today so we could put an end to this madness."

"And what does that mean to you?" Guanyu asked.

"You step down as abbot and turn yourself in for trial to the monastery at Two Bridges."

Guanyu laughed out loud. Delun figured that was a bad sign.

"Do you know what I think is madness?" asked Guanyu. "I see a monk who openly stands against his brothers, who cooperates with rebels looking to destroy the empire, who kills those very people he is sworn to stand side-by-side with. I see that monk demanding that an abbot step down.

That, to me, is madness. Delun, you have overstepped your authority and have sullied the reputation of the monasteries throughout the empire. By my authority as abbot of Kulat, I hereby banish you from the monastic system and sentence you to death."

Definitely not a good sign.

Legally, there would be a mess to sort out if the two of them ever ended up in front of an impartial judge. Unfortunately for the rule of law, the nearest impartial judge was hundreds of leagues away. Strength would decide the victor of this argument.

As if on cue, all six monks beside Guanyu began forming their signs. As Delun tracked their motions, he saw that four of them were signing attacks and two were signing shields. Apparently, this group had worked together before.

Guanyu spoke again. "This doesn't have to be hard. I suspect you have the girl hiding somewhere around here. Call her out and we can arrest you both. Otherwise they will attack."

When Delun didn't respond, Guanyu sighed. He made another dismissive gesture with his hand and turned away. The four monks with attack signs all aimed at Delun, and he swore. His fingers danced through the shielding signs, just barely getting to the third before the attacks darted at him.

Delun released his shield in time, but it was a thin defense against the combined powers arrayed against him. Kang stood among the attackers, and his strength alone almost cracked Delun's shield. Delun grimaced as he felt the pressure building, like being buried under boulder after boulder. He struggled to breathe, fought to expand his chest and bring in air.

He only had another second or two. Once his shield

dropped, the attacks would crush his bones into dust. He wasn't sure there would be enough of him left to bury.

Suddenly, Bai emerged from the trees and crashed into the line of monks. She dropped into the heart of the line, passing through their shields without problem. She was so fast, Delun could barely follow her movements.

Suddenly, the pressure against him nearly disappeared. As Delun came to his senses, he saw that several of the monks were on the ground. Two of them didn't look like they'd be getting up again, their heads at unnatural angles.

Delun knew Bai's strength. He remembered his fight with her all too well. But she was getting more comfortable with her power, and she *really* didn't like monks.

Behind the line, farther away from Delun, he felt an immense power gathering.

Now he understood how Guanyu had become the abbot of the monastery. Like Lei and Bai, he could draw power in from sources beyond himself. Against Delun's sense, he glowed like a second sun. A sun whose energy was becoming condensed and focused.

Kang and the remaining monks seemed to have the right idea. They scattered away from the road, finding cover in the forest.

Bai, so new to her power and so confident, didn't even think to avoid the attack.

Guanyu kept focusing his energy, bringing it to a point no bigger than a man's thumb. Delun cursed again. There was only one attack that strong, one that hadn't been seen in combat for over twenty years.

The Dragon's Fang.

Delun didn't know how Bai's gifts worked, but there was no way she could absorb that attack. No one could.

He yelled, tried to warn her, tried to convince her to get

out of the way. But she stood there, as stubborn and proud as the oldest of monks. He wanted to force her to the side, but she was too far away. There was nothing he could do in time.

As guilty as he felt, he had only one avenue of action open to him. He dove to the side, out of the way of the attack. He expected it to cut through Bai, and he didn't want to be in its way.

Guanyu released the attack, cutting through the air toward Bai like an arrow to its target. The abbot's aim was true, and the attack burrowed deep into Bai.

It was a testament to her strength that the technique didn't blow a hole through her torso. She stood there, somehow absorbing the tremendous energies. To Delun's senses she began glowing brighter and brighter, the power unbearable even to look at.

Delun couldn't tear his eyes away, though. He'd traveled the empire nearly from edge to edge and destroyed rebellions both serious and foolish. He thought he'd seen almost all there was to see, but this was something outside of his experience, outside even his imagination. The powers and abilities at play blasted his comprehension away.

Somehow, Guanyu found even more power. A normal man, even a trained monk, would have exhausted himself several times over by now. But the Dragon's Fang continued.

And somehow, despite all the odds, Bai stood.

Delun waited for her body to disintegrate into ash, to simply cease to exist. The powers within her were greater than any human body could handle.

Then it was over. The Dragon's Fang ended, and Bai still stood, the air around her shimmering with the latent energy she'd absorbed.

Bai screamed, an earth-shattering, piercing yell that broke Delun's heart. He'd never heard such pain before.

Beyond Bai, Guanyu's eyes were wide. Delun thought the abbot looked like he'd spent everything he had on the attack.

Still, Bai's body held far too much energy.

He saw her right hand come up, making the sign for the first attack. She started to release the power, sending the attack harmlessly into the sky, but it was too little, too late.

The air around Bai contracted, and Delun knew what was coming. He dove to the ground and signed the second shield, trying to dig himself as deeply as possible into the ground.

A second later, the world around him exploded.

35

B ai woke up in the middle of her worst nightmare.
Her head hurt, every heartbeat sending a fresh wave of pain down her neck and spine. She struggled to breathe, as though a boulder lay on her chest and she couldn't move it.

She had been here before.

As she came to awareness, a creeping dread washed over the pain.

Not again.

Light flickered in the corner of her vision. She glanced over and saw a man sitting next to a fire. He seemed familiar, but it took a moment for his name to return.

Delun.

With his name, dozens of other memories flooded her. He had been attacked by the monks and she had jumped in. She'd fought the monks and hurt a few of them. It had been easy.

Then she'd been hit with the other monk's attack.

From there, her memory failed her. It was as black as the deepest cave.

That, too, was horribly familiar.

She groaned, and Delun was by her side in a moment. "How are you?"

Bai couldn't get her mouth to work. Everything hurt and she felt drained. She wasn't sure which prevented her from speaking. Delun, thankfully, didn't seem to need her words. He returned to the fire and removed a small pot. He knelt again by her side and held her head up as he ladled some of the soup into her mouth.

Bai had never tasted anything more wonderful. The warm liquid coated her sore throat. After a few sips, she managed to chew some of the rice and vegetables inside. Exhausted by the effort, she lay back down.

Delun looked at her with concern but didn't say anything. Bai was grateful for his silence. She needed the time to think.

Calmer now, and with a bit of strength from the soup, Bai looked around. They were in the middle of a collection of downed trees. Something about their camp seemed unnatural, but Bai couldn't put her finger on what.

"What happened?" she croaked.

Delun stirred the fire with a stick, moving the coals around aimlessly. "How much do you remember?"

"I remember the fight, and being attacked by that one monk."

Delun jabbed at the coals. Bai sensed frustration in the movement.

"That was Guanyu," he said. "He's the abbot of the monastery, and much, much stronger than I expected."

Bai noticed the hint of failure in Delun's voice.

"You took a hit that should have killed you," Delun continued. He saw her expression and stopped her. "Yes, even you. I've never felt anything like that attack. Even you should have died several times over. I think you knew, near the end. You tried to release the power, but you had absorbed too much, too fast."

He left the rest unspoken.

Bai's stomach hardened to a rock. With a grunt, she pushed herself to her elbow and looked around. All the trees nearby had fallen in the same direction. She guessed if she followed their accusing trunks, she would find the place where she'd stood, a small patch of undisturbed ground among the destruction.

She had done it again.

"Who did I hurt?"

Delun threw his stick into the fire, watching it slowly catch. "I think you killed two monks in your initial attack. But I don't think your blast killed anyone. I was the closest, and I managed to shield myself. The monks were further away and were escaping as I came to. There were too many of them for me to attack, so I let them run and attended to you instead."

Bai accepted the news calmly. She was glad she hadn't hurt any innocents this time.

Delun turned the questions back to her. "Now, how do you feel?"

"Like someone threw me off a cliff."

"Not bad for someone who should be dead."

Bai gave a bitter laugh. She enjoyed Delun's perspective. "So, what happens next?"

"That depends on you. After this little skirmish, I'm less certain than ever that I can approach the monastery on my own. But you've been out for hours, and you look like death."

"Thanks." An idea occurred to her. "May I borrow some of your energy?"

"Are you certain that's wise?"

Bai gave a little shrug. "I don't know. But it seems worth trying."

Delun didn't look nearly as certain about that, but he gave his consent. Bai closed her eyes, feeling his strength. She decided to pull just a little to start.

A few seconds later, she heard a gasp. "Bai!"

She opened her eyes to see the panic on Delun's face. His mouth moved, but no words came out.

Panicked, Bai cut off the connection, and Delun toppled to the ground. When he looked at her, he looked furious. "You almost killed me!"

A protest was on Bai's lips, but she paused and reached out with her sense. She could barely feel Delun. Her mouth dropped open. "I'm sorry! I only tried to take a little."

Delun struggled to a sitting position. His eyes were wary. "Is that true?"

"I swear it. I thought it was only a trickle!"

She realized with a start that most of her pain and exhaustion had faded. It had worked. She stood up and took a few tentative hops. Her body felt sore in places, but she felt otherwise fine.

Delun shook his head. He whispered something under his breath, but Bai didn't catch it. "Sorry?"

He looked ashamed for a moment. "Your skills are remarkable." He paused and looked around. "We should rest for the night. No matter how good you feel, there's no substitute for sleep. And I don't have your ability to simply pull in energy. I'll need the time to recover. In the morning, we go to Kulat and attack the monastery."

He watched Bai closely. "Your ability to adapt seems to be increasing. But your body can only take so much. You will need to be even more careful in the city. Do you understand?"

Bai nodded, looking around the forest from a standing position for the first time. For hundreds of paces, trees were flattened, cracked, and broken. The damage was far worse than in Galan. She imagined the scene in the middle of Kulat and felt sick. She'd never let that happen.

She thought about the trials that lay ahead. As frightened as she was, she welcomed the challenge. She finished her bowl of soup, then lay down and fell asleep instantly.

BAI LISTENED to the thunder in the distance. A storm was coming in from the north, lightning already spiking against the sky. Such summer storms were often fierce. She and Delun walked quickly, trying to find a balance between covering distance and maintaining their energy for the fight to come.

She felt strangely calm. The dangers in front of her were more real than ever before, but she felt ready.

She thought of her mother, wondering what the woman would think of her now. Would she feel proud, or would she feel disappointed her daughter had ignored so much of her advice?

Delun grunted, bringing her attention to the present. Kulat was in sight. "Do you sense anything?"

She quested forward but found nothing.

Delun understood before she did. "They don't have their guards on the roads anymore." His voice was suddenly filled with fear. "We might be too late."

The monk began running, leaving Bai little choice but to follow along. She allowed energy to flow into her, giving her the strength and stamina to match Delun's pace. They passed into Kulat without challenge. Several people turned away from Delun's white robes, but there was no reaction otherwise.

Delun held up a hand. "There's no need for both of us to check what's happening. We'll need horses. Can you find your way to the monastery? As long as you don't draw power, they are less likely to sense you."

Bai didn't come to Kulat often, but she'd been here enough to find the enormous building. She nodded.

"I'll get horses and bring them to the monastery. You find out if the monks are still there. If we're too late, we can try to catch them."

Delun ran off. Bai continued toward the monastery. She didn't believe what she sensed, but she got closer until there could be no doubt.

Delun's fears were confirmed. Though the gates were shut, Bai could only sense two or three monks on the grounds. She inquired at a few nearby houses and learned the monks had left early that morning, before the sun had risen. Either they had forced Guanyu into moving earlier than he intended, or the approaching army was already close enough for the monks to move on them.

She didn't have long to wait before Delun thundered up on an enormous warhorse. He extended his hand toward her. "I'm sorry, but I assumed you didn't know how to ride."

She appreciated his thought. She'd never ridden a horse before. Grabbing his hand, she climbed up and held on tight to him as he turned the horse around and led it away. Within the narrow confines of the city, they couldn't ride fast, and Bai took the time to tell Delun what she had learned.

She felt a stab of guilt. If not for her need to recover, they could have made it the night before and stopped the monks before they left. Now, she worried they might be too late.

Delun's fears echoed her own. "We must trust in the questioner. Perhaps he managed to slow them, or stop them completely."

The hope felt thin to Bai. If the questioner had stopped the army, wouldn't the monks still be within their walls?

Once they passed the outskirts of Kulat, Delun kicked the horse into a gallop. At first, Bai held on, terrified. She'd ridden on plenty of carts before, but this horse was alive, its weight constantly shifting underneath her. It seemed unnatural.

In time, she began to relax, understanding the constant minute adjustments needed to stay balanced. The ground flew underneath them, and Bai marveled in the sheer freedom of the speed. She'd never moved so quickly in her life. Her relaxation melted into joy, and she threw back her head and laughed.

If Delun wondered at her behavior, he had the wisdom not to question her. He pushed the horse faster, driven by the fear they'd be too late.

As they rode, the storm caught up with them. It began as a light sprinkle, the small drops of rain cutting like sharp needles against Bai's face. Within minutes, the sprinkle became a heavy rain, the air cooling noticeably as the storm moved in. Small hailstones followed. Bai looked for shelter.

Delun didn't slow. He cast a shield over them and kicked the tiring horse again. Bai looked up and grinned with delight as hailstones smacked against the shield and bounced off. Combined with the rain streaming around the bubble, Bai could actually see Delun's shield. It kept them dry as they charged through the rain.

Her delight caught in her throat when she sensed what

was ahead of them. She spoke in Delun's ear. "Can you feel that?"

He shook his head.

"There's a fight. A big one."

Delun swore and pushed the poor horse even harder. Bai leaned over, wondering how much farther it could travel before it gave out. As they neared, she could feel the battle more clearly. Delun tensed up, and she knew he felt it too.

She'd never felt so much power in one place. She couldn't keep track of the number of people attacking and shielding, but they all seemed to be facing in one direction.

The battle had already started.

Delun's worst fears had come true.

They were too late.

36

Delun held on tightly to the reins as he guided the beast toward the battle. The animal must have had some sense of the danger ahead, because Delun could feel the tension underneath him. If given half a chance, the horse would spook in any direction except the one they were going.

He understood. Bai could feel the fight in front of them better than he could, but she didn't understand the significance. Lifetimes had passed since anything like this had happened. Monks very rarely fought in numbers, and they had never turned on the empire's forces before. No one alive had ever sensed anything like this.

Though they were approaching close enough for Delun to feel individual attacks, the battle reminded him more of waves crashing against a rock wall. His travels had brought him to the great sea to the north, where he'd stood on a cliff as the water boomed against the rock below. The day he visited had been relatively calm, but locals had told him that on stormy days, it wasn't unusual for the waves to send water sixty feet in the air.

That same power and intensity now stood before him. He could feel the shields held in front of the monks, protecting them from harm as wave after wave of attacks broke against the empire's armies. They weren't close enough yet to see the conflict, but Delun's imagination ran rampant. Against the coordinated power of the monks, he didn't see how the empire stood a chance. Even with Lord Xun's men outnumbering the monks dozens to one, the battle couldn't be even.

Trees rushed by them on either side as they galloped, silent witnesses to the tragedy ahead. They rounded a bend and found themselves confronted by pure madness.

Lord Xun's army stood in ranks on the road, prevented from large-scale maneuvers by the thick woods on either side. A group of nearly thirty monks stood in front of them, stopping thousands in their tracks. Bodies lay behind the monks, providing plenty of evidence the monks had been advancing into the ranks of the empire's troops. Arrows were occasionally lit up by the lightning above, but they clattered helplessly against unwavering protection. Running his eyes over the bodies, Delun didn't see a single white robe.

How did anyone beat a group of monks who had trained together so often? Delun noticed that several monks were sharing shield duty, with three at a time holding the shields overhead, preventing arrows from raining down on them. Two held the signs for shields but didn't release. Delun saw the reason soon enough.

The monks would cast shields over everyone, completely protecting them. Most of the monks used the protection to prepare attacks. When everyone was ready, the monks would attack as one. Some unfortunate soldiers, pressed up against the shields, would charge, but be immediately killed or driven back by the overwhelming attacks. There was no gap for the soldiers to exploit.

Delun had never seen such cold-blooded butchery. The monks advanced forward one step at a time, their coordination ensuring no single monk ever had to bear much strain. They would tire eventually, but given the intensity of the training Delun had seen in Kulat, he didn't think exhaustion would be a factor for some time. At the rate they were advancing, the empire's army would fall long before the monks.

Delun knew the two of them couldn't take on thirty monks. He and Bai were good, but not that good. He also didn't know how far he trusted Bai. She told him she felt fine, but her body had to be nearing a limit of some kind. Delun couldn't imagine otherwise.

Inspiration struck. They didn't need to take on all the monks. They just needed to bring those shields down. Then the army could help.

He was about to ready a blast when he realized his mistake. He could bring down the shields given enough time, but Bai could dart through those shields without problem. He turned to her. "Can you sense the monks casting shields?"

"Yes."

"Attack them!"

Delun kicked the horse to one last burst of speed. The poor animal had been ridden nearly to death, but too many lives hung in the balance for Delun to feel ashamed of his treatment of the creature. It would rest soon enough.

This close to Bai, Delun thought he could feel her bringing in energy from all around her. Mercifully, she left his own alone. He would need it soon enough.

A few monks noticed them as Delun's charge carried

them the last few hundred paces toward the battle. He reined the horse in as Bai leaped into the fray.

She moved with impossible grace. The monks looked at her with bemused grins, not knowing the storm was about to break on them as well. Bai fell through the shield, her aura increasing in intensity as she did. She passed the monks, looking astounded, not wasting even the second it would have taken to strike them. Before they could react, before they could overcome their shock, she had driven fists and feet into the monks holding the shields.

The shields collapsed and the infantry at the front of the line pushed forward. From his mount, Delun could see the look of fear on their faces. They had seen what happened to those in their position before.

But the shields had fallen, thanks to Bai. The monks hadn't finished preparing their next round of attacks. Confidence led to its own sort of weakness. One or two waves of energy crashed into the soldiers, but the attacks didn't prevent the soldiers from reaching the monks, swords slicing through flesh not even wet from the rain yet.

Delun dropped from the horse and joined the fray.

The monks' attack had been well-planned and well-executed. But it hinged on an assumption that Bai destroyed when she penetrated the shields without problem. The order that had once defined the monastic advance was gone, replaced by chaos.

That didn't mean the battle was over. Even though they were grossly outnumbered, the monks were strong. No matter how well-trained Xun's troops were, they still didn't train as much as the monks did. Combined with the monks' powers, the conclusion of the battle was still far from certain.

Arrows started falling around Delun, and he ducked

into the heat of the battle. In the confusion, many of the monks didn't attack him. He wore the white robes. It allowed him to get close.

He made his attacks count, but he still held back. He didn't want to kill monks if he could prevent it.

Within a moment, the currents of the battle brought him next to Bai. As she raised a fist against him, he realized he possibly blended in a little too well. The army would think him an enemy also.

Bai saw who he was a moment before she brought her fist crashing down. He cast a small shield over them to give her a short rest. "How are you?"

She didn't respond, leaping from his shield toward an exposed monk. Delun cursed and dropped the defense before she could take more energy from him. An arrow grazed his shoulder and he had to dodge a sword pointed at his heart. The monks were still fighting, but they were losing ground. A few feet away, Delun saw Kang step forward against the press of soldiers. He sensed the attack a moment before Kang released it.

Soldiers went flying backward like rag dolls, crushing their companions behind them.

The attack had been wide, pushing the army back, if only for a moment. Again, the narrow road helped the monks, as the army commanders found it nearly impossible to flank them. Guanyu had chosen his location well.

The moment was all the monks needed. Shields slammed down once more, and the soldiers quickly realized they couldn't reach the monks again. Bai had provided an opening, but Kang had slammed the door shut. Would Kulat have enough monks to continue the assault, or would they retreat?

Delun only had eyes for Kang. He prepared an attack

and thrust it out, launching a narrow weave of power at the enormous man. The attack was aimed at Kang's head, a killing blow.

But Kang leaned back, allowing the attack to drill into the trees on the far side of the road. He glanced over at Delun, a malicious grin on his face. "Hold the shields! Kill the false monk!"

Delun had hoped the man would at least be willing to duel him. His hands danced the signs for two separate shields as he felt a number of attacks being prepared around him. He didn't think he'd last long.

Then one of the shields protecting everyone fell. Delun glanced over and saw Bai standing over the body of a monk.

He cursed his temper. He'd thought only of fighting Kang. Bai had kept her vision focused on the larger goal: giving the army a chance against the monks.

The monks were better prepared this time. They had attacks ready, and the initial rush of the soldiers proved disastrous. Another shield appeared, further protecting the monks. Bai fought against the shield casters, but the monks were learning to protect their own.

He felt Kang preparing another attack, ready to drive the army back even further. Delun cast a shield to protect himself and dashed after Kang. He needed to stop the man before even more damage was done.

A heartbeat later, Delun ran into a solid wall of energy. His shield absorbed the blow, but his advance toward Kang halted completely. His eyes widened when he felt the reserve of strength behind the attack.

Kang was stronger than Delun had thought.

The large monk saw the look on Delun's face and laughed. "Did you really think I would reveal my true strength?"

With a dismissive gesture, Kang sent another attack toward Delun. Delun cast his second shield, but the strength of Kang's attack shattered it as though it was a toy. The blast knocked Delun onto his back.

Then the shields dropped again, just in time for a wave of arrows to barrage the monks.

Bai.

She was doing more to save the empire than Delun.

Many monks got shields up in time, but some did not, arrows killing several.

Without the shield protecting him, rain poured onto Delun's face. He coughed and sputtered, unable to breathe. He forced himself to sit up.

Chaos reigned everywhere. The monks, forced to contend with both Bai and an army, weren't sure to how fight, and every moment of indecision whittled their numbers down. Delun saw plenty of white robes around him, motionless in the mud.

He heard Kang's deep, booming voice. "Retreat!"

All around him, monks ran into the trees, retreating toward Kulat. Within moments, only Bai and Delun were left in the road, the only obstacles between the army and the city that had already seen so much suffering.

The next thing he knew, Bai was at his side. "Are you hurt?"

He shook his head. His breath was coming easier now and he was fairly certain he hadn't broken any ribs. He'd made a mistake in underestimating Kang.

Delun looked into the trees, trying to see how many monks ran for safety. Bai followed his gaze. "I don't think there were more than ten."

"It's still too many. Holed up in the monastery, they could cause tremendous damage."

Delun tried to stand up but his legs failed him.

Bai put her hand firmly on his shoulder. "You should rest."

She looked around them, and Delun joined her in noticing that Xun's army had surrounded them, arrows nocked and aimed. She whispered to Delun. "Although perhaps you could cast a shield."

Delun did, casting a small bubble of protection around them. It felt thin against the numbers they faced.

A man stepped to the edge of the circle. From the way he stood, Delun guessed he was Lord Xun. Delun was surprised and impressed. He hadn't expected the lord himself to accompany the mission. The lord saw Delun's white robes and made a dismissive gesture. "Kill them."

Before Delun could protest, the archers released. Arrows ricocheted off the shield. Delun grimaced; he could protect them for a few minutes, but then his strength would give out.

"Lord Xun!" he called.

The man turned around.

"We are not your enemies. We were the ones who brought the shields down so you could fight the monks."

The lord looked doubtful, but as he considered, the questioner joined him. Delun never thought he'd be so happy to see one of the men of shadows. "He speaks the truth, my lord. These are the two who urged me to warn you."

Lord Xun stopped and considered them more carefully. Delun saw the cold calculation in his eyes, but also the hate that resided there. This was a man who hated the monasteries. No wonder the Golden Leaf had found such fertile ground here.

"Kill them anyway." The order was issued without a hint of compassion.

Delun fought his way to his feet, bracing himself against Bai to stand. "We can save the lives of your men."

Lord Xun held up a hand to halt the archers.

Delun plowed forward before Xun could change his mind. He felt their lives hanging by a thread. "The monks will retreat to the monastery. With them behind those thick walls, you'll have little choice but to besiege. Perhaps you can starve them out, but by that time, other monks will have discovered you're attacking a monastery, leading to complete war. So you will need to attack, and that will cost hundreds of men their lives. We can fight them instead."

Xun didn't look convinced. "You two?"

"What have you got to lose? If we fail, you can continue on."

Xun looked around at his men. Delun was betting the lord didn't want to waste his army if he didn't have to. "I'll give you one day."

"Two," Delun replied. "We've been fighting them for days now. Give us one day to rest and one day to fight."

Xun nodded. "Very well. You have two days to bring down the monastery in Kulat. I'll be waiting outside the city."

Delun dropped his shield, utterly spent.

He glanced over at Bai. "I don't suppose you have any ideas for taking down a monastery in two days?"

"We could ask the Golden Leaf."

Delun laughed, his mission coming full circle. "You'll have to find them first."

Bai gave him a knowing smile.

"I know one of their leaders."

37

B ai looked between Delun and Yang, fighting to keep the smile off her face. At first, she had worried that one of them would try to kill the other, but that moment of concern had passed. The two monks glared at each other, uncertain who should speak first.

Delun hated Yang. Even if Bai hadn't heard Delun state as much on their way to this meeting, she would have known. The anger radiating off him almost took physical form.

It didn't require a stretch of the imagination to understand. Delun recognized Guanyu was a threat to the monasteries, but the rogue abbot's beliefs weren't that far removed from Delun's own. The fact that Delun fought against Guanyu was why Bai trusted him as she did.

But Delun viewed Yang as a traitor, a man working from the inside to bring down the monasteries. Bai had little doubt that Delun viewed Yang as an evil that needed to be destroyed.

Delun sat on the edge of his seat, across the table from Yang, his fists clenching and then unclenching when he realized what he was doing. A few moments later they would clench again.

Yang leaned back as far as his chair would allow. He looked to be a moment away from sprinting out the door.

Rebellions certainly made for strange allies.

Bai broke the tension, making the request Delun never could. "Yang, we need your help."

With an effort, Yang shifted his gaze from Delun to her. "I'm not sure how much I can help. The Golden Leaf organizes. We can't fight against the monks, not the way you intend."

Delun shook his head. "We don't want you to fight. We just need a way into the monastery. We'll do the rest."

Yang leaned back, looking off into the distance. "There's a cistern running under one part of the wall. But it's sealed almost as tightly as the front door. The thick iron bars are nearly impossible to break."

"Do you have any more black powder?" Bai asked. She'd heard of the ambush when Delun had ranted about the Golden Leaf earlier.

Yang looked uneasy. Bai felt her heart race a little. She'd heard rumors of black powder and what it could do, but had never come near any. Finally, Yang nodded, confirming what she had guessed. "There's not much left. Maybe a small barrel."

Bai had no idea how powerful the black powder was. "Would that bring down the wall?"

Yang laughed. "Not even close."

They sat in silence.

Delun would be noticed the moment he got anywhere close to the walls. The same would be true of Yang. Bai and Delun were willing to fight, but they needed a way in.

Delun suddenly looked up, his gaze focused on Bai. "Did Lei train you to use a weapon?"

Bai shook her head. They'd never trained in anything but empty-handed combat.

Delun reached into a pocket and pulled out a small knife. It wasn't long enough to be an effective weapon; instead, it was the type of knife carried for daily tasks. He handed the blade over to her. "I can't move energy into the weapon. Can you?"

Bai held the weapon gingerly, narrowing her eyes in concentration. She pulled in energy from the room around her, borrowing just a little from each person. She channeled the power into her hand, then into the blade. The blade felt as though it was beginning to vibrate in her hand. Both Yang and Delun looked at her with concern etched on their faces. For once, it appeared they agreed on something. "Hand that over, Bai."

She looked between the two of them, unsure why they were so worried. It had been an easy matter to put energy into the weapon. Delun held the blade like it carried a disease. Yang paled. The two men looked at each other. "I think I can use this," Delun said quietly.

"That changes everything," Yang replied. He looked at Bai. "Again."

"Would either of you care to tell me what's happening?"

They both looked at her as though she were a demon from legend. Delun answered her question. "Most monks can't imbue weapons with energy. That's good, because doing so is dangerous. If I use this, I could take down a house with a single cut." He leaned back. "I think I know how to get into the monastery."

Bai was grateful Delun had a plan, but she didn't miss the fear in his eyes. He was scared of her.

. . .

THE SUN HAD FALLEN by the time the three of them finished discussing their plan. Delun and Yang had done most of the talking. Bai didn't have the training they did, and most of her solutions were variations of the idea that they should charge in and see what happened. A brilliant war planner she was not, she decided.

When they were done, Yang left to meet his contacts in the city. Of the three, he had the most to do in the least time. Delun had wanted to join the other monk, further evidence of his lack of trust. But Bai had reminded him that the next day would be a long one. They needed what rest they could get. Reluctantly, Delun agreed.

The two of them went up to their room. They'd considered getting two rooms, but Delun wanted the two of them together at all times. He claimed it was so they could protect each other, but the truth was obvious enough.

He was too frightened of her to let her out of his sight.

She crawled into her bed while he climbed into another one. She waited for sleep to take her.

An hour later, Bai yawned, exhausted but unable to sleep. Her mind kept racing, imagining tomorrow. On the other side of the room, Delun seemed to suffer from the same problem. Bai could hear him tossing and turning.

Finally, she heard his voice, soft. "You awake?"

She nodded before realizing he might not see the motion. "Yes."

"There's one thing I can't figure out. Why are you doing this?"

"What do you mean?"

"You discovered your gift just a few weeks ago. You have enough training now that you don't need to worry about being attacked or threatened anymore. So, why are you here? Why are you risking your life when you don't have to?"

She felt her pulse quicken and blood raced to her head. "Why do you care?"

"Because tomorrow, I'm going to put my life completely in your hands. And I don't know why you're here."

Even without seeing him, she knew that wasn't the complete truth. Part, perhaps, but it wasn't the real reason he asked.

"I want revenge against the monks."

She imagined him frowning at that. "Why?"

She tried to articulate her feelings. "Have you ever felt like you don't matter?"

He shook his head. "No."

"I have. Most of the days of my life. I have spent my entire life hiding in corners and in shadows and cowering, because if I fight I only make it worse. I grew up scared of everyone." The anger in her voice surprised her. "The elders, powerful men, the wealthy. But you know who frightened me the most?"

Bai could tell that Delun knew the answer before she spoke it.

"It was the monks. Do you have any idea how it feels to know that there are people out there with powers you can't understand, with the strength to wipe out your house and your livelihood with a gesture from their hand? That fear runs deep, and in that fear, I wasn't alone. Not all of us feared the elders, but we all fear monks."

"But we protect—"

Bai couldn't keep the derision from her voice as she interrupted. "Are you so sure about that? I've spent time with you, Delun, and I think I know you well enough to understand that you fight for what you believe in. But there is blood on your hands. How many people have you killed to protect your vision of the monasteries? How many families have had to go days or weeks wondering where their father or brother has disappeared off to, never to find an answer? You may justify your violence with your belief, but you are no different. You believe that your strength gives you the right to destroy lives."

Bai realized that she had started to sit up in her bed. She couldn't believe she spoke so forcefully. "I understand Lei. I can see why he would hide in the mountains, away from the empire and the monasteries. But Galan was my home, and Guanyu will make the fear I felt look inconsequential. I will not allow it."

Across the room from her, Delun remained silent. She expected him to fight back, to argue and tell her how wrong she was. But his silence spoke volumes.

When he finally did speak, his voice was soft.

"Tomorrow, when we go into battle, I will be honored to fight by your side."

38

Delun looked out the window of the common room. A warm cup of tea sat in front of him, and he'd awoken early enough that the inn was still quiet. He cradled the steaming cup gently in his hands, basking in the warmth as it seeped into his fingers.

He took a slow, deep breath, trying to imprint this memory onto his heart forever. After all the training, conflict, and strife, this was what he truly lived for: a quiet moment and a deep feeling of peace.

He didn't sleep well the night before. Although he had been loath to admit it to himself, Bai's words cut him deeper than he expected. Combined with her unusual gifts, his mind had refused him rest.

The past few weeks had caused him to doubt most of what he cherished, but he had never doubted himself. Bai changed that. She forced his actions out into the light, casting them from the shadows and showing them for what they were.

He had never deceived himself. He had always known on some level the actions he had taken on behalf of the monasteries were horrible. But until last night, he'd always believed they were justified, not realizing the ripples he caused with every act of violence he engaged in.

He spent most of the night thinking about Bai's words, but he didn't have any answers to her unspoken questions. In the very early hours of the morning he had settled on a simple truth. All that mattered at the moment was that he give everything to stop the monks of Kulat before this disaster went any further. He would fight, and die if necessary, to prove that the monks were capable of more. He would fight to make sure that none of the children grew up with the fear Bai had described.

Delun didn't hold much hope for himself. The enemies they faced were strong. After the last battle, Delun was convinced that Kang was a stronger monk than he was, and Guanyu was on another level entirely. Lei might be able to beat them, but Delun didn't think he had a chance. If he happened to live through the battle, only then would he worry about his past and future.

So he sat in the common room, enjoying what he believed would be his last meal. His end didn't terrify him. He was a monk, and he had been trained to prepare for death his entire life. Now that the moment was finally at hand, he felt a profound peace, a certainty, that was beyond anything he had previously experienced.

His lingering questions were about Bai. He'd thought much about her the night before, and his thoughts only worried him.

As though his thoughts had summoned her, Bai came down the stairs, sat down, and poured herself a cup of tea.

Before she took a sip, she fixed her gaze on him. "What is it about me that frightens you so?"

Surely she hadn't added the ability to read thoughts to her list of gifts, had she?

"Your gifts frighten me. You seem almost perfectly designed for one purpose: to fight and kill monks."

She shook her head. "That's part of it, maybe, but I don't believe you're telling me the whole truth."

He cursed to himself. Over their past few days together, he'd seen this ability of hers manifest several times. The girl was one of the most intuitive people he'd ever met. At times, he wondered if that had some connection to her powers.

He could refuse to answer, but the truth was, he trusted her. Despite everything, he did.

"It's not just your powers, but what you represent," he admitted. "Twenty years ago, the monasteries learned that the Dragon's Fang was possible, that two-handed combat was possible. Now most monks can fight two-handed, and more than a handful are strong enough to attempt the Dragon's Fang. And now you appear, and the things you do shouldn't be possible. They go against everything we know."

"There's never been anyone like me?"

Delun shook his head emphatically. "No. I suppose one could make the argument that we're just learning more now, but my gut tells me that's wrong. I think that our gifts are changing, and the monasteries aren't ready."

She sat in silence, digesting his greatest worries. "I suppose that's something you'll have to figure out after we defeat Guanyu."

He smiled. With one statement, she had acknowledged his ideas weren't mad and had focused him on the task at hand.

She was remarkable.

She took a sip of her tea and smiled. "That's really good."

He nodded in agreement. He'd thought the same.

Last night he hadn't lied. He was honored to fight beside her today. If he was to die, at least it would be in good company.

They sat and drank their tea in companionable silence. The sun rose over a wet and muddy city.

It wasn't long before Yang arrived. He looked at both of them. "Everything is prepared."

They all shared some glances back and forth and then stood up. There was nothing left for them to say.

Judgment was here.

DELUN DISLIKED FORCING as much responsibility on Bai as he did. Unfortunately, the simple fact of the matter was that she was better equipped for this work than him. They crouched hundreds of paces away from the wall of the monastery, waiting for the signal that would give them permission to attack.

He wanted to ask Bai what she sensed but restrained himself. There was no point. He had asked her the question three times already in almost as many minutes. The signal would go off when everything was ready. Until then, it seemed unlikely Bai would sense anything unusual from the monastery.

When the boom rumbled between the walls of the city, shaking dust from the rooftops, Delun opened his eyes in surprise. It sounded like their friends in the Golden Leaf hadn't been entirely forthright about how much black powder they possessed. That explosion had been tremendous.

"Did it work?"

She had her eyes closed, her expression focused. "Yes. They are all approaching the explosion."

"Then let's move."

The two of them charged forward. The explosion had taken place opposite the front gate. With luck, it would distract the monks enough that they wouldn't notice the real assault. Bai led the way, carrying an enormous sledgehammer.

On her small frame, the weapon seemed foolishly outsized. But with her gifts, she handled it as though it were light as a feather. Even from this distance, Delun could sense the energy that flowed into the weapon. It glowed brightly in his mind.

They made it to the gate in short order, and they were close enough now that Delun could sense that their deception had worked. There were no guards at the gate. There weren't enough monks left to go around, and if everything went according to plan, townspeople were now firing arrows at the backside of the monastery, further distracting the monks. The monks would no doubt sense the two of them as they approached, but they only needed enough time to bring down the gate.

When they reached the gates, Bai swung the hammer with all her might, striking the thick wooden barriers with tremendous force. Under normal circumstances, that hammer would've done little but leave a small dent in the gate.

Augmented by enormous energies, though, the wood first splintered with a ear-splitting crack, then exploded inward, sending shrapnel throughout the courtyard. In an instant, one of the most defensible parts of the monastery was laid low with a single blow. Had he not been there to see it himself, he never would have believed the story.

A moment later they were in the courtyard, almost as surprised as the monks on the back walls.

Bai moved like lightning. She darted for the stairs, leaped up them in tremendous bounds, and reached the top of the wall in just a couple of seconds. She jumped into the gathering of monks, tossing them off the walls with abandon and taking full advantage of her additional speed. Delun shook his head, still unable to believe how quickly she could move with the energy coursing through her.

The monks had learned from their previous battles. Surprised as they were, once they realized who they faced, they altered their tactics. One eager young man struck out at Bai and quickly paid the price, but the other survivors of her initial assault remained far away. They gave up ground willingly and sent short bursts aimed at the walls and ground around her, trying to trip her up. The ideas weren't poor, but Bai handled the distractions with ease. Lei had trained her well in the short time they'd been together.

Delun realized too late he'd been paying too much attention to Bai's fight and not enough to his own surroundings. He sensed Kang's attack just before the enormous monk released it. Unprepared, Delun dove to the side as the attack blasted through the place he had stood. Before he could reach his feet, another blast caught him full in the chest, causing him to roll end over end. Delun kept his limbs loose and tucked in close to his body, only coming to a stop when he hit the inner wall of the courtyard. He looked up just in time to see that both Kang and Guanyu faced him. Delun cursed as twin attacks flew towards him. He hadn't even been able to give them a decent fight.

Then Bai was there, absorbing the energy from the attacks. The two monks had learned their lesson, though. They cut off their attacks immediately, unwilling to give Bai any more energy to use against them.

Delun struggled to his feet, feeling a bit wobbly. How many times would she save him before she failed?

Beyond her, Guanyu and Kang conversed for a moment. Then Kang left, running through the broken gate and into Kulat.

Delun uttered another curse. Clever as they were, they knew either of them was stronger than Delun, and by separating and going into town to threaten civilians, at least one of the two invaders would have to give chase. If both gave chase, the monastery would be safe and prepared for another attack. If they split, they could be defeated individually.

Bai was about to go after Kang, but Delun put a hand on her shoulder. He hated what they'd been forced into. They couldn't both leave the monastery. Delun wasn't sure he could defeat Kang, but of the two warriors, Bai had the better chance of standing up to Guanyu. Delun knew he was hopelessly outmatched against the abbot.

For all his years of training, when the moment came, he still wasn't enough.

He cursed the world. But he would still do what he could.

"You fight him. I'll follow Kang." Bai looked doubtful for a moment, then nodded. The two of them separated. Delun looked at her one last time before he left.

He didn't think he would see her again.

DELUN DIDN'T HAVE to travel far to find Kang. The monk had stopped only a few hundred paces away from the front gate, not too far from where Delun and Bai had waited in hiding earlier.

Kang stood in the middle of the street, waiting for him.

"I wondered if you would choose me, or if you'd send the girl. Do you still think you have a chance?"

Delun didn't respond, channeling his energy into both a shield and an attack. He ran at Kang, hoping to close the distance so that Kang would have less time to respond.

Kang seemed content to let him approach, forming an attack with each hand. The other monk was so confident he didn't even think he needed a defense. Delun came face to chest with his opponent, throwing a jab up at the man's face.

Kang slid to the side and back, releasing one of the attacks he'd formed. Delun spun away, releasing his shield and using that as a weapon, slamming it across Kang's face. Few monks ever considered the shield as a weapon, and it caught Kang by surprise. The blow knocked him back a few paces.

That gave Delun the space he needed. He aimed and released the attack, catching Kang off-balance. The technique struck true, energy crashing into the man and sending him flying several feet backward.

Delun felt a flush of victory. Perhaps he wasn't the strongest, but he was still more experienced than the other monk. Strength wasn't everything. He resisted the urge to push the attack. There was too much distance to cover, and overconfidence had felled plenty of monks.

Kang rolled onto his back and smoothly to his feet, wiping a trickle of blood from the corner of his lip. He smiled at Delun.

"Not bad."

Delun's pride turned to horror. His attack should have broken ribs, at least. The blast had been strong enough to kill many men, and Delun hadn't held back. He'd been willing to kill. Yet the tower of muscle stood as though he'd been pushed over and nothing more. There wasn't a hint of pain in the man's voice.

Delun knew then he was in for trouble.

Kang moved with surprising speed. Delun, distracted, hadn't prepared more attacks, a novice mistake. A meaty fist drove into Delun's stomach, punching the air from his lungs. With his other hand, Kang made a sign for an attack directly in Delun's face. The technique wasn't strong, but it still snapped his head back and made his ears ring. Delun stumbled and fell, blind and deaf from the blast.

Delun struggled to his feet. He had one trick left to play, but the moment had to be perfect. Right now, Kang stood confident, but he hadn't dropped his guard.

"I don't want to kill you, Delun. You're a strong monk, and I know our beliefs aren't that different. Surrender and live. I'll speak to the abbot for you."

For a moment, Delun felt the pull of temptation whispering in his ear. Perhaps he could do more from inside the movement than opposing it. He did want the monasteries to be stronger than they were. It was no more than Kang and Guanyu wanted.

He almost surrendered.

But the memories of Bai's voice in the night and the massacre of Kulat were too fresh. The temptation pulled, but it couldn't convince. He formed the sign for an attack.

Kang actually looked disappointed. Before Delun could react, he was hit by two attacks. The first took his feet out from under him and the second caught him in midair, flinging him down the road. Delun groaned and coughed up blood. He could feel his energy fading. If he waited for his moment too long, he might never have a chance.

Kang stepped forward. He formed several signs, focusing his attack tighter and tighter. It would be the killing blow.

Delun tried to catch his breath. He didn't want to die, but he could barely move.

"Last chance," Kang said.

Delun grabbed the knife in his pocket, pulling it from its sheath. He didn't know how strong the attack would be, but the blade was still filled with energy. It was a last-ditch effort, but he had nothing left to give. Delun whipped the blade out, willing it to expel energy.

It worked.

A razor-sharp line of energy snapped from the blade.

Kang hadn't been off-guard, but he hadn't expected an attack from a weapon. He shifted his weight, turning away from the cut. The energy sliced through his left arm, cutting it off near the shoulder.

Delun didn't wait for Kang's reaction. Summoning every bit of strength he had, he screamed and fought his way to his feet, tackling Kang to the ground. He sat on the man's chest, holding the now-inert knife in his hand, stabbing repeatedly at Kang's chest. Red wounds blossomed across the man's white robes, but none were fatal. The knife wasn't long enough to pierce beyond the barrel-chested man's muscles and reach his organs.

Kang caught Delun's hand with his right hand, freezing the smaller monk in place. Kang's eyes were filled with cold fury. He twisted sharply and Delun lost his grip on the bloody knife. With a roar, Kang pulled Delun toward him, then drove his forehead into Delun's nose, sending stars through Delun's vision.

Kang tossed him away with one arm and Delun crumpled to the ground.

Despite the loss of his arm, Kang stood smoothly. The only hint that he'd been injured was the way he wobbled slightly as he stepped forward. Delun lay on his back, unbelieving. He knew he hadn't wounded Kang enough for immediate death, but there was no way the man should be standing.

Kang was the strongest monk Delun had ever met.

Kang began signing an attack. "You're not enough to stop me."

Scenes flashed in front of Delun. The men he'd killed. Bai's words. The worlds he'd destroyed. He couldn't leave like this.

He felt the flame of anger flicker inside. If he was going to die, it wouldn't be silently. He could at least take Kang with him. It wouldn't atone for the wrong he'd done, but it was a start.

Delun formed the signs for an attack as well, pulling all his energy, leaving nothing behind. It would probably kill him, but he was dead anyway.

They released their techniques at the same time, two waves of energy crashing into one another.

Kang's immediately overwhelmed Delun's, and the attack came closer and closer to Delun. Delun groaned, pushing with everything he had. There was nothing left after this attack, nothing at all. He either won or died.

Kang's attack couldn't quite make contact, Delun's power just enough to keep him alive.

Delun could feel Kang's soul through the attack. He sensed the hatred of people who didn't respect the monasteries, the white-hot belief Kang held in the superiority of his strength. In a way, it was like looking in a mirror.

Inch by inch, Delun's attack advanced on Kang. The other monk was losing blood. A lot of it. He grew weaker by the moment. Like Delun, he held nothing back.

But his spirit was weaker.

Kang's attack suddenly shattered, and Delun's blow hit Kang in the chest, knocking him onto his back.

One last time, Delun fought his way to his feet. He felt the familiar pangs of giving too much, deeper than he'd ever felt them before. Once he closed his eyes, he was certain he would never open them again. But perhaps Bai would be proud of him.

That would be enough.

Kang was suffering too. His reserve of strength had given out. Delun's attack hadn't been fatal, but Kang had given all the energy that provided life. He was blinking his eyes, struggling to keep them open. He fought to meet Delun's gaze.

"Kill me. Let me die at the hands of a monk, at least."

Delun considered denying him, as one last punishment, but couldn't bring himself to.

Kang closed his eyes, breathing softly.

Delun picked up his bloody knife. He didn't have the strength to kill the man in any other way. He offered his opponent a short bow and drew it across Kang's neck.

The monk would never open his eyes again.

39

B ai watched Delun leave, then turned to Guanyu. She'd felt this man's power before, knew well who she faced. This man wasn't just a monk, he was one of their best.

Her heart raced and her palms sweat, but she forced herself to stillness. Delun had believed she was the best suited to fighting Guanyu. That had to mean something.

A breeze blew through the open door of the courtyard, ruffling the robes of the monks lying dead or unconscious around them. A few leaves skittered across the ground. Guanyu started circling, his pace calm. To Bai's sense, she could feel the way he pulled in power, just the way she did.

She remembered a little from their earlier fight. He had formed an attack more focused than anything she'd felt before, more dangerous than anything Lei had trained her for. Her memories had gone blank shortly after. He'd beaten her on the road, but she still stood.

"So, you're the one I've heard so much about. The girl who killed her own mother."

Bai clenched her fist, holding in her response. She wouldn't have killed her mother if the monks hadn't pushed her. None of this suffering was necessary. But her words would change nothing.

Instead, she closed her eyes and breathed power into herself. Across the courtyard, she could hear Guanyu speaking to himself.

"Interesting."

When she opened her eyes, the world looked sharper. Guanyu appeared relaxed, but she saw through the facade now. There was worry in his eyes.

He opened his mouth to say more, but Bai hadn't come to trade words with Guanyu. As far as she was concerned, this man was the architect of the greatest pain in her life. She leaped at him, trying to drive her fist into his face.

Guanyu shifted his weight, avoiding her blow easily. He sent a small blast at her feet, trying to throw off her balance. She felt the wave, and it did move her a bit, but not so much she couldn't adapt. She landed and flung herself back at Guanyu, swinging again. The abbot shifted once more and watched her sail by.

Undeterred, Bai came in again, this time leading with a series of quick, short jabs. The monk blocked one, dodged another, then snaked his own fist at her. She saw it coming and leaned backward, stumbling a few paces but remaining unharmed.

The exchange encouraged her. She was faster than Guanyu. She stepped forward, aiming a kick at his shin. In response, he stepped back, allowing her foot to pass just in front of him. As soon as the danger was past he stepped in and drove a kick into her unprotected side.

The kick wasn't much, but it sent her stumbling back a few paces again. Filled with energy, she barely felt the pain.

Guanyu nodded, as though he had seen everything he needed. "You haven't been training long, have you?"

The question was odd enough to stop Bai in her tracks. She looked into his eyes and didn't see the worry that had been there just moments ago. That lack of worry frightened her more than the massive well of power he drew upon. What had he learned?

Guanyu stepped forward, his fists and feet moving quickly. Bai's senses were sharp enough that she could see them all coming, but after blocking the first two strikes, the third slammed her head to the side. Guanyu didn't waste the opportunity, following her as she stumbled backward, pummeling her face and torso with his fists. He finished with a kick to her chest that slammed her into the wall.

Bai shook her head. She felt dizzy. The energy still coursed through her body, and there wasn't much pain, but she didn't feel right, like the sights and sounds around her weren't quite lining up.

Roaring, she filled herself with energy, bringing the world back into sharp focus. She leaped at Guanyu again, jabbing and launching short kicks. She was certain that she was faster than him, but it didn't seem to matter. No matter how fast she punched, she wasn't able to connect. She landed one glancing blow, but found his foot in her stomach yet again.

Bai fell down and coughed, seeing the blood on her hands. She didn't feel anything, though.

Guanyu squatted about a dozen paces from her. He looked completely at ease, in his element.

"You were foolish to believe them, you know."

She frowned, confused.

"What did Lei and Delun tell you? That you were something special? How did they convince you to attack this monastery?"

Bai fought her way to her feet, spitting out the blood that was pooling in her mouth. "This was my choice."

Guanyu didn't even get out of his squat. "Then you are a fool."

Bai leaped, aiming a kick at Guanyu's head. She yelled and snapped her leg at his face, but he shifted and her kick missed again. She tried to land, but his wrist wrapped around her ankle, tripping her up and sending her crashing to the ground. Guanyu formed a fist and smashed it into her torso.

This time, the energy drained out of Bai, as though Guanyu had somehow poked a dozen holes in a bucket, the water pouring out. She tried to summon more but couldn't find the focus.

As soon as the energy vanished, the pain hit. Her eyes rolled up in her head, the agony and dizziness almost too much to take. Her limbs refused to move, and she could feel the deep bruises her body had sustained. She struggled to breathe, and her eyes went wide, realizing just how much danger she was in.

This time Guanyu squatted down right next to her. "You understand now, don't you? The power you drew in masked the pain in your body. You have gifts. I'll grant you that. Some of them are unique." He leaned down even closer, until his face was right next to hers. "But you are nothing special."

Guanyu's eyes ran down her body and she shivered involuntarily. She'd seen that gaze before, and nothing good had ever come from it. His voice kept hammering away at her new identity, chiseling it away one piece at a time. "You are faster, and perhaps, with real training, you might have been a danger to me. But you don't have a lifetime of experience. You've survived on surprise, speed, and your gifts. You were never prepared for a real fight."

When he grabbed her, running his hand down her body, she broke. She found the strength to swing an arm at him, but he deflected it easily. Her arm flopped back to the ground, weighing more than she would have believed possible.

Just like that, she was the girl she had always been, scared and afraid. There was nothing she could do. Her body wouldn't respond to her commands. Her eyes darted back and forth, looking for someplace to hide. She could feel the dark corners of her mind where she used to hide from the world.

Guanyu grabbed her by her hair, pulling her toward the gate of the monastery. Her head erupted in fire, and she swiped at him, but couldn't reach.

As her arms fell back, useless, she saw the bracelet she had given her mother.

She saw her mother's hand, cold and lifeless, and a spark was lit somewhere deep inside her, someplace Guanyu's words hadn't reached.

She wouldn't be afraid. Not of a man like this. She forced her body to relax, to focus on the energies moving within. The spark was weak, liable to burn out at any moment. Her rage was like a soft breeze, blowing the spark into a small fire.

Bai closed her eyes, focusing on that feeling of power in her core. At that moment, she realized a new truth.

She would never hide again.

Something inside her unlocked, and she could feel the energies flowing around her once again.

She surrendered, opening herself up completely.

Power flooded into her, and she felt better than ever before. Stronger. Faster.

Part of her knew it was a lie, but she didn't care. She would push herself over the brink if it meant preventing Guanyu's victory.

Guanyu noticed, but he'd gotten too close, too sure of his victory. She scrambled to reach his hand, the one he had wrapped around her hair. She grabbed the wrist, then pulled and twisted until her feet were under her. Guanyu reacted, tried to get away, but Bai's lock on his wrist was unbreakable. She threw, sending him tumbling through the dirt. As he rolled, she stood tall, feeling a tremendous strength well up inside her.

Bai saw the glint of fear in his eyes. He had beaten her twice, but she kept standing back up.

She wouldn't hide, and she wouldn't back down.

Nothing Guanyu did could stop her.

Fear made Guanyu attack. Wisely, he avoided energy attacks, knowing those were next to useless against her. Instead, he came in himself, his fists a flurry of strikes and blocks.

Bai saw the gaps in his defense, the moments of weakness. They seemed so obvious, his movements too slow.

She jabbed a fist into his nose, then one into his stomach. Both caused him to stumble back.

Bai didn't take advantage of the momentary weakness. She'd hurt him, but now he was more dangerous than ever. Blood leaked from his nose and he wiped it away with the sleeve of his robe.

She still saw his fear, but it was being replaced by anger.

She could sense it building.

Up until this week, Guanyu had believed himself the

master of his world. He had strong followers capable of changing the course of history. He had an incredible strength to personally draw on. No doubt, he considered himself wise. He'd had everything, and she'd been nothing.

He didn't believe her. She understood him now, as clear as day.

For the first time, his hands started moving, collecting the energy for a serious attack. Bai had felt the process from him before. Lei had told her about the attack but had never demonstrated it. She suspected her teacher wasn't even capable.

The Dragon's Fang.

The energy focused tighter, until it was nothing more than a small glowing ball of light to her senses.

That attack had almost killed her last time. She remembered the incredible sensation of power flowing through her, her inability to control it. She had destroyed an enormous swath of forest. If it hit her here, she didn't want to imagine the consequences. She didn't think the walls of the monastery would be protection enough for Kulat.

Guanyu's move forced her to attack. As fast as she was, Guanyu had been right. She didn't have enough training. He avoided her punches, remaining a step ahead of her the whole time.

Frustration almost caused her to launch a foolish strike, but she held back, trying instead to get too close to Guanyu for him to use the attack. But he kept as much distance between them as possible.

She sensed him getting ready. She only had one chance.

Bai leaped, cocking her fist back and driving it at Guanyu. He sidestepped easily, smiling, confident in his victory.

He released the Dragon's Fang into her unprotected side.

For a few moments, it felt as though she was being covered by several warm blankets, a soft pressure wrapping around her entire body. But within the space of a heartbeat, that gentle pressure turned into something more intense as the blankets grew heavier and heavier, crushing her.

Her body couldn't take much more. Already, she felt as though she was a piece of fabric, tearing apart at the seams.

No!

She refused to end this way. No monk would kill her. No monk would terrify her, ever again.

Bai focused her will, just the way Lei taught her. She didn't try to control the energy, but guide it.

Time slowed down and she shifted some of the energy to her legs, throwing herself at Guanyu.

He shifted his weight, preparing for her attack, ready to keep retreating.

But she pushed against the enormous power of the Dragon's Fang, the attack that threatened to destroy her also giving her the strength to fight against it. Her body felt large and bloated and ready to explode.

Bai channeled the energy into her fist and arm. All of it.

Guanyu must have predicted her attack, because he started to react.

Bai had too much strength. Powered by the Dragon's Fang, she was too fast. With a scream, she drove her fist toward his face. He couldn't avoid it.

Her fist connected.

She averted her eyes, knowing she had succeeded when the Dragon's Fang instantly vanished.

It was over.

40

Delun stumbled to the monastery. He wasn't sure what good he would be in a fight. Kang had almost destroyed him. But he had to try. Given the energies emanating from the building, Delun guessed Bai and Guanyu were in the heat of their fight.

Just as he made it to the gate, the energies suddenly disappeared. It was disorienting, as though the sun had suddenly blinked out of existence. Delun stumbled, then found his footing and entered the courtyard. Bai was there, on her knees, over a prone body.

She had done it.

Delun knew that of the two of them, her skills had been their only chance. But there had been no way of knowing. Despite her incredible gifts, she had only trained for a few weeks. It hardly seemed enough.

And yet, it had been.

Delun approached, soon getting his first view of Guanyu. When he did, he blanched, feeling suddenly sick. Vomit rose up in his throat, and he was grateful he hadn't eaten more of a breakfast.

"Is that him?" he asked, feeling foolish as soon as he said it. Who else would it be?

Bai nodded.

"That's…" He couldn't find the words.

Bai nodded again, then got to her feet. She wobbled, and Delun wondered just how much the fight had taken out of her. From the bruises he could see, and from the tattered state of her clothing, it looked like she'd taken quite the beating.

Delun looked one last time at the corpse. "That *is* Guanyu?"

There was no easy way to recognize him. Bai's final attack had taken care of that. But the look on her face brokered no argument. Delun raised his hands in surrender. "Sorry."

The two of them faced each other, silence between them. Delun's thoughts had stopped with the sight of Guanyu's body. Truthfully, he hadn't expected to survive. The idea of the future seemed daunting.

She eyed him warily. "So, what comes next?"

He shook his head, unsure of the answer. Then the tone of her voice registered.

She viewed him as a threat.

Was he?

A few weeks ago he had chased her up a mountain. She was dangerous to the monasteries. He couldn't think of another person, living or dead, who could harm monks like she could. In her own way, she was as dangerous as Guanyu.

She had killed one of the monasteries' most powerful abbots after only a few weeks of training. If she continued to improve, just how dangerous would she become? If she set her sights on the monasteries, what could any of them do?

She would never be weaker than she was now. Guanyu had almost beaten her.

His duty was to kill her.

He pressed the palms of his hands to his eyes, shaking his head.

She had risked her life and saved his several times.

He trusted her.

He would not give her another reason to hate the monasteries.

Delun looked off into the distance. "I suppose I need to speak with Xun. The danger has passed, but the situation will take a long time to repair."

Delun saw her relax. She remained wary, but less so than before.

"What about you? Will you return to Lei's village?"

Bai nodded. "For a time, perhaps. I do not think I am meant to live there for long."

"What will you do?"

"Study. Continue training. I'd like to make amends for the harm I've caused. I'm not sure how."

Delun turned to fully face her. He bowed deeply. "It's been an honor."

She returned the bow.

Then she turned and walked out of the monastery, never looking back.

Delun sat across the table from Yang. This time, instead of an inn, they were inside the monastery. Delun tapped at his tea cup, unsure of how to proceed. Yang looked equally uncertain.

Lord Xun had left the city a week ago. The army had eventually marched into Kulat, but there had been little to do. With the monastery defeated, tensions had dropped almost overnight. Delun hadn't said anything, but he suspected Yang and the Golden Leaf had a fair amount to do with that.

"I appreciate you meeting with me," Delun began.

"It seemed," Yang struggled to find the right word, "wise."

Delun nodded. "Kulat cannot be without a monastery. Given that all of Guanyu's edicts have been erased, your status as a monk is currently unquestioned. As the only surviving member of the monastery, it would make sense to elevate your role. But you understand my concerns."

Delun wondered at the change within him. First he'd let Bai leave, and now he sat across from Yang, a monk who had actively worked against the monasteries.

Yang took a deep breath. "Ask what you will."

"Did you plan the black powder attack?"

Yang shook his head. "No. The attack was planned by several other members of the Golden Leaf. I did not want our movement to resort to violence, but when I was incapacitated by Bai's actions in Galan, the others took the opportunity to act."

Delun rubbed at his chin. So much came back to Bai and that fateful afternoon in Galan.

"Why should I not kill you?"

Yang laughed. "I appreciate your directness. I'll answer in kind. Because you can't afford to. Killing me would send the region back into an uproar, as I'm sure you suspect. Granted, Xun is close and you've got more monks on the way, so the uproar would be short-lived, but the tension would live on."

Yang had said nothing Delun hadn't already figured out for himself. "And if I put you in a position of authority?"

"I would lead the monasteries in charting a new path. Guanyu and his followers had to be rooted out, but I do not see a future without the monasteries. We need to do better. Kulat can be the model the others follow."

"You have ideas?"

"Focus on the study of our gifts. We're seeing people with new gifts more frequently now, and the old ways of training won't be enough. There are too many questions we don't ask. We should open our doors and our books to anyone interested in our lives or our studies. Pay for some of the food we consume."

Delun's eyes narrowed. "Do you also sense that the nature of our gifts is changing?"

"I think they've always changed. But they are changing faster now, and instead of embracing the change and adapting, the monks are retreating to comfortable traditions."

Delun leaned back, letting the ideas sink in. Some of Yang's ideas were more radical than others, and he would definitely drive the other abbots mad. But Delun also didn't see how any of the ideas violated the spirit of the monastic tradition. Yang also wanted to lead the empire, just in a very different way.

Still, old habits died hard.

"If you continue to plot the fall of the monasteries, I'll kill you myself."

Yang smiled at that. "I would expect no less."

"Then I shall raise you temporarily to the role of the abbot of Kulat. Your peers will most likely make it official within a month."

Yang bowed. "I am honored. And what of you?"

Delun sipped at his tea. "I will continue my work."

Yang hid his surprise well, but it was still there. "Even after all you've seen?"

"My methods might change, but I still serve the monasteries."

Yang studied him. Delun felt like the other man understood.

Yang raised his tea cup. "To a new monastic era."

Delun joined him. "To a new era."

EPILOGUE

TWO YEARS LATER

Outside of Jihan

Bai followed the monks at a distance. There were two of them, focused on a merchant's daughter, a beautiful woman trying to get home before the sun set. The streets were dangerous at night, now more so than ever.

She'd had her eyes on these monks for a while now. Rumors of them had surfaced over and over, two young monks who had forsaken their vows to protect and serve the empire.

She forced herself not to spit as she thought of them. They were symptomatic of a larger problem plaguing the empire.

Perhaps it had all started in Kulat.

Guanyu, for all his failings, had shown the monks what they were capable of. Their teachings didn't have to bind them.

The monasteries were not as they once were. Besieged on all sides, many of the younger monks had started ignoring their vows.

Anyone could see the split coming. On her more hopeful days, Bai believed that the rifts could be healed. Kulat, after all that had happened, had become a beacon of a new way forward. The monks there were well-loved, and the area was at peace.

Someday, Bai hoped she would be able to return.

Her life was here now, where she could do the most good. The places where the split between the different monks caused problems.

As the streets emptied, it became more difficult to follow the monks without being spotted. With an ease born of the last two years of training, she leaped to the rooftops in a single bound, landing softly on the tiles and walking as quietly as a cat. She closed some of the distance between her and the monks. At the same time, the two monks were closing the distance between them and the woman.

Bai didn't know exactly what they had planned, but she suspected she wouldn't approve.

A moment later she heard one of the two monks yell, "Halt!"

The woman, surprised to see two monks behind her, obeyed. That was her first mistake. But obedience of the monks ran deep in many well-to-do families. They still believed that all monks were there to serve them, despite ample evidence to the contrary.

Bai crept closer, making sure she was near enough to drop on them with a moment's notice.

The two young monks didn't even bother pretending. One of them released an attack that pinned the woman against a wall. The other stepped right up to her. She tried to scream, but the second monk pressed his hand tightly against her mouth.

Bai had seen enough. She dropped down from the roof,

lashing out with her foot as she dropped. The monk who'd been right next to the woman collapsed, never even realizing he'd been in danger.

The other monk launched an attack at her, but she absorbed the blast without problem. A well-aimed kick at his groin dropped him to the ground.

She turned to the woman. "Are you okay?"

The woman nodded mutely, still trying to understand what just happened.

"Go home, tell everyone what happened here."

The woman nodded again, and after a gentle push, finally ran home. Once Bai was sure the woman was out of sight, she turned back to the two monks, both of whom were getting to their feet.

She assumed a fighting stance and smiled.

Her work was just beginning.

WANT TO KNOW MORE?

If you enjoyed this story, I'd like to invite you to join my newsletter. Subscribers get free stories, access to early releases, and so much more.

www.waterstonemedia.net/newsletter

THANK YOU

Thank you so much for reading!

I hope you enjoyed *Heart of Defiance*. I've had a lot of fun writing in this world, and I plan on continuing the story soon.

Until then, if you just can't get enough fantasy, might I suggest the Nightblade series? The first book, *Nightblade*, can be found wherever you like to buy your books.

Finally, if you enjoyed the story, I would appreciate it if you would leave a review wherever you purchased the book. Reviews mean the world to authors and help others find the book as well.

With gratitude,

Ryan

ALSO BY RYAN KIRK

ABOUT THE AUTHOR

Ryan Kirk is the bestselling author of the Nightblade series of books. When he isn't writing, you can probably find him playing disc golf or hiking through the woods.

www.waterstonemedia.net
contact@waterstonemedia.net

 facebook.com/waterstonemedia

 twitter.com/waterstonebooks

instagram.com/waterstonebooks

Printed in Poland
by Amazon Fulfillment
Poland Sp. z o.o., Wrocław